DANGEROUS PLEASURES

DANGEROUS PLEASURES

BERTRICE SMALL

THORNDIKE
CHIVERS

This Large Print edition is published by Thorndike Press, Waterville, Maine, USA and by BBC Audiobooks Ltd, Bath, England.
Thorndike Press, a part of Gale, Cengage Learning.
Copyright © Bertrice Small, 2008.
The moral right of the author has been asserted.

The text of this Large Print edition is unabridged.
Other aspects of the book may vary from the original edition.
Set in 16 pt. Plantin.
Printed on permanent paper.

LIBRARY OF CONGRESS CATALOGING-IN-PUBLICATION DATA

Small, Bertrice.
   Dangerous pleasures / by Bertrice Small.
      p. cm. — (Thorndike Press large print romance)
   ISBN-13: 978-1-4104-1242-3 (alk. paper)
   ISBN-10: 1-4104-1242-3 (alk. paper)
   1. Widows—Fiction. 2. Single mothers—Fiction. 3. Contests—Fiction. 4. Sexual fantasies—Fiction. 5. Large type books. I. Title.
   PS3569.M28D365 2008b
   813'.54—dc22
                                 2008040550

BRITISH LIBRARY CATALOGUING-IN-PUBLICATION DATA AVAILABLE

Published in 2009 in the U.S. by arrangement with NAL Signet, a member of Penguin Group (USA) Inc.
Published in 2009 in the U.K. by arrangement with NAL Signet, a member of Penguin Group (USA) Inc.

U.K. Hardcover: 978 1 408 43204 4 (Chivers Large Print)
U.K. Softcover: 978 1 408 43205 1 (Camden Large Print)

Printed in the United States of America
1 2 3 4 5 6 7 12 11 10 09 08

For all those women who seek to find
themselves.
May your journeys prove less dangerous
than Annie's,
but just as pleasurable.

PROLOGUE

Already the week sucked, and Monday had only begun. A call from her mother before nine a.m. didn't bode well. Annie Miller knew better than to answer her phone when Phyllis's number popped up on the caller ID. But her mother would keep calling until she had said whatever it was she had to say this morning. Just back from dropping her youngest at nursery school, Annie reluctantly picked up the handset. "Morning, Mom!" she said cheerfully, hoping to defuse the complaints that were sure to come.

"I just don't know what I'm going to do about your father," Phyllis's disapproving voice said without further ado.

"What's the matter? Is Dad all right?"

"He's never home!" Phyllis replied.

"But, Mom," Annie responded, "three months ago you were complaining that when he retired he'd be underfoot all the time, and you wouldn't be able to get

7

anything done. Why isn't he home?"

"Golf!" Phyllis sighed dramatically. "Golf! Golf! Golf! All day long. Every day. It's all he does anymore. Plays golf. Comes home to eat dinner, watches television, and then goes to bed. It's as if I'm not here at all. And he won't even go to church on Sundays now because he has an early tee time!"

"Have you spoken to him?" Annie ventured.

"I've tried," her mother answered. "He says it's his retirement, and he gets to do what he wants to do. You have to speak to him, Anne Elizabeth. He listens to you."

"What do you want me to say to him, Mom? He's worked hard all his life, and it is his retirement. Besides, it's probably just a phase. When he's gotten it out of his system you two can do something nice together. Maybe plan and take a nice trip."

Her mother sniffed derisively.

"Look, Mom, when the weather gets cold in a few months he won't be able to play golf all day," Annie reasoned.

"You always take *his* side!" Phyllis said angrily. "I'm going to call your sister! She'll understand!" And the phone went dead.

Annie sighed. "Yeah, sure," she muttered to herself as she put the handset back in its cradle. "Call the corporate lawyer for sympathy." Annie picked up the full laundry basket from the kitchen counter, where she had left it earlier, and headed for the washer, where the first load was in a final spin cycle.

The phone rang again, and seeing that it was the high school, Annie wondered if she had forgotten a meeting today. "Hello?"

"Mrs. Miller, it's Mrs. Long from the principal's office. I'm afraid Nathaniel is going to be sitting detention this afternoon." The principal's secretary sounded sympathetic, and almost embarrassed to be delivering such news.

Annie was astounded. Her oldest son, Nathaniel, and detention were two words that had never in his entire school career been spoken in the same sentence. "What on earth did he do?" Annie asked Mrs. Long.

There was a short pause, and then Mrs. Long said, "He called Mr. de Reeder a damned fool." Then she lowered her voice. "Not that the entire faculty doesn't agree with Nathaniel's assessment, of course." There was a humorous lilt to her words.

Annie sighed. "But Nathaniel should not have said whatever he was thinking. Please tell my son to apologize to Mr. de Reeder before school is out. And tell him to walk home. I won't be picking him up. And, Mrs.

Long, thanks for calling."

"Um, one more thing, Mrs. Miller," the high school secretary said apologetically. "Amy will also be sitting detention this afternoon."

"What has my daughter done?" Annie wanted to know. Amy had been so difficult of late, but then, she had always been Daddy's girl.

Mrs. Long couldn't refrain from giggling. "Well, the ninth-grade girls have had this dare going all spring," she began. "Some of them have been found out, and some of them have gotten away with it. Amy and another girl in her class were the last two to take the dare, and I'm afraid they got caught today."

"Caught doing *what?*" Annie asked nervously.

"Not wearing underpants, and wearing very short skirts," Mrs. Long said.

"Oh, my God!" Annie exclaimed. "And this was the dare?"

"Yes," Mrs. Long answered. "Please don't be too upset, Mrs. Miller. Girls this age are prone to do silly things. It isn't that unusual. They so desperately want to be accepted. No real harm done. The school nurse gave them each a pair of new briefs to put on when they were caught."

"How were they caught?" Annie asked, wondering if she really wanted to know.

"Ms. Franklin, the field hockey coach, noticed it when they were at practice."

"Tell my daughter to walk home with her brother," Annie said wearily.

"I will, Mrs. Miller," the high school secretary said. "You have a good day."

Annie sighed as she hung up. It didn't get any easier.

Just after eleven the middle school called. The twins, Lily and Rose, had freed all the animals in the science lab because caging animals was inhumane, the middle school assistant principal told Annie. Unfortunately several of the mice had found their way into the school's lunchroom, causing a stampede among the luncheon workers that had resulted in a sprained wrist for one of them. There would be a disciplinary hearing in the middle school principal's office Wednesday morning at ten a.m. It was requested that Mrs. Miller attend this hearing. Until then the twins were suspended from school, and they would be sitting detention that afternoon.

"Tell them to walk home," Annie said grimly, wondering what was next as she went out the door to pick up her youngest child at nursery school.

William Bradford Miller, named after his maternal grandfather, was four years old. Known to his parents as Whoops, he was Wills to everyone else. And Wills, it seemed, had brought balloons to school today for all of his friends, his teacher, Mrs. Gundersen said as she handed Annie the packet of extrasensitive sheepskin condoms.

"It's not the first time this kind of thing has happened," she told Annie laughingly, attempting to ease her embarrassment. "I get this kind of thing at least twice a year."

"I don't know how he could have possibly gotten hold of them," Annie mumbled, wondering if she could make Whoops walk home. Where had he gotten them? Nathaniel?

"Oh, you know little kids. Nosy." Mrs. Gundersen chuckled. "Aren't you, Wills?"

She ruffled his hair fondly. "See you Wednesday."

"Lunch and nap for you, buddy," Annie said.

"No nap!" Whoops said mutinously.

"Nap for both of us, kiddo," Annie told him as she strapped her son into his car seat. Yep, if today were any indication, the week was really going to suck.

CHAPTER ONE

Some days, like today, Annie Miller doubted
if she could continue to do it alone until all
the children were grown. But then, what
choice did she have? She hadn't said anything to them, but she wondered if they
remembered that two years ago today their
father had stepped off a curb in London
and been hit by one of those big red buses.
He was dead by the time he had reached
the hospital, and they had called her. It
amazed her that Nat, her larger-than-life
husband, could have been so easily killed.
Had he lived he would have told her, and
anyone else who would listen, that the bus
got the worst of it. And then he would have
laughed that big, booming laugh of his.

Annie let the tears come. She was alone,
and there was no one to see her cry. God
forbid that anyone think she couldn't handle
it. She knew what they said about her. They
said she was brave, a trooper, a wonderful

mother, devoted to her family. They said that Nat would have been proud of her, approved of everything she was doing. No one ever saw Annie Miller cry or show any sign of weakness. "That Annie Miller," she had heard a woman in church say of her, "she's one strong woman." Sometimes, Annie thought wryly. Only sometimes. At other times she wanted to run away, because it was all just too damned much for one woman to handle by herself.

They had met in college. He was a senior. She was a sophomore. Their story was the all-American fullback and the cute, perky cheerleader. Nat had asked her to marry him just before he graduated, but even at twenty-two Nathaniel Miller was a careful man. He wanted Annie to finish her education while he got a master's degree in business and then found a good job. And they had followed his plan carefully. Annie graduated and worked for a year before they were married in 1988. Nat Junior had been born in 1990, Amy in 1993. The twins, Rose and Lily, had been born in 1997. They had planned for four children, and felt quite foolish when a very romantic New Year's Eve had resulted in the little boy she and Nat laughingly dubbed Whoops during Annie's surprise pregnancy.

She had been born and raised in Egret Pointe. He had come from the city, but he loved her small town, and so they had settled there, buying an old colonial house on a dead-end street called Parkway Drive. They moved in just in time to set up the nursery for Nathaniel Junior. Nat claimed not to mind the long commute into the city and back each day. At least he didn't have to drive it, which had always been a relief to Annie. He took the six-thirty a.m. bus in, and a five-o'clock bus home five days a week.

Nat had been an account executive with a large public relations firm. He had been in London overseeing the opening of his company's new office when he had been killed.

Although his death had been ruled accidental, Annie had later learned from her husband's insurance company that there had been a rash of incidents going about London where people waiting to cross busy streets were being pushed into oncoming traffic. But if Nat had been pushed, no one came forward to say so, and no one had ever been charged. So the death was ruled accidental and the insurance company paid on Nat's policy.

Annie had been shocked to find that the

insurance policy Nat had wasn't enough for everything she would have to handle in future years. Her husband's company, however, had, in a burst of generosity, paid off the mortgage on their house and turned over his retirement fund to her. With her father's help Annie had invested almost all of it in funds that paid her an income. Her in-laws, her parents, and her sister helped out as best they could, but both sets of parents were retired now. Annie felt guilty taking anything from them.

She lived frugally, which wasn't difficult for her, but the children, particularly Amy, had a hard time with the tight budget that ensued after their father's death. Nathaniel had caught on quickly and gotten an after-school job he worked full-time in the summer. He was able to buy his own clothing now, and had a little pocket money for himself, for which Annie was glad. Girls, however, were a different animal. To be accepted, to be popular, girls needed fashion on the cutting edge. Amy was fourteen going on fifteen, and right now it was all about her.

Nathaniel was impatient with Amy. "You've got enough clothes," Annie had heard her son saying to his sister one day. "You don't need to wear something new to

16

school every damned morning. You might try concentrating more on your studies instead of on what some skanky little actress is wearing."

"You don't understand," Amy whined.

"What I understand," Nathaniel said, "is that Mom needs a new winter jacket. The one she's wearing she got seven years ago. But if you nag her enough she'll probably spend the money on you."

The twins, who cared only for animals, made fun of their older sister.

"Oh, Lily, do you like my jeans? They're by Poo-Poo originals. Paris wears them *all* the time," Rose said one evening in a falsetto voice, dancing about the room.

"Oh, Rose, do you think I'd look good in pink hair with purple stripes? *Teen Fashions* says it's the latest trend," Lily had replied, fluffing her hair as she pranced around.

Amy's answer to all of this was usually to burst into tears, run upstairs, and slam her bedroom door.

Annie shrugged to herself as she thought about her children. She wished she could give Amy anything she wanted, but she couldn't. Thank goodness Nathaniel understood the situation, and that the twins were right now low-maintenance kids. As for Whoops, he didn't realize that almost all of his toys and most of his clothing were hand-me-downs. He was a good-natured little boy.

But college was coming up for her oldest son, and Annie didn't know how they were going to make up the difference between tuition and the scholarships Nathaniel could gain. And she had no doubt he would get scholarships. But would they be enough? They would be getting letters from the acceptance offices any day now. Nathaniel had, of course, applied to several schools, including one of the state universities. But he had applied to Princeton and Yale as well. He had done a tour last summer of Ivy League schools with several of his classmates, and fallen in love with both places. Annie prayed her son would be refused or wait-listed. There just wasn't enough money for him to go to an Ivy League school, and she couldn't bear to disappoint him if he was accepted at either.

"Hello! Anyone home?"

"In the kitchen," Annie called to her sister, Lizzie. "What are you doing here, and in the middle of the day, and the middle of a workweek?" she asked her sibling.

They were a year apart, and had often been taken for twins in their youth. Both women were tall, although Annie was heavier now. Both had bright blue eyes and rich chestnut-colored hair. Annie's was pulled back in a horsetail and held with whatever she could find, which today was a rubber band. Lizzie's hair, however, was cut fashionably short, with a wisp of bangs swept to one side of her head.

"I came to take you to lunch," Lizzie announced.

"Why?" Annie wanted to know, immediately suspicious. Her younger sister was a corporate litigator with a big firm in the city. It wasn't like her to drive all the way out to Egret Pointe to have lunch. Such a drive out and back would mean a day of work lost.

"Because, like you, I remember what today is, even if everyone else has forgotten," Lizzie told her older sister.

Annie burst into tears. "Oh, Lizzie, thank you!" She sniffled.

"Mom's picking up Wills at nursery school," Lizzie continued. "We can pick him up after lunch. Okay? Go put something decent on, Annie."

"Could we stop at the cemetery after lunch?" Annie asked her sister.

"Sure. We'll get some flowers for the grave," Lizzie replied.

"I'll only be a few minutes," Annie said, heading for the stairs.

19

"I know," Lizzie murmured, resigned. It had always taken her at least thirty to forty minutes to dress and get ready to go out, but Annie could do it in ten minutes and look just as good. *No fair!* Lizzie thought.

Ten minutes later Annie descended the stairs again. She was wearing a pair of perfectly tailored pale beige cotton slacks and a white cotton sweater. There was a Navajo cornrow bracelet on her right arm, and turquoise earrings clipped to her ears. A touch of blue eye shadow, a bit of blush, and pale coral lipstick had completed her preparations.

"How do you do it?" Lizzie said. "You look great, as always."

"It's all at least five years old," Annie told her sister. "After Nat died I realized I wasn't going to be able to be Talbot's best customer anymore. I take really good care of what I have. The kids need more than I do. They're growing."

"Speaking of my niece," Lizzie said with a grin, "there's a box in the back of the car for Amy. I forgot to bring it in, so don't let me go back to town with it."

"You spoil her," Annie said, and she kissed her sister's cheek. "Thank you!"

"I got her a couple of those little dresses that are becoming so popular with girls her age. Short. Flirty. Baby dollish," Lizzie told her sister. "I figured with spring in full swing, and the end of school in another month and a half, she could use them."

The two sisters exited the house and got into Lizzie's Porsche convertible.

"Where are we going?" Annie asked.

"I thought the country club," Lizzie answered. "It's near."

"I don't have a membership there any-more," Annie said softly.

"I do," Lizzie replied as she swung the silver Porsche out of Parkway Drive and down another tree-lined street and gunned the car out onto the road that led toward the Egret Pointe Country Club. "Oh, shit!"

"What's the matter?" Annie asked.

"Cop car," Lizzie said, and automatically pulled over. "I wasn't even doing the speed limit yet. These damned cops think anyone who doesn't drive an SUV, van, or sedan must be looking to drag race."

"Hey, Lizzie, thought that was you," the patrolman said as he walked up to the driver's side of the car.

"Hey, Glenn, you going to give me a ticket?" Lizzie wanted to know.

"Nope, just wanted to say hello. We don't see you a whole lot around here these days.

You weren't home last Christmas," Glenn said.

"Got invited to go skiing in Aspen with some clients," Lizzie answered him.

"Married yet?" Glenn drawled, smiling down at her.

"No time," Lizzie responded candidly.

"Hey, Glenn!"

"Hey, Annie. Didn't see you sitting there." Annie laughed. Glenn never saw anyone or anything when Lizzie was about.

"You married yet?" Lizzie asked the policeman.

"Waiting for you, honeybunch," he told her.

Lizzie colored. "We've got a reservation," she said.

"Enjoy your lunch," Glenn replied, and walked back to his patrol car.

"He's been sweet on you since high school," Annie said as they once again headed toward the country club. "He's a good man."

"I know," Lizzie answered. "I'm just not ready."

"You were forty-one in February," Annie noted.

"And you'll be forty-three in December," Lizzie remarked. "You're a widow with five kids and a modest — no, meager — income.

I'm a lawyer with a seven-figure income, a Porsche, and a three-bedroom, two-and-a-half-bath co-op, all paid for in full. I win!"

"But I've been loved and cherished, while you live a cold corporate existence," Annie countered. "I think I win."

They were both laughing when Lizzie pulled into the country club parking lot.

"Not so cold," Lizzie said. "My nights can get pretty hot sometimes."

"Too much information!" Annie said with a grin. "But I'm surprised that you would risk your reputation, when in your business reputation is everything. There aren't too many good women litigators, sis."

"Not to worry. I have the Channel to satisfy my wicked desires and keep me sane. As far as the wide world knows, I'm celibate: a prim, no-nonsense attorney with a killer instinct," Lizzie replied. "The other partners love me," she said smugly.

The club dining room was practically empty. They sat at a table overlooking the golf course. Lizzie ordered a salad plate, and Annie a club sandwich. Their lunch and their iced teas came quickly. When they were alone again Lizzie spoke.

"You know, now that Nat has been gone two years, you ought to get the Channel. It can be anything you want. It doesn't just have to be mindless and guilt-free sex. You devote yourself to the kids, Annie, and I know from Mom that you don't have any social life outside of school events. You need something for yourself."

"Basic cable is all I can afford," her sibling answered. "And it's all I can do to keep up with that. They keep raising their rates all the time. If I could afford something special I'd get the Disney Channel for Whoops. And don't go offering to give it to me for my birthday," Annie cautioned her younger sister. "I see that look in your eye. I'm too tired to watch much television these days anyway."

"If I do something for the kids, will you let me help?" Lizzie asked.

"Like what?"

"Remember Stoneledge Lake?" Lizzie said.

"Our old camp in Vermont? Is it still in existence?" Annie smiled, remembering the summers she and Lizzie had spent there.

"It's still there. It's better than ever, and I would love to send the girls this summer," Lizzie said. "Amy is almost too old, but she won't be fifteen until the fall, and if she likes it next year she could be a counselor in training. But the twins are the perfect age for Stoneledge Lake. I'm going to Tuscany for a month in August. I've rented a villa that's staffed. I'm taking Mom, and I'd love to take Nathaniel as a graduation gift. If he needs to come back before we do for college that's fine, but he's been the man of the family since he was sixteen. I think he could use a break, too."

"Oh, Lizzie, that is so generous of you!" Annie said, and she felt her eyes beginning to tear. "But it's too much, really!"

"Oh, pooh! I can afford it, and who else have I got to spend my money on except my nieces and nephews? Look, I'm getting Mom off Dad's neck so he can golf to his heart's content. If the girls go to Stoneledge Lake and Nathaniel goes to Italy with us, you are left with only one little boy to look after. It will be like a vacation for you." She scooped up the last bit of coleslaw from her lettuce.

"I don't know how Amy is going to feel about camp," Annie began.

"She'll hate the idea. Remember how we bitched and complained to Mom and Dad the first year we went? But Amy's at that age where you and she are going to be at sword point more often than not," Lizzie remarked. "You need a little bit of a break from her, sis. Let me tell the kids of *our* summer plans, okay? Amy will take it better coming from me than coming from you. I told Mom I'd stay the night, so I don't have to go into the city until the morning."

"One kid," Annie mused. "The girls will be away for eight weeks, right?"

Lizzie chuckled. "Eight glorious weeks!" she answered. "I've got plane tickets for three the night of July thirty-first."

"I'd have Nathaniel for a month before you took off," Annie said. "He's got a summer job lined up, but only for a month. I thought he would need August to get ready." She smiled almost to herself. "Just me and my boys. And then a month with just one. Lizzie, I don't know how to thank you!"

"The look on your face just has," her sister responded.

"The twins are going to be over the moon, but I know Amy had a summer of hanging out with all her friends planned," Annie said slowly. "Oh, the fights we would have had. Thank you for saving me, Lizzie!"

Throwing caution to the wind, they ordered dessert, sharing a tartufo between them before leaving the club to drive to their parents' house. They found their mother feeding her youngest grandson ice cream. Whoops was looking extremely pleased with himself as he mongreled down the dessert.

"Thank heavens you're here!" Phyllis said. "Doesn't this child take a nap anymore?" she demanded to know, her gaze fixing itself on Annie.

"He does if you put him down and tell him that's it," Annie replied.

"Well, I asked him if he took a nap, and he said no. I am utterly exhausted chasing after him! Take the little barbarian home." She sagged against the counter.

"Thanks, Mom, for picking him up," Annie said, giving her parent a kiss on her cheek. "It was nice to be out for lunch with Lizzie."

"Are you going to accept your sister's help for the summer?" Phyllis wanted to know. "Isn't she just the most generous woman?"

"I am going to accept her help, Mom, and you are one hundred percent right. She is the best sister anyone could have! Hey, isn't this a first? You and I agreeing on something," Annie teased her mother.

"Go home!" Phyllis said with a fond swat at her elder daughter. Then she turned to Lizzie. "I serve supper at six o'clock sharp. Your father likes to see the world news."

"I'll be back in time," Lizzie said. "I just want to see the kids and tell them our plans. I thought it might go down easier if I told them."

"Yes," Phyllis agreed. "Especially with Amy."

"Amy's just like you, Mom," Lizzie said with a laugh. "See you later."

As they returned to Parkway Drive, Annie said, "You know, you're right. Amy is like Mom. I never realized it, but now I know why we don't get on easily."

"But I'll bet Mom never went to school in a short skirt without her drawers," Lizzie said, laughing. "Did you tell her about Amy?"

"I did not!" Annie said. "She would have said it was all my fault."

The twins were already home, and greeted their aunt enthusiastically. Nathaniel and Amy came off the high school bus a few minutes later.

"I have exciting news," Lizzie said. "Come into the den and let me tell you."

"You've found a man, are getting married, and I'm going to be your bridesmaid," Amy guessed, looking hopeful.

"What do I need a man for?" Lizzie demanded of her eldest niece. "No. It's even better. I'm sending you, Lily, and Rose to Stoneledge Lake Camp for Girls this summer. Remember? Your Mom and I went there for five summers. It is such a cool place. Tennis, field hockey, soccer, riding,

28

swimming, trips. You know, the whole camp experience! You leave June twenty-eighth!" She smiled broadly.

The twins began to whoop delightedly. They flung themselves at Lizzie, thanking her, hugging her. Amy, however, was obviously confused by her good fortune.

"Why are you sending us away?" she asked. "Is someone dying? Is that it? You don't want us to be here when they die?"

"Good grief, Amy, you are such a drama queen," Lizzie replied. "No one is dying. I just thought it would be a cool thing for my nieces to follow in their mother's and aunt's footsteps."

"You aren't sending Nathaniel to camp," Amy noted.

"Nope, he's coming with me and your grandmother to Italy," Lizzie said.

"Italy?" Amy said.

"Yep, museums, ancient ruins, history," Lizzie murmured, winking at Nathaniel.

"Ewww," Amy groaned. "I'd rather go to camp."

"That's just what I thought!" Lizzie said. "You see how alike we are, kiddo? Oh, there's a box in the backseat of the Porsche for you. Go get it, and give us a fashion show. Rose, Lily, you and I will be going camp shopping one Saturday soon, okay?"

"You don't have to bribe us," Lily said.

"Yeah," Rose agreed. "We think camp will be great. Thanks, Aunt Lizzie!"

"Museums? Ruins? History?" Nathaniel said, grinning at his aunt.

"A villa in Tuscany. Wine. Italian girls as ripe as the grapes, a hot little car," Lizzie murmured seductively with a twinkle.

"Better," Nathaniel said. "Thanks, Auntie. Oh, Mom, I got accepted at State, wait-listed at Yale, *and* I got accepted to Princeton! I'm going to Princeton!" He looked so happy and hopeful.

"That's wonderful," Annie said slowly, "but, Nathaniel, going to Princeton depends on the kind of aid or scholarships you get. You know that, honey." She felt terrible. She felt awful. Her beautiful son deserved to go to Princeton if that was where he wanted to go.

"I'm being given an alumni scholarship, Mom, for ten thousand dollars. I have to keep my grades up, of course, but if I do it's good for the four years."

"Is it ten thousand for the four years, or every year?" Lizzie asked.

"Ten thousand a year for the four years," he answered her.

"That's very good," Lizzie said, looking to her sister.

"Princeton is thirty-three thousand a year," Annie said.

"He should be able to get almost enough aid to cover it," Lizzie said, looking meaningfully at her older sister.

"We can't make any decision, Nathaniel, until we work out the logistics of the financing," Annie responded quietly. "Lizzie, you had better get going. You know Mom and her six-on-the-dot supper hour."

Lizzie took the hint. "Walk me to the car," she said, taking her sister's arm.

"Don't even offer," Annie said softly as they finally stood by the Porsche.

"Let me make up the difference between the aid and the scholarship," Lizzie said. "We can wait till he has all the aid packages."

"I can ante up five thousand a year, but no more," Annie told her sister. "If he gets ten more in aid it's still not enough. And he's going to need pocket money."

"He'll get an on-campus job," Lizzie said. "Look, my firm gives scholarship aid to partners' and employees' kids with good grades. Nathaniel has very good grades, and helping a kid at Princeton is just up our corporate alley. Don't be so proud, Annie, that you deny your oldest son his dream school. You know damned well that if Nat

31

were alive he would move heaven and earth to make it happen for his oldest son."

Annie was silent, and then she finally said, "Okay, but only because I don't think Amy will go anyplace expensive. God, Lizzie, I really owe you big-time."

Lizzie Bradford hugged Annie. "Family is everything," she said. "Even a cold-ass corporate bitch like me knows that." She slid into the driver's seat of her car. "I'll call you in a few days." And then she was gone.

And suddenly life was smooth for Annie and her family. Her sister's firm came up with ten thousand dollars in scholarship money for Nathaniel's first year at Princeton, renewable as long as he kept his grades up. And the guidance counselor at the high school worked with her son so that when graduation day arrived, Nathaniel's first year's tuition at college was taken care of, and Annie's small fund could be kept for any shortfall in the following years. Her son graduated as his class's valedictorian. School was over until September. Summer had begun in earnest.

The morning of June twenty-eighth came, and Annie drove her three daughters to a central meeting point some forty miles from Egret Pointe, where the camp bus had come to pick up the girls going to Stoneledge

Lake Camp. Lily and Rose were still wildly enthusiastic. Amy, however, was having serious second thoughts until she heard her name called. She turned to find herself face-to-face with the most popular girl in her class, Brittany Cowles.

"Hi, Amy! You're going to Stoneledge? It's my third summer."

"My first, but then, duh, of course you know that. My mom and aunt went for five summers," Amy responded nervously.

"You're a legacy? That is so cool! Come sit with me on the bus. Maybe we'll be in the same cabin," Brittany said. "Hi, twins!"

Amy turned. "Well, Mom, I gotta go." She gave her mother a quick kiss and hurried to join Brittany.

"Brittany Cowles is one of the most popular girls in high school," Rose informed her mother. "I hope Amy doesn't act all slobbery and dorky around her."

"We're waiting to see how she behaves before we admit she's our sister," Lily told Annie. "Listen, thank Aunt Lizzie for us again."

"I will," Annie said. "Have a great time. We sure did."

The twins hugged their mother and climbed onto the bus. Annie watched it pull out of the IGA parking lot, and then, getting into her own car, drove home.

The house was so quiet with the girls away. She got letters, and to her relief all three of her daughters were having a marvelous time. The twins were doing everything the camp offered. Amy's letters were full of *Brit this* and *Brit that.* But she was having a good time. July seemed to speed by, and in a few days Nathaniel would be on his way to Italy with his aunt and his grandmother. It would be just Annie and Wills.

Lizzie came by a few days before they were to leave. It was the weekend, and she had come out to Egret Pointe to help Phyllis, who couldn't seem to decide what she wanted to take with her. "She's driving me crazy. It's Tuscany. It's going to be August. What the hell is there to decide?" Lizzie grumbled.

Annie laughed. "She's done nothing for the last month but talk about it," she told her sister. "She's so excited she hasn't complained once about Dad and his golf."

"I had forgotten what she's like. I hope she doesn't ride Nathaniel. I want this to be a wonderful trip for him," Lizzie said. "His passport came, didn't it?"

"It came," Nathaniel said, joining them. "Ma, I was just on the computer. You've got an e-mail. It's from someplace called the

Spa, and it says you've won."

"Junk mail probably. Delete it, sweetie."

"No!" Lizzie almost shrieked.

"It's junk mail," Annie repeated.

"I don't think it is," Lizzie told her sister.

"You ladies figure it out," Nathaniel told them. "I've got to get to work." He bent and kissed his mother's cheek. "See you later."

"Come on," Lizzie said, dragging her sister into the den, where the computer was kept. Seating herself before the PC, she clicked the mouse on the message. "Omigod! Omigod! Omigod!" She gasped as she read it. "You've won, Annie! You've won the grand prize!" Then she sat back. "I can't believe it. You've won!"

"What are you talking about?"

"I entered you in a contest," Lizzie began. "Remember you told me you couldn't afford any extras on your cable bill? Well, the Channel Corporation — they're the people who own the Channel — are the ones renovating the old Gardener estate as a women's spa. They were having a contest. The big prize was a week at the spa, all expenses paid. There were some smaller prizes, among them one hundred free subscriptions to the Channel for a year. I was trying to win one of those for you. But this e-mail says you've won the grand prize! Eight days, seven nights, and you've got a free year's subscription to the Channel! I can't believe it."

"You entered me in a contest?" Annie said. *"Why?"*

"You need to live your fantasies," Lizzie told her sister.

"I don't have any fantasies," Annie replied.

"Every woman has fantasies," Lizzie answered softly. She took her sister's hands in hers and looked into Annie's pretty face. "Sis, Nat is gone. He isn't coming back. It's been two years. And in that time you've devoted yourself mind, body, and soul to the kids. You are a spectacular mom, but you've lost yourself in the process. The Channel lets you live your fantasies, mild or wild. It's just for you. And you need something just for you. Trust me on this one, Annie."

"I can't accept this prize, Lizzie. It's for the third week in August. Sure, the four older kids will be away, but what am I going to do with Wills? A spa vacation with a four-year-old? Not going to happen." The phone rang, and Annie picked it up. "Hello? Oh, hi, Mavis. What? You're kidding? When? Wills? He'd love it! Yes, of course I'll let him go. I trust you and Ted. He's going to

36

be thrilled! Look, my sister's here. Can we talk later? Okay. And thanks so much, Mavis. Bye." Annie slowly set the telephone back in its cradle and turned to look at her sister. "Talk about spooky."

"What is it?" Lizzie asked, cocking an eyebrow.

"Mavis and Ted Iaonne have been planning a trip to Disney World in Orlando for a couple of months. Their little boy, Mark, is one of Wills's friends. They were in nursery school together, and are starting kindergarten in September. They were taking their nephew, who's two years older than Mark, with them. He fell out of a tree this afternoon and broke not one, but both of his legs. He's not going anywhere. They want to take Wills with them."

"What a great trip for Wills," Lizzie said. "When?"

"That's the spooky part," Annie replied. "It's the third week in August."

"But that is perfect!" Lizzie enthused. "Now you can accept your prize, and I don't know anyone in this world who deserves a week at a spa more than you do, sis!"

"What about this Channel of yours, though? It's not for kids, is it?"

"Nope, only ladies," Lizzie said. "Don't

worry about the kids gaining access to it. They give you a special remote. It's programmed to your touch, and *only* your touch. Even if one of the kids got it, it wouldn't work for them."

"What do you fantasize about?" Annie asked her sister.

Lizzie laughed. "Extraordinarily kinky sex," she said with a grin. "And sex in the Channel is guilt-free, disease-free, complication-free. I can be anything I want, and have any man I want. After a long day of being a tough bitch, it's nice to come home, shower, and slip into the Channel for an evening of diversion."

"I wonder why they're opening a spa, and why here in Egret Pointe?" Annie considered. "There must be more exotic locations."

"The Channel Corporation is a privately held company," Lizzie said. "Egret Pointe may not be exotic, but it is charming and has an air of old-world exclusivity about it. The Gardener estate was falling apart. No one has lived up there for years. That quirky Grecian temple architecture isn't for everyone, and the zoning isn't for multiple houses. It was residential, but no one wanted to buy it because of all the zoning restrictions. The town board rezoned it for the Channel Corporation because they agreed to renovate and rebuild it. It's called the Spa at Egret Pointe. I hear it's absolutely gorgeous, and ultra-, ultraplush."

"Just the place for a tired widow with five kids," Annie said wryly.

"Hey, you won. That's all that counts. Accept your prize and enjoy every minute of it. Get massaged, salt scrubbed, manicured, pedicured, and facialed to your heart's content. They will feed you and cosset you to bits and pieces, and you deserve it!"

"I'll bet they have aerobic classes for the already skinny ladies who live on mineral water and lettuce leaves," Annie said with a chuckle.

"Who cares? Take a meditation class. Do a little tai chi," Lizzie told her. "And you can feel totally superior knowing that you are much better off than all the other women there. So you're widowed and have five kids, but you're loved, and despite it all you are content with your life."

"I suppose," Annie replied.

"You aren't content?" Lizzie was surprised. "What do you want then?"

"I'm a little bored with being the Widow Miller, and a lot bored with being held up all over town as a paragon of motherhood. I must be more than just that," Annie said.

"Gee," Lizzie said, "I always thought you were happy."

"I was. I am. But my husband is gone. My oldest son is off to college in the fall. Three more years and Amy will be gone too. In ten years I'll be down to one kid, in my mid-fifties, and when Wills is gone what's left? I'm stuck in a big house in constant need of repairs. Alone. With no life."

Lizzie shook her head. "I never thought of it that way," she remarked.

"Of course you haven't," Annie answered. "You have a career, and you will always have a career if you want it. The law won't leave you, but your kids do, and that's the way it should be. But it doesn't make it any easier."

"You've got a college degree," Lizzie said.

"In history," Annie noted.

"You could teach," Lizzie suggested.

"I'd have to go back to get teaching credits and to get certified," Annie said. "Besides, I don't want to teach."

"You have work experience," Lizzie replied. "When Wills is set in kindergarten get something part-time. People are always looking for help."

"I worked in Dad's insurance office for a year before Nat and I married," Annie responded glumly. "I typed letters, sent out forms, and filed. I am barely computer literate, and only because Nat insisted. I'm not big on technology."

"There has to be something you can do, and earn a living at the same time," Lizzie insisted. "And now that you've started thinking about it, something is bound to come to you or just fall into your lap. It always happens that way."

"How you can be such a tough litigator and believe in coincidence continues to astound me." Annie laughed.

"You don't have to make any decisions now," Lizzie said. "Right now the only thing you have to do is decide what you are going to take to the spa."

"What does one take to a spa?" Annie asked her sister. "I'm a spa virgin."

"Did they suggest anything in the e-mail?" Lizzie queried.

"They said comfortable and casual clothing," Annie replied.

"Okay, you'll be there seven nights, so I'd say three pairs of nice slacks, five tops. You can mix and match. Maybe two pairs of sweatpants and a couple of tees. The usual amount of underwear, a few scarves to make the slacks seem a bit dressier at dinner, that great cornrow bracelet, and some of your turquoise earrings. Nightgown."

"I wear pj's now," Annie said. "After our

41

little Whoops it seemed less provocative, and it was always more difficult to get out of them for sex. It gave him time to put a condom on, instead of just pushing up my nightie and jumping aboard." She grinned. "After Nat died I never switched back. Never saw any reason to do it."

"Take a nightgown," Lizzie said softly. "This spa experience is going to be a whole new beginning for you. Oh, better take a bathing suit or two. There's a pool, and I'm sure they'll have an aquacise class."

"Me? In a bathing suit?" Annie laughed. "I don't think I own one anymore."

"Then we'll go buy you a couple," Lizzie told her older sister.

"I'll look like a whale, and all that cellulite I'm sporting these days . . ." Annie groaned. "Don't make me get a bathing suit. Please!"

"Exercising in the water is wonderful. I do two classes a week at my gym. There's no strain on your muscles in the water. And it's good for your heart," Lizzie said briskly. "What size are you now?"

"Don't make me say it," Annie pleaded piteously.

Lizzie looked sternly at her sister. "Size, please!"

"Sixteen," Annie admitted.

"You don't look it," Lizzie told her. "Get

42

your credit card, sis! We're off to the mall to buy you a bathing suit. They'll all be on sale now. Oh, I just *love* sales!"

CHAPTER TWO

"Mrs. Miller?" the smartly uniformed man at the door asked.

"Yes," Annie replied.

"I'm Karl, your chauffeur from the spa. I'll take your bag." Picking it up with a smile, he waited while she locked the door, and then he ushered her to the standing white limousine, opening the door so she could get in. Then he put her bag in the trunk. "It will just be a few minutes," he told her as he slid into the driver's seat.

"Thank you," Annie said. And then she sat back to enjoy her first taste of luxury. The vehicle was cool and dim. The leather seats were unbelievably soft. She was on her way, she thought as they pulled out of Parkway Drive. Had she forgotten anything? She didn't think so. Dad knew where she was in case of emergency, and so did the camp. Wills was off with the Iaonnes. The lure of Disney World had proved too great to permit him any fear of being without his mother. Lizzie, Phyllis, and Nathaniel had called from their villa in Tuscany already. The flight had been perfect. The dog, the two cats, and the rabbit were at the vet for the week. No, she had not forgotten anything. Suddenly her time was her own, and Annie realized that she was really looking forward to it. She couldn't wait to see what had been done to the old Gardener estate.

The limo glided along the shore road, and then swinging right toward the water, it stopped before a pair of decorative black iron gates flanked on one side by a gatehouse and on the other by a stone pillar to which was attached a bronze plaque with gold lettering that read THE SPA AT EGRET POINTE. Her driver honked once. A man emerged from the gatehouse, peered at the limo, then went to open the gates. Her car rolled past the gatekeeper, who tipped his cap to her politely as they passed.

The road wound down and around. There was lush old-growth greenery on both sides of it, obviously well cared-for, well trimmed. Someone must have been taking care of the estate grounds all these years, Annie thought. Maybe the man at the gate? And then they were pulling up before what looked like an ancient Greek temple. The limo came to a stop, and immediately a young man was opening the car's door and handing her out of the limousine.

"Mrs. Miller, I'm Devyn, your PA as long as you are with us," he said, smiling. He was of medium height, blue-eyed, blond, and obviously fit, by the look of the arms that protruded from beneath his short-sleeved shirt. He was wearing tight white slacks and a white tee. "Karl will take your luggage inside."

"What's a PA?" Annie asked.

"Personal assistant," Devyn said with a grin.

"My God, just like a rock star." Annie laughed. "What does a PA do, Devyn?"

"I do whatever you want me to do, ma'am," he told her earnestly.

"Oh." A few decidedly wicked thoughts, very un-Annie-like came to mind. Lizzie would definitely approve, she decided.

"If you'll allow me to escort you inside, you'll need to register, even if you are our grand-prize winner," Devyn told her, and, his hand beneath her elbow, he led her into the Greek temple. "Ms. Buckley, who is currently overseeing the opening of the spa, is waiting to greet you. Actually she's a bigwig with the Channel Corp., which is why I think they sent her to do this. The company

46

really wants this to succeed."

The lobby was both intimate and elegant. The carpeting was deep green, and so plush Annie thought she might sink up to her knees in it. The chairs and couches were in shades of ivory and green, both solids and stripes. An elegant stained-glass dome in the lobby's low ceiling allowed natural light to flood the room. But there were also lamps set upon Brazilian rosewood tables too. Annie registered at the marble front desk.

"Welcome to the Spa, Mrs. Miller," the girl at the desk said. She was pretty and perky, and dressed in a flattering pale rose-colored raw-silk blazer. "You are, as you can see, our very first guest. We hope your stay will be everything you wish it to be. Devyn has your keys, and he'll get you to your suite," she chirped.

"Thank you," Annie replied. A suite, no less. She turned, and coming across the lobby toward her was a vaguely familiar woman, her hands stretched out in welcome.

"Annie, do you remember me? I'm Nora Buckley, and for the interim I'm the general manager here at the spa. I wanted to welcome you officially as the grand-prize winner of our contest. With all the entries we got, it's amazing that a woman from Egret Pointe itself would win." She smiled.

Nora Buckley. Of course, Annie thought. There had been some sort of scandal a few years back. Nora and her husband had been in some kind of fuss over their divorce. Nora had fallen into some kind of mysterious coma, but she had recovered. There had been another woman involved, Annie recalled. The husband had ended up in the local poky after an altercation with the girlfriend, and he had died in the night. The gossip had been all over the country club. Everyone had said the husband was a shit and Nora was victimized, but in the end it had all worked out for her.

"Of course I remember you," Annie fibbed. "The club, right?"

Nora Buckley nodded, a faintly amused smile on her lips. She was a beautiful woman with one of those ageless faces, that flawless pale, creamy skin that redheads seemed to possess, and limpid gray-green eyes. "Yes, the club," she replied.

"Didn't you used to work at that antique shop in town?" Annie asked.

"Yes, I did, but then I was offered a job with the Channel Corp. It was too good an offer to turn down," Nora responded. "I don't recall ever seeing you there."

"Too pricey for me," Annie told her, "but my sister met you there several times. She's a lawyer, and has the income for antiques. I remember she always said the owner of the shop was very knowledgeable, and very dishy, if I may quote her."

Nora laughed. "Yes, Kyle is very dishy. I did love the place, but when opportunity knocks it's always smart to answer. I did find him a lovely older lady to assist him. Kyle has an eye for women, and it wouldn't have done to have some young thing in there with him. She would have spent more time on her back than at the front desk." And Nora laughed again. "Bad for his business," she noted. "But enough of my past. I'd like you to have dinner with me tonight, Annie. Part of the perks of being our grand-prize winner. It will give me a chance to answer all your questions about the Spa."

An efficient young woman hurried up and said, "Ms. Buckley, the press limo and the other guests are just coming through the gates."

"I must go," Nora told Annie. "I'll see you tonight at dinner. Eight o'clock. Devyn will bring you to my private dining room." Then she hurried off.

"If you're ready to go now . . . ?" Devyn said, and she nodded.

49

He led her to a small open elevator, ushering her inside and closing the gate behind them. "You've been given the penthouse suite," Devyn said. "There's only one here at the Spa. Most of the rooms and other suites are in the wings of the main building. They did a really terrific restoration. You should see the before pictures. They're on display in the library." The elevator stopped, and, opening the gate, Devyn led the way across the carpeted corridor to a large double mahogany door with brass fittings. "This is your key card," he said, showing her how to insert it. "Don't even think about it. Just put it in and get it out quickly."

Annie heard a faintly audible click, and the door swung open. It was then that she noticed it had no knob. "Where's the doorknob?" she asked Devyn.

"Isn't that just the greatest security measure?" he said. "The door opens when you use the key card. You can't open the door from the outside without that card. We've got terrific security, but places like this attract all kinds." He preceded her into the suite.

Be cool, Annie told herself as her gaze swept the room. *Try not to behave like a geek.* "Oh, my!" she said softly.

"Yeah," he echoed her admiration. "It

really is pretty neat, isn't it?"

Annie laughed. "How old are you?" she asked him.

"Old enough to work at the Spa," he told her, grinning. "Why?"

"You remind me of my son," she lied. "First job?"

"Yeah, first real one," Devyn admitted. "After I graduated college I backpacked around a bit. But it was time to find a job. I majored in English, of all things in this day and age. Didn't want to teach, and then a friend of my father's said that the Channel Corp. was hiring. My brother says that even though they're a privately held corporation they're solid, and a foot in the door is a foot in the door. They gave me and the rest of the guys they hired a quick course in hotel management and manners, and here we are." He moved across the living room in which they now stood with her bag. "This is your bedroom," he told her, flinging open a door. "I'll put your luggage here. Would you like me to send a maid to unpack for you?"

"No, thank you," Annie said, swallowing back a giggle.

"This is for you," Devyn said, handing her a small gold button. "It's my call button. You can clip it to whatever you're wearing.

Just press it when you want me. I'll give you an hour to unpack and get yourself acclimated. Then I'll be back to pick you up. I've scheduled a manicure, pedicure, facial, and massage for you this afternoon." Then with a quick smile he was gone out the door of the suite, closing it behind him.

Annie stood very still and looked all about her. The living room of the suite was beautiful. The thick carpet was cream colored. So was all the upholstered furniture, a couch, and two extra-large club chairs, one with an ottoman. The fabric on them appeared to be a nubby textured silk. And there were large multicolored pillows in purple and green, both solids and patterns. There was a fireplace on one wall of the living room. The tables and the chests were of the same beautiful Brazilian rosewood she had seen in the lobby. The lamps were ceramic, palest green, with floral designs. She slid out of her shoes. It seemed almost sacrilegious to walk about on this carpet in shoes.

A pair of louvered doors caught her eye. Walking over to them, she folded them back to discover a little wet bar, a microwave, and a small fridge. Curious, she opened it. Inside she found six small bottles of San Pellegrino water, a round of Brie, a little net of Gouda, and a rectangle of extra-sharp cheddar. The cabinet above held a single box of whole-grain crackers and some white plates and crystal glasses. Annie closed the fridge and then the painted louvres.

On the coffee table was a crystal bowl of fresh peaches, plums, and apricots. On a small sideboard was a vase of pale lavender roses. She saw a card with the roses and, reaching for it, opened it. *Congratulations to our winner! Enjoy your stay with us!* The card was signed, *Mr. Nicholas, CEO, the Channel Corporation.* The card smelled faintly of sandalwood. *My goodness,* Annie thought. *Wait until I tell Lizzie about all of this.* Annie smiled. She'd save the card to show her sister.

A wall of windows ran across one end of the room. There were draperies on either side of the expanse of glass, cream silk with a tiny green sprig, and delicate sheer curtains that she discovered could be drawn aside, which led her to a door. There was a terrace beyond the door and, stepping out on it, she found it was at the top of the front facade of the temple-like building. The terrace was furnished with wicker furniture with green, white, and rose cushions, glass tables, and great pottery urns with trees and flowers. The view was spectacular. All of the bay was visible to her eye. *God,* Annie thought, *this is paradise for certain.* She turned and went back inside. It felt strange to be in a beautiful place and not besieged by five kids. She quite liked it, Annie decided.

Having inspected the living room, she decided to check out the bedroom. As in the living room, the carpet was cream colored. A chair rail divided the wall. Below it the wall was painted pale green. Above the chair rail was a beautiful hand-blocked wallpaper with a cream background and pink lilies with green leaves. The windows were hung with Jefferson swags in a fabric that matched the wallpaper, and sheer cream curtains in a check pattern. The furniture was country French provincial in a warm golden brown walnut. The bed was king-sized, and canopied in pale green watered silk, its bed curtains a pale green and cream stripe. There was a small pink marble fireplace opposite the bed, and a door opened onto the large terrace outside her windows.

Slowly Annie unpacked her suitcase, utilizing both the elegant bureau and the closet. Then, taking her little toiletry case, she went into the bathroom. It was huge. It had a sunken bathtub, a commode, a bidet, and a large glassed-in shower. A beautiful shell-shaped sink was set into a marble counter-top; her little case looked shabby on it. The floor was tiled in large squares of dark green porcelain.

A large gilt mirror hung over the counter and sink. Curious, she opened the sink cabinet's drawers and discovered a supply of everything she could possibly want or need. Creams. Lotions. A natural tooth-paste. A toothbrush. A beautiful carved wooden comb and a boar's-bristle hair-brush. Then she noticed a small card on the counter. It read, *Please Accept These Toiletries as Our Gift.* Was there anything she needed from her own case? Annie queried herself. And then she put the little nylon case back in her suitcase. *Why not?* she thought. *I'm the grand-prize winner, aren't I?*

Finished unpacking, Annie went out on the terrace and sat down. She had never in her whole life known luxury like this, and she liked it. She liked the peace and quiet. She liked not being importuned by her children or the animals they had. She had never in her entire life taken a vacation alone. Until she went to college, vacations were always family affairs at their cottage down at the shore, except, of course, for those few summers she and Lizzie had spent at Stoneledge Lake Camp for Girls. But they didn't count. Being at camp with your younger sister wasn't a vacation. And after her freshman year in college Annie had come home and spent the summer helping her mother get Lizzie ready for college; and after that she had just come home every summer. Lizzie didn't come home.

Lizzie went to Europe with friends the summer between her freshman and sophomore years. She did a two-month bicycle tour across New England the following summer. And the last summer she was in college, before law school, Lizzie was the au pair to the children of the man who was the senior partner in the law firm in which she now was a partner. While in law school she didn't come home except briefly at Christmas. Yet she was still their mother's favorite.

So Annie never went anywhere alone, because Phyllis cried that she couldn't let both her girls leave her, and because Annie was the oldest she had to stay home with her mother. Her father had rolled his eyes in sympathetic amusement, but Bill Bradford had learned long ago to save the battles for the important stuff. Annie would have to fight for herself. But Annie had been content to remain at home. Or had she? she wondered now. Maybe she just hadn't wanted to fight with her mother. Phyllis never fought fair. She flung threats and guilt about with wild abandon. "But this is my summer, thanks to you, Lizzie," Annie said softly.

"Mrs. Miller? It's Devyn. Time to get going." He came out onto the terrace. "Hey, you aren't ready."

"Sure I am," Annie said. "What are we doing?"

"You're not in your Spa robe," he told her. "It's in the bathroom closet, ma'am."

"Unless there's some rule about it, call me Annie," she said. "That 'ma'am' is a killer, kiddo. Okay, give me a minute. What should I wear beneath the robe? I don't want to make a faux pas."

"Just briefs and your Spa slippers will do," he told her. "I'll wait in the living room for you."

Just briefs? This really was going to be an adventure, Annie thought, amused. Dressed in what was considered appropriate, Annie followed Devyn to the elevator. "Tell me I'm not going to have to walk through the lobby in this getup?"

"Nah," he said. "We're going to the terrace level. The house is built on the hillside, and so we can utilize what would otherwise be a basement. The treatment rooms all look out on the gardens and lawns. Ah, here we are."

Her soft Spa slippers, which were emitting the smell of lavender, didn't make a sound as she followed him down a subtly lit carpeted corridor. Devyn stopped before a door with a brass number one on it. Opening it, he ushered her inside, where two pretty young Asian women waited.

"Mei and Pei," Devyn said. "They'll be doing your mani and pedi. I'll get you something to drink. It's important to keep the toxins flushed from your body."

"I think the toxins got me long ago," Annie said with a chuckle. She settled herself in a large chair.

Almost instantaneously Mei and Pei began to work on her. The toenails on one foot were pared and filed before being smeared with cream and her foot plunked into a stone basin of perfumed hot water. Annie winced.

"Too hot?" Pei wanted to know, and when Annie nodded the girl reached for a china pitcher of cold water and poured a little into the basin. "Better, yes?"

"Better," Annie agreed as Pei took up her other foot and began to work on it as Mei was following a similar program with Annie's hands.

Devyn set a cut-crystal goblet next to Annie. "Pomegranate juice," he said. "It's excellent for the heart. Your mother has a small heart problem, and those things are hereditary, you know." He stood attentively by her side.

"How do you know my mother has heart disease?" Annie asked him, surprised.

"The contest entries asked for a brief health history," he told her. "It's the kind of thing we need to know in advance. Anyone making reservations at the Spa has to fill out a health history so they can be treated accordingly. We're not a one-size-fits-all establishment. Each of our guests is treated individually."

Annie was silent. *Interesting,* she considered, *and very smart marketing.*

"The reason I booked your first spa treatments today is that I knew you would be having dinner tonight with Ms. Buckley. You'll want to look your best, Annie."

"You are very good at your job," she told him with a smile, and then she took a sip of the juice. It was delicious, and very refreshing.

"Thanks," he told her. "When the girls are finished we'll do your massage, and then your facial last. You'll have some time to rest before dinner."

Mei massaged her hands until Annie was

almost purring. "No polish for you until you go home," the manicurist said. "You got pretty hands, and now look good."

Pei finished up with Annie's feet, and Annie thought they had never felt so good. The two young women packed up the tools of their trade and hurried from the room, passing a tall and muscular man with a brush cut who was entering as they left.

"This is Lars," Devyn said. "He'll be doing your massage."

"A *man?*" Annie's voice squeaked.

"Massage is my profession, Mrs. Miller," Lars said quietly. "Men, women — a body is a body." He unfolded a large padded table, fitted a face cradle at one end, and flipped over it a silk sheet he took from a small cupboard in the room. He set a large pink towel at the foot of the table. "Take off your robe and roll your panties down to make a bikini bottom. Then get facedown on the table. I'll wait outside until you're ready."

"I'll go back up to the suite, Annie," Devyn said. "I'll see that your garments are pressed immediately so you're all ready for tonight."

The two men left the room. Annie slowly unbelted her soft full-length terry robe, and laid it aside. Carefully she rolled her briefs down to the required formation and, reaching for the towel, climbed onto the table. She placed the towel over herself as best she could. She was about to get her first massage. And by a man. She hadn't been touched by a man since Nat died. What if she got aroused? Then she laughed softly at herself. Lars wasn't likely to know if she creamed her pants.

There was a knock on the door, and the masseur's voice called out, "Are you ready, Mrs. Miller?"

"Yes, I am," Annie said back, and she heard the door open and close again.

"Are you comfortable?" he asked her. "Face cradle adjusted all right?"

"I'm fine," Annie told him.

"Your skin is a little dry," he noted. "I'm going to use almond oil on it." She heard him uncork something, and then the sound of hands rubbing together. The hands slid strongly up one side of her back and then the other. "And you're tense. Let me guess. You've never had a massage before. Try to relax, Mrs. Miller. I'm really very good at what I do." His fingers dug gently into her shoulders.

She tried to take his advice. His voice was impersonal, professional. He wasn't here to seduce her. His job was to massage her and help her to let go of her tensions. The Spa wasn't a hotbed of licentiousness. It was a place to renew her body, her mind, and her spirit. Nat would fully approve. For the first time in her life she was free for eight days and seven nights from children, pets, and making meals. She had better make the most of it, because God only knew when she would have such pampering and luxury again. Annie drew a deep breath and let it out in a whoosh.

"That's it!" Lars said enthusiastically. "Let that stress go, Mrs. Miller."

"Do I get a massage every day I'm here?" Annie asked him as he worked.

"Twice a day if you want," Lars told her. "I've been assigned to you and you alone for your stay, Mrs. Miller."

"Annie, please. I may have five kids, but 'Mrs. Miller' makes me sound so old," she told him. God, she was being touched by a strange man, and she was really beginning to enjoy it. It felt so good to be touched again by someone who wasn't hanging on her leg whining, or nursing on her breasts. Not that Nat had ever massaged her like this, but still, it did feel good. Very, very good.

He chuckled. "Five kids, huh? Well, if it wouldn't offend you, I have to say you're in great shape for a lady with five kids."

"I'm overweight," Annie answered him.

"You won't be by the time you leave here," he told her. "Five or six pounds is all you need to lose. You're a big-boned woman."

"Like my dad," Annie said ruefully. "My sister is like mom, and she's half my size."

"Genetics," Lars replied. "It'll get you every time. I'd like to do your buttocks, if it wouldn't freak you out. The glutes can always use a little loosening up."

"Maybe tomorrow," Annie said, nervous again.

"No problem! I'll hold the towel up now, and you turn over," Lars instructed her, and when she quickly rolled over he dropped the big towel down over her, and then, going behind Annie, he began to work on her neck and shoulders.

Annie closed her eyes and actually began to relax. Had he seen her breasts? she wondered. But then she put the thought from her mind. He hadn't seemed to be looking, and why would he? He had told her quite plainly that massage for him was a business. The strong fingers digging into her neck and her shoulders felt wonderful. And when he was through with them he did her arms, massaging each of her hands until they felt devoid of muscle and bone. Then he moved on to to her legs and feet. Annie grew so relaxed that she actually dozed.

"Annie."

She heard her name being called, and opened her eyes.

Lars was standing next to the massage table. "You're through now, and I'm glad that you got a little catnap. By the time you go home we're going to have you all loose and relaxed. And we'll teach you how to do it at home without us."

She sighed deeply. "That was wonderful," she told him. "Where do I go to get my facial?"

"Janka will be right with you," Lars told her as Annie sat up, clutching the towel to herself. "I'll get your robe." And when he had brought it to her Lars helped Annie into the soft garment, standing behind her so she felt more comfortable. Taking the towel back from her, he took the face cradle out and folded his table. "See you tomorrow," he told her, and briskly departed.

At the same time an elegant woman in a white uniform dress came into the room. "Mrs. Miller? I am Janka, your facialist," she said in an accented voice. She pushed a button on the door wall, and a panel across the room opened up, allowing a comfortable chair, much like a dentist's chair, Annie thought, to slide out into the middle of the room.

"Please be seated, Mrs. Miller, and let us see what we have to work with today."

As soon as Annie settled herself in the chair, Janka pushed another button and the chair was slightly elevated. Janka moved behind her, slipping a broad terry headband about her head. She then tucked a hard yet comfortable bolster beneath Annie's neck. Two moistened cotton pads were carefully placed on her eyelids.

"Cucumber lotion," Janka said. "It lessens the swelling. Everything I will use on your skin is natural and has been formulated without animal testing."

"My twin daughters would appreciate that," Annie murmured, but Janka didn't reply. Instead a bright light was snapped on that Annie could see even from beneath her eye pads. Janka's fingers began to move slowly and gently over Annie's face.

"The light," Janka explained, "is part of a large magnifying glass that allows me to see your skin closely. How old are you?"

"I'll be forty-four in December," Annie answered.

"Children?"

"Five," Annie replied.

"Amazing!" Janka said. "You've got gor-

65

geous skin, Mrs. Miller. It's firm, smooth, and there isn't a crow's-foot in sight. *Yet.* You're a little dry, but we can take care of that. And before you ask, because I sense it on your lips, I'm Hungarian."

"I've never been to Hungary," Annie said, for want of anything else to say.

"Not a lot of Americans have until recently. My country is beautiful, and we welcome all peoples of goodwill. And full purses," she added, and laughed uproariously at her own humor.

Annie laughed with her, and then she settled back for the next hour as Janka creamed, steamed, massaged, creamed some more, slid hot stones over her face, and finally smeared a mask made from avocado over her skin. And when the mask was removed, Janka delicately drizzled fragrant rose oil over Annie's face, gently rubbing it into her skin with a supple, light touch.

"I'll see you in a few days," she said. "And when I do I will give you some tips on how to keep that beautiful skin of yours in peak condition."

"Thank you," Annie said, slipping from the facial chair.

"Perfect timing!" Devyn said brightly as he entered the room and escorted her back into the corridor toward the elevator. "I've had all your slacks pressed, so whatever you want to wear tonight at dinner, you'll look perfect."

The elevator doors opened up, and they stepped inside.

"Your dinner is at eight," Devyn continued. "I'm bringing the makeup artist and hairstylist to you at seven fifteen."

"I don't need a makeup artist or a hairstylist," Annie said. "I can put on my own lipstick and brush my hair all by myself."

The elevator doors opened again and, slipping the key card into the lock, Devyn opened the door of the suite for her. "Every woman can put on her lipstick and brush her hair," he agreed, "but when you see what Judi and Mr. Eugene can do for you, you'll change your mind. You nap now, and I'll be back later, okay? I've turned the bed down for you." Then with a grin he was gone.

Annie walked slowly into the bedroom. The elegant clock on the fireplace mantel struck once. Annie looked at the timepiece. Four thirty. She was starving, she suddenly realized. She hadn't eaten since breakfast. And there on her bedside table was an individual serving bowl with a creamy pale peach something in it. Picking up the spoon, she took a mouthful. Yogurt. Freshly made yogurt, with generous bits of fresh apricot in it. "Devyn, I think I may take you home with me," Annie said aloud as, sitting down on the bed, she ate the yogurt and sipped at the iced green tea in the glass next to the bowl.

When she had finished she swung her legs up and stretched out on the bed. It was incredibly comfortable. It had been an amazing day, Annie thought. Could she stand an entire week of such pampering? Yeah, she could, she decided as she fell asleep.

Devyn gently shook her awake at the appointed time. Together they picked a pair of fawn-colored silk slacks and a cream-colored shirt with three-quarter sleeves and a boat neckline. She dressed quickly. Mr. Eugene, the hairstylist, decided her hair would look best in a French braid. He quickly accomplished it. Judi, the makeup artist, said Annie's beautiful skin shouldn't be covered with too much makeup. She quickly put a light foundation on Annie, some blush, and a touch of smoky blue eye shadow to her eyelids.

"The cornrow bracelet and some turquoise earrings," Devyn decided, handing her the pieces. "You're gorgeous, Annie!"

Mr. Eugene and Judi murmured their

agreement.

Annie turned to look in the mirror over the bureau. Was that her? She looked younger. Not tired. She did have a shape. She turned her head slightly. The makeup was so subtle it didn't look as if she were wearing any. And she loved her hair! It was casual but elegant, pulled back from her face. "Wow!" she said. "Not bad for an old broad with five kids. Not bad at all."

"You should look like this all the time," Devyn told her.

"With my brood? I'm like the old woman in the shoe, kid," Annie said, mocking herself slightly. "But I want to look like this all week so I can remember that there is an attractive woman beneath the mother and the chief cook and bottle washer." She turned. "Thank you," she said to Mr. Eugene and Judi.

"Gotta jet," Devyn said. "The boss lady will be waiting for you." He led her from her suite down the corridor and around a corner, and there was another large double rosewood door. "Ms. Buckley's apartment," the young man said, and rapped.

The door was opened by a smiling gentleman. He couldn't have stood any taller than five feet, seven inches. He was impeccably dressed in a dark gray pin-striped suit with a white shirt, and a striped gray tie. His hair was beautifully styled, wavy and gray. The hand he held out to her was perfectly manicured. "Mrs. Miller? I am Mr. Nicholas, CEO of the Channel Corporation. You may go now, Devyn. I will escort our guest back to her suite after dinner."

"Yes, sir," Devyn said respectfully, and disappeared back down the hall.

Mr. Nicholas took her hand and, raising it to his lips, kissed it. "I may call you Annie, mayn't I?"

"I thought I was having dinner with Ms. Buckley," Annie said, slightly confused as Mr. Nicholas drew her into the apartment.

"You are," Nora Buckley said, coming forward. "But Mr. Nicholas very much wanted to meet you, Annie. This spa is a brand-new undertaking for his corporation, and he's anxious that it succeed. You're our everywoman."

"And how do you like it so far?" Mr. Nicholas wanted to know as he drew her to a creamy beige couch, where they sat down.

"Well," Annie said, "I've only been here a few hours, but from what I've seen, it's just lovely. My suite is gorgeous. And I've been pampered to bits all afternoon. I love it, and the thought of spending the week here is just wonderful!"

"Your PA is satisfactory?" Mr. Nicholas wanted to know.

"Devyn is a darling," Annie enthused. "He's just a little older than my oldest son, and he has made me feel so comfortable. When I got back from my treatments this afternoon he even had something for me to eat. I hadn't eaten since breakfast this morning, and I was starving. I think he's doing a terrific job!"

"I'm delighted to hear it, Annie," Mr. Nicholas said, smiling. Then he took an aperitif from the tray a white-coated house-man was holding out and offered it to Annie.

"Thank you," she said, and sipped. A dry but sweet sherry, she thought.

"Have you any suggestions yet as to how we might improve our services?" Mr. Nicholas asked her casually, sipping from his own cocktail glass.

"I think my introduction into the facilities was perhaps a bit too fast," Annie said. "Not that I haven't enjoyed every moment so far. But I think it would have been a bit nicer if, after I was shown to my suite, I were served a light lunch before being hurried off for my various treatments. And there was no music. Relaxing music always adds to any pleasurable experience, in my opinion. But, of course, I'm no expert."

"No, no," Mr. Nicholas said. "We're catering to women, and we want to get it right, my dear. As Nora has so cleverly put it, you are our everywoman."

Annie laughed. "Believe it or not I find that flattering, although I'm not certain just how true it is. I do know, however, that when you're stressed out, easing into a comfortable situation is nicer. You want to enjoy every moment of it."

Mr. Nicholas set his drink down. "I must be going now," he said. "This is, I know, to be a ladies' evening, but I did want to meet you, my dear." He took her hand, bowed in a very courtly manner, and kissed it again. "Good night, Annie." Then, turning to Nora, he repeated his good-byes and, going to the apartment door, exited.

"What a charming man," Annie said. "His accent, I couldn't quite place it."

"It has a slightly Brit quality to it," Nora told her guest. "But actually I know very little about Mr. Nicholas, other than that he is a generous employer, and very understanding."

"Dinner is served, madam," the houseman said.

"It must be nice to work for someone like that. I worked only a year before Nat and I were married. In my father's insurance office. It wasn't very exciting, like running a spa must be," Annie noted as she sat down at a small, perfectly set dining table.

"Actually, I run the Channel," Nora told her guest, "but Mr. Nicholas wanted me to get the Spa up and running before I hired anyone for this venture."

"My sister loves the Channel," Annie said.

"Thousands of women do," Nora replied. "You don't get it, do you?"

"I haven't got the money for frills. My husband was relatively young when he died. His insurance policy wasn't particularly big. We get by. Just," Annie explained.

"I know how that must be. When my husband was attempting to divorce me he cut me off entirely in his effort to force me to sign an agreement that would have been very much to my detriment, and that of our children," Nora said.

"He died, didn't he?" Annie remarked.

"Yes, poor Jeff," Nora murmured. "The young girl he was dumping me for dumped him. He assaulted her and was arrested. Jeff never knew how to treat people. He fought with the police. With the judge arraigning him, the result was no bail. He died that night in the Egret Pointe jail of a cardiac, they said."

"Were you divorced then?" Annie asked, unable to stem her curiosity.

"No," Nora replied softly. "The children and I got everything." Then she smiled. "As part of your prize you've won a free year of the Channel. Let's enjoy our dinner, and then I'll tell you all about it. You have it in your suite and should learn how to program and access it while you're here."

"I don't really understand what the Channel is all about," Annie admitted.

Nora smiled warmly. "Let's have dinner first," she repeated. "I hope you don't mind, but I've ordered for us."

As if on cue the silent houseman in the white jacket appeared from a small alcove, wheeling a serving trolley. Stopping it by the table, he lifted off two small plates with rounds of ripe, juicy tomatoes alternating with thin slices of fresh white mozzarella, and placed them before the two women. The salad, topped with fresh basil, was dressed with a subtle combination of oil and vinegar.

"Tomatoes are good only at this time of year," Nora said as she began to eat.

When they had finished their salad, the houseman who had taken his trolley and disappeared after serving them returned again. The little vehicle made absolutely no noise as it came across the lush carpet. After taking the salad plates and putting them on the lower half of the trolley, the houseman lifted two steaming plates from the top shelf and set them before the diners. "Will that be all, madam?" he asked Nora.

"Thank you, Fritz. I'll call when we're ready for dessert," she replied.

Each plate contained a generous slice of what looked very much to Annie like prime rib. She hadn't eaten prime rib in ages, and her slice was barely cooked, just the way she liked it. There was a perfect ear of summer corn on the plate, along with a serving of French-cut green beans and several thin slices of yellow squash.

"You look as if you haven't seen a good meal in ages," Nora teased.

Annie shook her head. "I haven't. You've cooked for kids. You know what it's like. Burgers, spaghetti, baked ziti, chicken fingers. Getting veggies into them is a constant battle. They think French fries count. This plate is so beautifully arranged it's almost a crime to touch it, but I'm afraid I'm shameless when it comes to rare beef." And then Annie set about demolishing the food on her plate.

"This is the kind of meal we will serve you here at the Spa. Your sister filled out a page of your likes and dislikes. Everyone who books in will have to do that," Nora explained. "We will personalize as much as we can for our guests. You need to lose a few pounds. We've set you up with a high-protein, good-carbs diet."

"I noticed no bread," Annie admitted.

"People tend to fill up on bread before a meal, and then, no matter how good the meal, they don't finish it. Our proportions are perfect. You won't feel hungry, but you also won't eat too much. Hopefully when you see the changes we can make for you, you'll feed yourself that way when you get back home," Nora concluded.

Annie had to admit when she had finished her meat and vegetables that she was no longer hungry. And while she always enjoyed a good glass of red wine with beef, she hadn't missed it. The Pellegrino water had been fine. She looked questioningly at Nora when the houseman removed their dinner plates, replacing them with small dessert-filled plates containing a meringue filled with raspberries and peaches.

"We use a sugar substitute in the meringues, and egg whites. Nothing more," Nora explained.

"You ought to have a small shop here at the spa where guests can purchase things like these meringues, and the marvelous lotions that were used on me this afternoon," Annie suggested. "And they could buy those great soft terry Spa robes you have in my suite. A shop could be a real moneymaker." Then Annie laughed. "Listen to me, would you? It sounds just as if I know what I'm talking about."

"You very well may," Nora told her.

Annie shook her head. "I'm no businesswoman. A year typing and filing in my father's insurance company is hardly experience. I'm a housewife, a mother."

"That's just what I once was," Nora told her. "I didn't even have a checking account in my own name. But Mr. Nicholas said he saw something in me, and he gave me the opportunity to try to be something different. By the way, keep it under your hat that I run the Channel. It's not public information. I'd be besieged by every woman in the world if it were known." She smiled warmly again.

They finished their desserts along with cups of pale green tea, and then, leaving the table, they sat together watching an August moon rise over the bay. Annie realized that she hadn't felt this relaxed, this genuinely comfortable, in ages. Obviously the Spa was working its magic on her.

"Let me tell you about the Channel," Nora said. "At least, what I can tell you."

"What do you mean?" Annie looked curious.

"Well, even I can't tell you exactly how it works," Nora began, "but it does."

"But what exactly is it?" Annie wanted to know.

"Well," Nora said, "I suppose the best way to describe it is to tell you that it is only available for and to women. You can obtain it through your local cable company. We provide you with a special remote. The Channel can't be accessed by your own television's remote, so you never have to worry about your children getting into it. And your special remote is sensitive to your skin and your touch only, so if any of the kids got ahold of it, it wouldn't work for them."

"Parental controls." Annie chuckled. "I like that! Okay, I've got access to the Channel, and I've got the remote. Now what?"

"Well," Nora said, "then, holding the remote, you think of your wildest or most dearly held fantasy, and press the A button. Turn on your television and that fantasy will be there waiting for you, and before you realize what has happened you will find yourself in the middle of that fantasy, actually living it."

"You're joking, of course," Annie said skeptically.

"No," Nora told her, "I'm not joking. Back when I was first introduced to the Channel there was only the remote. My friends couldn't say exactly what the Channel was. No one can. I called the cable company and ordered it for the evening, like you would order pay-per-view. I couldn't believe what happened to me next. There was my fantasy. I was there, and living it not with my son-of-a-bitch husband, but with a sexy man who thought I was terrific. But I've had several changes instituted since I became head of the Channel," Nora said. "Now you can program two fantasies at a time, and live whichever suits you that evening. And you can get a yearly subscription to the Channel, too. This is a tough world in which we women now live, and we deserve a little fun. The Channel is our dirty little secret, Annie. You will love it, I promise you, but you won't believe any of this until you've tried it," Nora concluded.

There was a soft knock on the apartment door, and the silent Fritz hurried to answer it, opening the portal to admit Mr. Nicholas.

"I've come to escort you back to your

suite," he said, smiling. "Have you explained everything to her, Nora?"

"Everything except that the Channel is online from eight p.m. until four a.m. When it's time to release your fantasy for the evening you'll hear a chime giving you a two-minute warning," Nora said. "Have fun!"

"What are your fantasies?" Annie asked Nora boldly, and Mr. Nicholas chuckled.

"My beautiful apartment, and a Caribbean island where I play pirate with a girlfriend of mine," Nora said with a grin.

Mr. Nicholas took Annie's hand and tucked it in his arm. "Come along, my dear," he said. "Nora, I will want to speak to you before you retire."

"Thank you for dinner," Annie said as he led her from the room and back to her own suite. "Nora didn't say where my personal remote is, Mr. Nicholas."

"You'll find it by your bed, but it will work on either the screen there or in your living room," he answered her. "Good night now, my dear." He bowed and was gone.

CHAPTER THREE

Annie shut the suite door. It couldn't be true, she thought. But that didn't mean she wasn't going to try it, and, going into the bedroom, she reached for the remote by her bed. Then, putting it down, she undressed slowly, took a quick shower, and put on the elegant nightgown she had bought at Lacy Nothings just for her spa stay. Fashioned of pale green silk and delicate lace, it fit her like a glove. It had cost a week's worth of groceries, but then, no one was at home this week, she thought, soothing her conscience. You couldn't come to an elegant place like the Spa with a worn pink cotton sleep shirt, could you? Of course not, she reasoned.

The king-sized bed had been turned down. There was a single dark-chocolate mint on one of the pillows. Annie climbed into the bed. Beneath her the feather bed shifted gently. Half seated against the pile of pillows, she drew up the down comforter and reached for the remote on her night table. There were three buttons on it. One said, OPEN/CLOSE. The other two were marked A and B. Pressing OPEN/CLOSE saw the wall opposite her bed open to reveal what appeared to be a flat-screen television. She had briefly read the suite's instructions earlier with regard to the lights. Now she tried it. "Lights off," she said, and immediately the bedroom darkened. Now, that was really cool, she thought. Maybe her electric bill at home wouldn't be so high if she and the kids could do that, she thought, smiling.

Her mind now turned again to the remote in her hand. A fantasy. She had to think of a fantasy. Had she ever had a fantasy? Her father was a practical man. Her mother was a no-nonsense type. They had been good parents to her and to Lizzie, but she couldn't ever remember a time when they had played pretend with their children, or even encouraged their imaginations. They had encouraged learning. And they had taught manners and ethics. But they had discouraged both of their daughters from anything that smacked of fancy. Annie had grown up knowing her future was already mapped out for her. She would be a wife and a mother, because that was what respectable women became.

Lizzie, on the other hand, being younger, had broken the mold when she turned around after college and got into law school. She hadn't even told their parents she was applying, but, Annie thought, Lizzie's summer adventures should have given them some hint that Lizzie would not follow the prescribed plan. However, their mother was too busy planning Annie's engagement party. And there was a wedding date to set, a trousseau to be assembled, a wedding dress and bridesmaids' gowns to find, a reception to plan. And Dad smiled benignly, went to his office, and wrote the checks required of him. No one was paying a bit of attention to Lizzie.

Sometimes, Annie thought as she sat in her luxurious bed, *I wish I had been that focused, but I didn't know what I wanted to be, and I loved Nat.* A fantasy. She had to think of a fantasy. She remembered her grandmother Mumford, her mother's mother, reading fairy tales to her when she was younger. She had a wonderful big, thick book with beautiful old-fashioned colored pictures in it. Grandmother had died when Annie was sixteen. Annie and Lizzie had helped clean out the old woman's house. Annie had found the book and kept it to read to her own children one day, which she had done now and again. Were any of the fairy tales in that book fantasies worth living? If indeed this Channel thing were actually real. But Lizzie said it was, and Lizzie wasn't a woman to lie.

Cinderella? No. She had already had her happily-ever-after with her prince. Rapunzel? Nah. Who wanted to sit around in a tower all day combing her long golden hair? Definitely not Sleeping Beauty! Snow White? Annie had always thought there was something creepy about that girl and seven little men. And then she remembered her favorite of the fairy tales her grandmother used to read to them. It was "Beauty and the Beast." There was something lovely about a girl who loved her parent enough to sacrifice herself — and a love so great that it could overcome evil. It might be fun to be that girl. Why not? Annie pressed the A button.

She felt a slight tingling sensation, and then she found herself in a coach traveling through a dark forest. Shivering, she pulled her woolen cloak about her. Peeking out of the coach window as the vehicle slowed, she could see a walled and towered castle ahead of them. The coach passed through open iron gates, which were closed with a bang behind them. They finally came to a stop, and the coach door was flung open. A gloved hand reached in to assist her out. Taking it, she stepped from the carriage.

The man who held her hand towered over her. He was dressed all in black, and a silk and leather mask hid his features from her, covering his face to just below his nose and above his mouth. "You will be Mistress Anne, the merchant's daughter. You understand that your father has given you to me in exchange for his debt?"

"Yes," Annie answered. Her heart was beating furiously. This was really quite exciting, she thought.

" 'Yes, my lord,' " he corrected her. "I am the master of this castle and the lands about it. You must learn respect, Mistress Anne, and I shall teach it to you."

"Yes, my lord," Annie replied with a small smile.

"You find this situation amusing?" he demanded harshly. His voice was deep and dark. "I can see you have much to learn, and there is no better time than now to begin your lessons in obedience, Mistress Anne. Come!" His grip on her hand tightened, and he half led, half dragged her up the broad stone steps and into the castle.

I can stop this at any time, Annie thought

to herself. Lizzie had told her she could if her fantasy frightened her, or wasn't as much fun as she wanted. But right now Annie was so intrigued by what was happening to her that she didn't want to end the fantasy. This tall man was rather exciting in a fierce way. So this was the Beast of legend. She wondered what was beneath that silk-and-leather mask he wore as she stumbled along behind him. Where was he taking her? Was it to his great hall? All castles had great halls, didn't they?

But the Beast did not take her to his great hall. Instead he led her down a narrow flight of stone stairs into a little round chamber lit only by a single torch. From the chamber's low ceiling hung two golden chains, to which were attached a pair of golden manacles. *I can end this at any time,* Annie told herself again as the Beast roughly pulled her arms up and fastened the manacles about her wrists. To her surprise the manacles were lined in the softest silk. Hanging, her toes just grazed the floor. *I can end this.* But she didn't want to end it. Never in all her life had she faced such a creature as the Beast, and to her surprise she found it was exciting her sexually. Well, her husband had been dead for over two years, and she hadn't had even a single date.

The Beast said not a word. Instead he walked about his victim, observing her. Then, unfastening her skirt, he let it drop to the stone floor. He undid the three petticoats she had worn beneath the red velvet skirt, and they fell into a heap. Annie squealed as two big hands slid beneath her chemise and up her legs. He slowly drew her white silk drawers to her knees, and then his hands slipped back up to fondle her buttocks briefly before he removed the garment entirely.

"You have a nicely rounded bottom, Mistress Anne. I think it will take well to punishment," the Beast said softly. He stepped back to observe her again as she hung in just her chemise. Then, hooking his fingers into the dainty ruffled neckline, he ripped the garment off of her before she divined his intent.

Annie gasped, surprised. She was hanging stark naked before a strange man. She blushed, embarrassed. What a sight she must be, with her forty-something body full of cellulite and boobs that were beginning to sag. She decided to end this ridiculous fantasy right now. But for some reason she didn't understand, she couldn't. Something inside her wanted to know just how far she was willing to let this go.

"Have you ever seen yourself entirely naked, Mistress Anne?" the Beast asked her.

Annie realized she should respond as the merchant's young daughter. "N-n-no," she said.

"Your father had no looking glass in his house?" the Beast queried.

"My father thought such things would only produce foolishness and vanity in a woman," Annie heard herself say. *Good lord!* She was becoming the girl in the fairy tale, although the fairy tale had never been quite like this.

The beast's mouth quirked in an almost smile, and Annie saw the beginnings of a scar at the left corner of his lips. "You shall see yourself now," the Beast told her, and with a wave of his hand the wall opposite her became a mirror.

She stared, surprised at the image revealed. The body in the mirror was not hers. It was the body of a young girl of about twenty. It was a voluptuous body, with full hips and firm round breasts. Her belly was flat, her thighs were nicely fleshed, and there wasn't a dimple of cellulite to be found. Annie smiled at the image in the glass. She gazed down at herself, and realized that the mirror did not lie. "What, my lord, do you mean to do to me?" she heard herself asking. "I was told I was to housekeep for you for a year in order to repay my father's debt to you."

The Beast smiled a cruel smile. "I mean to have your virginity of you, Mistress Anne. Your father misunderstood me. You are to be my mistress, and not for just a year. For as long as it pleases me that you be. But first you must be punished for your earlier insolence toward me." Reaching out, he drew on a thick chain, and Annie found herself being drawn upward. "Spread your legs for me," the Beast commanded her, and, realizing it was futile to resist him, Annie obeyed.

Each of her legs was manacled to the wall. The Beast stood beneath her, looking at her well-furred mons. With the thumb and forefinger of one hand he spread the lips of her labia wide. With his other hand he conjured a long feather with a stiff pointed tip from the air, and began to ply it with delicate touches to her clitoris. After a moment a burst of pure, hot lust overwhelmed her, making it almost impossible to breathe. Annie moaned, and then she came.

The Beast said nothing. Instead he directed the feather to the opening of her now wet vagina. The feather swirled just inside her, and she moaned again. It had been so long. So damned long since she had been fucked. Yet she couldn't betray Nat. But her husband had been dead two years. And this was a fantasy, wasn't it? How could her secret fantasy betray anyone? The feather ran along the edges of her labia, and then attacked her clitoris again. Her body arced with a second clitoral climax.

Then, to her complete surprise, his head was between her outspread legs. His lips kissed the moist skin. His tongue began to explore every nook and cranny of her soft coral flesh. He nipped gently at it, and Annie squirmed, although she wasn't certain whether she was trying to escape him or get closer. His mouth closed over the bud of her clit and he sucked strongly. She screamed softly as he worked her into a fierce frenzy of desire. "Please!" she whimpered to him. *"Please!"*

He ceased immediately, releasing her legs, and, reaching for the chain, he lowered her to a point where he could face her. He took her face between his thumb and his forefinger and smiled into her blue eyes, sensing her need. "You do not yet understand, Mistress Anne," he told her. "I am the master here. In time you will be fucked. But you lack discipline." He lowered her further until she was on her knees. "Bend yourself forward," he said. "You will receive five strokes of my tawse."

"You are going to beat me, my lord?" Annie said. She was definitely going to end this fantasy right now. Well, maybe not this moment, but shortly.

"No, I am not going to beat you, as you so quaintly phrase it, Mistress Anne. You are simply to be disciplined by having your bottom smacked with five strokes of the strap. It is to be hoped you will learn quickly that I am your master, and such discipline will become unnecessary in the future." Then, without another word, he raised his arm, and the leather tawse met Annie's flesh for five quick strokes. "Excellent!" he said approvingly as he hung the strap back on the wall by the torch holder. "You did not cry out. This bodes well for you, Mistress Anne, and for our future relationship." Then he raised her back up so that she hung with the tips of her toes again just barely brushing the floor. "I will leave you briefly, Mistress Anne. Take this time to consider well your future behavior. You must learn to obey me instantly and without question." And, taking the torch from its holder, he left her hanging in the dark within the small chamber.

I can end this now, Annie thought again.

But did she really want to end it? It was dark, and it was perverse, but it was the most exciting thing that had ever happened to her. Right now her entire body was throbbing with a ferocious sexual need to be fucked as she waited, hanging from her restraints in this dark room, for the Beast to return. The mask, she suspected, hid facial scarring, but the rest of him seemed quite normal. He was very tall, probably between six-foot-four and six-foot-six inches. He was big boned, but lean and hard. What did he look like naked? How long before she would find out?

It had been a very long day. Unable to help herself, Annie felt her eyelids drooping as she waited for whatever was to happen next. She started awake suddenly, fully aware that someone was in the chamber with her. "Who's there?" she whispered, and then a soft gag was tied around her mouth. Her heart beat wildly at this new and total feeling of helplessness. She whimpered beneath the gag.

She tensed as hands began to caress her. The hands were warm and big. Was it the Beast? It had to be, and yet her instincts said that there was more than one person here. That was confirmed when both of her breasts were grasped and suckled upon simultaneously. The mouths on her nipples bit and licked and drew strongly. Her fires, banked slightly by her doze, began to reassert themselves. Her body shuddered with her desperate need to be satisfied.

Then a hand pushed between her thighs to burrow between her labia. Fingers thrust hard and deep into her vagina. They kept thrusting back and forth, back and forth, until Annie was dizzy and almost nauseous with her need. Again she whimpered behind the gag. The fingers withdrew briefly, only to return thicker as they reinserted themselves into her fevered body, driving deep, forcing her to a climax.

A strange voice whispered hotly in her ear, "You'll take well to his cock, my girl. Your cunt is big, but nicely tight."

"Aye," the second unfamiliar voice agreed. "She's going to please him well if she will just learn to obey her master. Do you understand, girl? He'll not fuck you until you are obedient to him. And he has a fine big cock, a full foot in length it is, to please a lass such as yourself. We've left your virginity intact for him. Don't keep him waiting long."

"If you do," the first voice said, "he'll give you to his soldiers, and they'll be rough on a pretty creature like yourself."

She felt the gag being removed from her mouth, but before she might say a word the two men were quickly gone from her prison. Annie drew several deep breaths to clear her head. Where was the Beast? Had he allowed these two men to come into her little prison and assault her? Had that been part of his discipline? She had to ask him, but he didn't return. And then she heard the chime pinging, signaling she had only two minutes left in the Channel. Where was the Beast?

"My lord!" she called out. "My lord!" And Annie felt the manacles containing her wrists dissolving, and she awoke amid a tangle of her silk nightgown and the down coverlet. *No!* she thought desperately, but the little digital clock on the bedside table said four oh one. The Channel was closed to her. She grabbed for the remote and pressed the A button again, but the flat screen was quickly obscured by its mobile wall. She pressed the open/close button, but the wall remained tightly shut, and an automated voice said, "The Channel is now closed. It will reopen tonight at eight p.m."

"Damn!" Annie said irritably. She caught herself. It had been a dream. And then her gaze touched on her wrists. A faint but distinct imprint of the manacles was there. "Omigod," she whispered softly as she saw it, and then she felt a faint soreness in her vagina. It had been real! But how could it have been? Did it really matter? It had been real! And it had been exciting, and she wanted to go back to her fantasy. It was going to be a very long sixteen hours. She could hardly wait. Would the Beast fuck her? Was his penis really twelve inches long? Nat's eight had been the biggest — the only — penis she had ever known. Nat had been almost as tall as the Beast, and as big a man.

She was suddenly overcome with a strong sense of weariness. Closing her eyes, she fell asleep.

It was eight a.m. on a rainy August morning when Devyn awakened her by gently shaking her shoulder until Annie's protesting eyes opened. "Good morning," she said to him with a rueful smile. "It's morning, right?"

He grinned boyishly. "Yep, rainy, but morning. I've brought you a glass of pomegranate juice. When you're ready, I'll show you to the dining room. The other invited guests arrived last night while you were at dinner with Ms. Buckley. And you got to meet Mr. Nicholas. He's pretty much a recluse, you know. He's so busy that very few people get to meet him. I think he's one cool dude."

"I agree," Nora said, letting Devyn plump up her pillows so she could sit up. She sipped at the juice he had brought. "This is really good."

"Bath or shower?" he asked her.

"What's my schedule today?" she asked him.

"Massage, of course, but we'll set the time up after we decide on the rest of what you're going to do," Devyn said. "You've got lots of choices, Annie. The dining room serves breakfast until ten a.m., so there's no big rush."

"Bath then," she told him. Sipping her juice, she watched him as he went into the glamorous bathroom. A moment later she heard the tub running.

"Rose? Lavender? Summer lily?" he called to her.

"Lavender this morning," Annie replied, knowing he was referring to the bath scents she had seen lined up near the big tub last night.

"Water temp?" he asked.

"You can adjust the water temperature?"

"Sure. What do you like?"

"Hot, but not too hot," she answered him.

"One hundred and five degrees then," he said. "If it's not right we'll adjust it after you get into the tub."

Annie shook her head. This was so much better than she had ever imagined — and to think she had been hesitant about accepting her prize. Finishing her juice, she swung her legs over the edge of the bed, then hesitated a moment. She didn't have a robe, and her sexy nightgown was a bit revealing. "I'm sure it will be just perfect," she said. "Scram now and let me take my bath. I can smell the lavender from here, and it's just delicious." She slid back into the bed and pulled up the coverlet as he exited the bath.

"Enjoy," he told her. "I'll wait in the living room for you."

Annie waited until he had left the bedroom, and then she scampered into the big bathroom. Shucking her nightgown, she stepped down into the tub and slid into the water. It was absolutely wonderful, and she sighed with the soreness from her adventure. Her arms had been stretched by her weight as she hung. Her butt ached a little from having been smacked with a leather . . . what had he called it? A tawse?

Allowing time for a five-minute soak, Annie then washed quickly and got out of the tub. Drying herself and then wrapping a towel about her body, she walked back into the bedroom to dress. She brushed her hair free of the French braid she had been given last night and, pulling it back, slid an elastic about it. Then she joined Devyn out in the living room of the suite.

He whistled. "For a lady with five kids, you are really hot," he told her with a grin.

"Thank you, sir," Annie responded. "Now show me my choices for today." She sat down on the couch next to him.

He held out his clipboard to her.

Annie took it and scanned the printed page. "I'll take the nature walk at ten a.m., do a half hour of reflexology at eleven thirty, have a massage at two o'clock, and get my hair washed and a scalp massage at four. You said some other guests came in last night. Who?" She handed him back the clipboard, and he wrote her choices and times on it before answering her.

"Some of the Channel Corporation's more important clients and a couple of travel writers were invited," Devyn said. "There's going to be a get-together about five thirty tonight in the main lounge. I'm supposed to take you there. Don't forget, you're the grand-prize winner." He stood up. "Ready for breakfast, Annie?"

The dining room was light and airy. It had windows on three sides, and the windows were positioned in such a fashion that it appeared they were aboard a ship and surrounded on all sides by water. It was a wonderful illusion. Devyn was to take his meals with her at breakfast and lunch. At dinner she would be seated with the other guests. The waitress placed a glass dish of fresh summer fruits before her. It was followed by a plate of scrambled eggs and sausage. A delicate china cup was filled with fresh-brewed white tea.

"Part of your weight-loss program," Devyn told her as he wolfed down his waffles and bacon. "Sorry. They put you on low carbs, high protein. The good carbs."

"How about getting me an English muffin?" Annie said hopefully.

He shook his blond head. "No breads, and only natural sugars," he told her.

She took her nature walk with two other women who had managed to get up early enough. It was led by an enthusiastic woman Annie recognized immediately as her twins' Girl Scout leader. She acknowledged Annie with a smile, and congratulated her on being the grand-prize winner. Her companions exchanged pleasantries but said little else.

The reflexology session was wonderful — fifteen minutes for her hands, and fifteen minutes for her feet. The woman doing the reflexology suggested that she book an hour next time, saying she could feel the built-up tension in Annie's extremities. Lunch consisted of a delicious chicken salad, fresh tomatoes, and coleslaw, followed by an absolutely delicious dessert.

"What is this?" Annie asked Devyn. "It's sweet. It's yummy!"

"Apricot Whip," he told her. "Egg white whipped into a meringue consistency with fresh ripe apricot puree folded in. No need for sweeteners. The apricots are local, and very sweet themselves, since they've been allowed to ripen naturally in their orchard."

"I'm in love," Annie said as she scraped the last of the Apricot Whip from her dish. "Can I have this every day?"

"I'll ask," he said, grinning boyishly at her.

At two p.m. she was stretched out on Lars's massage table, purring as his fingers dug into her shoulders. She was more relaxed with him today. At four o'clock Mr. Eugene was washing her hair and massaging her scalp with talented fingers. Scalp massage, he explained, stimulated the hair follicles and kept the scalp healthier. He then dried her hair and put it in a French braid. At five p.m. Devyn had her back in her suite preparing for the get-together. There was a dress laid out on her bed.

"That's not mine," Annie said.

"Ms. Buckley sent it over. She said she

thought you might want to wear it tonight at the get-together. It's one of those perks of being the grand-prize winner."

Annie nodded. "Okay," she said, and he left her to dress. The dress was simple, and very sophisticated. It was black silk that complemented her shape when she put it on. It was sleeveless with a boat neck. Annie slipped a single strand of pearls over her head. *Wow,* she thought. *I don't think I've ever looked so grown-up or so good.* Fortunately she had brought a pair of black patent-leather sandals for evenings. She stepped into the living room. "Well," she said to Devyn. "What do you think?"

"You look great!" he told her. "A little lipstick and eye shadow and you're ready to go, Annie. You don't even need blush tonight. You've got your own natural color."

"I can do my makeup," Annie told him.

"Nope, this is your week to be pampered. Judi should be here any minute," he replied as a knock sounded on the door.

The makeup artist hurried in and, seating Annie down, quickly added the smoky blue eye shadow to her lids and a pinkish coral lipstick to her mouth. She agreed with Devyn that Annie needed nothing more tonight. Escorted by her PA, Annie departed her suite to join the get-together. Devyn left her at the entrance to the main lounge.

"It's just the ladies," he said. "If you need me, just call."

Annie stepped into the room, and immediately Nora Buckley came forward.

"Here's our grand-prize winner now, ladies," she said, smiling, and drew Annie into the small group of women. "Her name is Annie Miller, and she is the mother of five children ranging in age from eighteen to four. Annie, two of these ladies are doing articles on the Spa for national publications, so I hope you'll answer their questions."

"Of course," Annie said with a smile.

"Mrs. Miller, I'm Carole Kramer of *Pampered Woman* magazine. How does your husband feel about your spending a week at the Spa?"

"I'm a widow," Annie said.

"Okay, then how do your kids feel about Mom running off for the week?"

"My oldest son is in Italy with his aunt and grandmother. My three daughters are at camp, and my little boy is off at Disney World with his best friend," Annie said. "But they know where I am, and they were very enthusiastic about it. This was perfect timing for me. I never won anything before, and I couldn't have accepted this prize if everything hadn't fallen into place so nicely."

"Your husband must have left you pretty well fixed that you could send your son to Italy and your daughters to camp," Carole Kramer said a bit rudely.

"Actually he didn't leave us well fixed at all. Who expects to get killed stepping off a curb in London?" Annie asked sweetly. "The girls are at camp and Nathaniel is in Italy courtesy of my sister, who's a partner with Devers, Gordon, and Williams in the city."

Carole Kramer looked very abashed at Annie's explanation.

"I'm Susie James from *Chic* magazine," a younger woman with red hair said. "How do you like the Spa so far, Mrs. Miller? Is it everything you expected?"

"Well, having never been to a spa before, I didn't know what to expect, but I'll bet The Spa at Egret Pointe is head and shoulders above a lot of other spas. I especially love having a personal assistant. Makes me feel just like Lindsay Lohan," Annie replied.

Everyone laughed.

"Yeah," Susie James said. "That is a rather delicious touch." Susie turned to Nora. "Are they trained to do everything we want?" she asked pointedly.

"Absolutely!" Nora said. "Whatever your wish is, your personal assistant has been told to cater to it. Has yours been uncooperative?"

"No," Susie James answered. "I just wanted to know how far I could take it."

"As far as you want," Nora responded.

"The Channel is for women only," Carole Kramer said. "And it's available in all of our rooms and suites. But the PAs are male. Do they know about the Channel?"

"Of course not," Nora said. "At least, not the truth. They've been told it's an inspirational health and holistic channel for our women only. Since they're unable to access it, they can't prove otherwise."

"Have you accessed the Channel, Mrs. Miller?" Susie James asked Annie.

"Not yet," Annie lied, "but I certainly will before I leave. My sister has it and loves it. So do some of the women I know. I just haven't come up with a fantasy yet, but I guess I had better, since part of my prize is a year's subscription to the Channel."

"I would think a widow would have a lot of fantasies — unless, of course, you have a boyfriend," Carole Kramer said acerbically.

"There has been no one since my husband," Annie said. "He was the love of my life, Mrs. Kramer. He was a great husband, lover, and father."

"If your sister and some of your friends have the Channel," Susie James said, "why haven't you gotten it too?"

"I can't afford extras. We have basic cable. If I could pay for something other than that, it would be the Disney Channel for my little boy, Wills," Annie answered her.

A white-coated houseman came into the room with a small gong, and struck it. "Dinner is served," he announced.

"Oh, but I still have some questions for Mrs. Miller," Carole Kramer said.

"Me too," Susie James echoed.

"She'll be here for the next few days, ladies, and so will you," Nora Buckley said. "Annie, come and sit with me tonight. Elise, you too. Annie, this is Elise Van der Veer, the wife of the famous jeweler." Nora led the way into the elegant dining room with its water view and, after seeing the other women seated, joined her two chosen guests.

"I've been admiring Mrs. Miller's pearls," Mrs. Van der Veer said, smiling.

"Annie, please. My maternal grandmother left them to me. They were her mother's before that. I just love them."

"Elise," Mrs. Van der Veer replied. "I thought you handled yourself very well with that wretched Kramer woman," she said

105

low. "She has all the sensitivity of a jelly. How long have you been widowed now, my dear?"

"Just over two years," Annie said.

"And this is your first respite, isn't it? Well, I should certainly say that you more than deserve it. Where are your girls camping?"

"Stoneledge Lake. My sister and I went there as girls," Annie answered.

The older woman smiled. "My great-grandparents founded Stoneledge Lake back in nineteen hundred and one," she told Annie. "It's a lovely spot, and as I was there as a girl myself, I have to say it was a lot of fun, too. How kind of your sister."

"Lizzie is a wonderful woman," Annie agreed. "She was the one who entered me in this contest."

"Where is your home?" Mrs. Van der Veer wanted to know.

"Right here in Egret Pointe," Annie said, laughing.

"Gracious, this whole thing has been quite serendipitous for you, hasn't it?"

"It really has," Annie agreed. "I didn't know what I was going to do about Wills, my five-year-old. My dad is home while Mom is in Tuscany with Lizzie and Nathaniel, but he's a golfer." She smiled ruefully. "But then my son's little friend's cousin couldn't make the trip to Disney World, and they had paid for two children, so Wills was invited. Problem solved! I really was very lucky, wasn't I?"

The evening continued on with good food and light conversation. Annie's mind kept wandering, as it had much of the day, to her naughty fantasy. She had lied earlier about accessing the Channel because she hadn't wanted to talk about her fantasy, and she had suspected that both Carole Kramer and Susie James would have asked. But she was very eager for the evening to end so she could get to bed and go back to her wicked little illusion. She was dying to know what would happen tonight. Would the Beast have his way with her? She remembered what the two unknowns had said to her in the darkness of her cell: He wouldn't fuck her until she was obedient. But Annie didn't know if she felt like being a complacent fairy-tale heroine.

Looking around her at the other women, she wondered what their fantasies were. The elegant and at least seventy-something Elise Van der Veer, the sour Carol Kramer, and the perky Susie James. What were their fantasies? And the three other women who were now chatting with the others — who were they? And what did they conjure up in their imaginations that translated to the Channel? And there was another thing: What had Susie James meant when she asked Nora if the personal assistants were trained to do *everything?* Did *everything* mean even sex? She blushed at her own thoughts.

After dinner Nora led them out onto a lovely stone terrace set up with lounges. Stretching out, they listened to a violin, cello, and piano concert of delightful baroque music as a moon rose over the bay. The evening was warm, and there was a light breeze that kept the mosquitoes away. Finally the party of women broke up for the evening, each going to her own room or suite. Devyn was there to escort Annie, but she left him at the door saying, "I can take it from here, kid. I'll see you in the morning. Good night."

" 'Night, Annie," he said cheerfully. "Sleep well."

"I will," she told him, and, entering her suite, she closed the door behind her. She wanted to rush, but she didn't. She was excited to get back into the Channel, but she was already sensing a potential addiction to it. She would prepare herself for bed in an orderly fashion. Removing her elegant black dress, she carefully hung it up. She put her pearls away in the little chamois bag they came in. She set her sandals in the closet. She hadn't worn stockings tonight. Her legs had a light tan, and it had sufficed. Stripping off her bra, she put it in the drawer. Her briefs she consigned to the small white plastic garbage bag she had brought to serve as a laundry container.

Going into the bathroom, she peed and then tried the bidet. The warm water bathing her was delicious. God, she loved this place! After drying herself off, she washed her face and hands, then brushed her teeth. Returning to the bedroom, she put on her silk-and-lace nightgown that had been neatly laid out on the turned-down bed. She set the chocolate aside on the nightstand and climbed into her bed. Then, picking up the remote, she pressed the open/close button, watching as the wall slid open to reveal the flat-screen television. For a long moment she held the remote. Should she press A and return to her fantasy of Beauty and the Beast? Or should she program another fantasy for B? She recalled a favorite novel of hers, *The Kadin*. It might be fun to be a sultan's sex slave. She had to remember to ask Nora how to delete a fantasy when she got bored with it.

But the Beast had been so intriguing last

night. Her thumb pressed A, and Annie found herself once again hanging naked in the darkened cell. Her body was immediately hot with her rising desires. The door to the little chamber opened, and the Beast entered, carrying a torch that he placed in the iron holder on the wall. He turned and looked at her. Reaching out, he examined one of her breasts.

"I see the marks of my men on you," he said. "They should not have been so rough, Mistress Anne."

"Did you send those men to assault me?" she asked him.

His big hand smacked her bottom with two sharp slaps. "You must ask my permission to speak, Mistress Anne." Then he sighed. "You understand nothing of obedience, do you? But are you capable of learning, is the question we must answer."

"May I speak?" she asked him.

" 'May I speak, *my lord,*' " he admonished, smacking her buttocks again.

"May I speak, my lord?" she rephrased her query, wincing.

"Be brief, Mistress Anne," he said.

"Did you send those two men?" she questioned him.

"Aye," he told her.

"May I speak, my lord?" she asked again.

"Excellent! You can learn," he praised her. "Aye, you may speak."

"Why did you send them?" Annie asked.

"You must be taught, Mistress Anne, that I now own your body and soul. You must be taught and brought to perfect obedience to my fancy. I can and will do whatever I choose with you. If it pleases me to permit two of my men to fondle you, to frig you, then I shall have it done, because you are my possession. And after I have had your virginity, and taught you to please me, I may share you with my friends. Or if you cannot be brought to an exquisite refinement of sexual pleasure, I shall simply give you to my soldiers for their delectation, as I have the other young women who have come into my possession and disappointed me. Are you capable of understanding what I have just told you, Mistress Anne?"

"Yes, my lord, I am," Annie told him. God, he was masterful! Arrogant, too, but perhaps she could change that. She imagined that the other girls had struggled to please him, and wept when he had been displeased. She would be different. She would learn, but she would also be strong without defying him. She imagined such an attitude would intrigue him.

The slight smile again. "You already

comprehend that you may answer my questions without requesting permission to speak. Excellent!" he said.

"May I speak, my lord?" Annie said.

"Nay. For now I would enjoy the beauty and the symmetry of your body in the silence of this chamber," the Beast said. Grabbing the chain, he raised her up a few feet. "I am told your cunt is large, but tight. Let us see if my men speak true." Reaching into the pocket of the shirt he wore, he drew out a phallic dildo.

Annie had heard of such things, but she had never seen one. Her blue eyes widened. A question formed on her lips, but she bit it back before she made a sound.

Seeing it, he nodded his approval, telling her, "It is made of ivory, and replicates my own organ when fully aroused. I will not insert it all the way, for I do not wish to disturb your virginity, which my men tell me is lodged quite tightly. I simply wish to see if you are actually capable of accepting my penis. When I decide to fuck you I will not dally about. Open your mouth now and suck on it while I prepare you. You will also be taught to suck my cock before I inject you with it. Sucking a cock is a great skill, Mistress Anne. You have a most luscious mouth, and I anticipate that you will excel at this art," he told her, and he pushed the phallus between her lips.

It stretched the edges of her mouth almost painfully, and Annie struggled briefly to find her breath. It touched the very back of her throat, and she fought down her gag reflex. Finally comfortable, she sucked on the ivory dildo, becoming more and more aware as she did so of his fingers playing between the folds of her labia, teasing at her clit, pinching it, and then he pushed his fingers a tiny way into her vagina. She was squirming against his hand, desperate for more.

He smiled his faint cruel smile and withdrew his hand from between her thighs. Then he chained her legs to the wall, spreading her wide. "You are an eager little bitch, Mistress Anne," he said softly as he drew the ivory phallus from her mouth and began rubbing it against her throbbing clitoris. "Shall I give you a little taste? But just a little, mind you, my pet." Slowly he inserted the head of the dildo into her vagina.

Annie shuddered, moaning with her need, and tried to force her body down upon the ivory, but she was restrained tightly.

The Beast laughed. "Do you want more, Mistress Anne? You may answer," he told her. "Do you want more?"

"Yes!" she gasped.

"You must beg me for it, my pet," he said in a soft, deadly voice. *"Beg!"*

"Please, my lord! Please!" Annie whimpered.

"Please, what, Mistress Anne?"

"Please give me more!" she begged him. *"I need to be fucked!"*

He reached out and stroked her thick chestnut hair as he inserted the phallus but an inch more. Then he slowly twirled it about within her vagina. "That is enough now," he told her, withdrawing it and setting the ivory aside. "My men say you took three fingers, and you took nicely to the phallus tonight. I shall very much enjoy having you in my bed. You are learning obedience quickly, Mistress Anne." He freed her legs once more, and then, reaching down with his hand, he released his penis from his trousers. It had been twitching and swelling until he found it uncomfortable to be so constrained.

Annie's eyes widened. Her lips formed a small O of both surprise and admiration. He was enormous, but then, given his height and frame he would be. The men who had come to her in the dark had said it was a foot long, and it certainly looked it. She could not take her eyes from it, for she found it both an object of power and of beauty.

"You are staring," the Beast said. "Remove your gaze from my cock, wench! You are not yet permitted to look upon it." He slapped her lightly upon her cheek to gain her attention, and then he sighed. "I can see you must be strapped again to instill obedience in you, Mistress Anne."

"I want you," she whispered desperately. She could just imagine that great penis filling her, making her scream with pleasure, making her come until she was weak.

"Tsk, tsk. But another infraction, you wicked girl!" He smacked her butt several stinging blows, and then, taking his tawse from its place on the stone wall, he laid it across her buttocks until her bottom was burning. As he punished her his cock grew larger and larger until it was hard and thrusting straight from his trousers.

Unable to take her eyes from it, Annie moaned more from her need for him than from any pain she felt from the leather. She had never in all of her life imagined such delicious, such wicked torture, and she was loving every moment of it. Nat's passions had been born out of his love for her, and hers for him. This was entirely different. It was depraved, perverse, and yet she wanted it. *My God!* What emotions had she been suppressing all of these years?

"You will have to relieve me, you wicked little bitch." He groaned as he lowered her to her knees. The straw beneath them was rough. "Open your mouth, Mistress Anne, and suck me. You will do so until I bid you to cease."

Obediently she parted her lips, and he pushed his penis between them, pulling his foreskin back as he did. Annie began to suck him. She pulled strongly on his length. Her tongue slid around the head of the penis. The ivory phallus had prepared her for his size, but not quite his length. Still, she drew him in deeper. She wished that her hands were free so she might touch him, but she knew her mouth was doing its job when he moaned low.

His voice was thick as he praised her. "That's it, my pet. I knew you would be good at this exercise. You are not yet ready to be fucked, for you have still not attained perfect obedience, but you are close, I suspect." His fingers dug into her head as she sucked him.

And then Annie felt him stiffen, and she knew he would climax within the warmth of her mouth. She sucked harder, swallowing the fierce, thick bursts of cum that he released to her, and she couldn't stop sucking even after she had greedily sipped every drop of his juices.

He groaned, retrieving his penis to place it back in his trousers. Then, bending down, he tangled his fingers in her hair and pulled her head up, kissing her hard. His mouth took hers in a fierce, possessive embrace. His tongue thrust deep into her mouth, caressing hers for the longest moment. Annie kissed him back hungrily. She had needed this more personal contact. The Beast was only a man, and she suddenly realized that she meant to tame him even as the girl in the fairy tale had tamed her Beast. But first she must gain his trust. The mouth on hers drew away. He pulled her up again so that her feet grazed the floor, and then he left her without another word, taking his torch with him.

Annie hung from her golden shackles, her bottom, her vagina, and her mouth sore from the Beast's ferocious attentions. She had learned in her Human Sexuality class in college that gentle punishment was sometimes used to increase sexual pleasure. It had always seemed odd to her, for she and Nat were lovers in every sense of the word. They needed nothing but each other for their mutual pleasure. Yet she had to admit to herself that she was enjoying his torture. Again she wondered why she felt this way. However, she had to admit to herself that the Beast was not cruel. She wondered what would happen to her next. The evening was, she sensed, only half over. It certainly couldn't be any later than midnight. What more was to come?

The door to her prison opened and closed quickly. And then Annie felt herself being bathed with a fragrance-filled soapy sponge. Every inch of her was washed, and then buckets of warm water were splashed over her. Her body was carefully dried with soft cloths. The door opened and closed again as a small figure scuttled through, carrying several pails and cloths. Annie hadn't been able to decide whether the creature was male or female.

Then, to her surprise, the Beast returned. He set his torch in the holder and, reaching into his tunic, he drew out a beautiful bejeweled collar, fastening it about Annie's neck. Lined in the softest silk, the collar settled upon her collarbone. Next the beast attached a delicate gold chain to the collar. Releasing her from the manacles, he said, "You will come with me, Mistress Anne. If you remain obedient for the next hour or more you will be given your own chamber in a tower, and not returned to this dungeon. If, however, you are disobedient, you shall be whipped publicly and brought back here. You may answer me now. Do you understand?"

"Yes, my lord." Annie said.

"Excellent, my pet. Come along now." And the Beast led her by the chain from the little round cell and up the stairs.

She was naked. As they exited the dungeon into a main corridor of the castle Annie looked nervously about, but the servants they passed paid her no attention at all. But then they entered the great hall, and it was filled with rough men sitting at trestle tables beneath the high board. As they passed between the tables many of the men reached out to touch her, pinching her buttocks, grabbing at her breasts. The Beast ignored them, and Annie took her cue from him, hurrying behind him although she was a little frightened. *I can end this at any time,* she reminded herself.

"You will sit on the dais at the side of my chair, by my feet," the Beast said as they reached the high board.

Annie saw there was but one high-backed oak chair set behind the high board, directly at its center. Reaching it, she obeyed his instruction. At least she was not so easily available to the hot eyes and crude remarks of the soldiers in the hall. The meal was served. Annie could see the servants coming up to the other side of the Beast's chair and offering him bowls, plates, and platters of food. She had seen a gold plate and a bejeweled gold goblet before she had seated herself at his feet.

"Open your mouth," he commanded her now and again.

Annie would obediently raise her head up and open her mouth to receive some tidbit of food. Once she raised her head to his command and he transferred some sweet wine from his mouth to hers. It was a most sensual experience. When he had finished eating and the dishes had been cleared away from the high board, the Beast pulled Annie up and settled her into his lap, where he fondled her breasts absently as a minstrel played his lute and sang. Now and again he would put a sweetmeat into her mouth. He began to frig her, pushing three fingers deep into her vagina slowly, then increasing the rhythm until she was whimpering softly. He withdrew the three fingers and sucked on them as his eyes met hers. "You taste delicious," he told her. "And you have really been very good, Mistress Anne. You have exhibited perfect obedience tonight. Would you like to be rewarded? You may answer all my questions without further permission."

"Yes, my lord," Annie said softly. "Thank you."

"Would you like to be fucked, Mistress Anne?" His eyes still held her in thrall.

"Yes, my lord."

"Here on the high board before my men, for all to see?" he said wickedly.

"If it pleases my lord, aye," Annie answered him, for she realized it was what he wanted. And he thought she would protest such a thing.

"And afterward, if it pleased me to let my captains fuck you?" he pressed her.

"Yes, my lord. Whatever pleases you pleaseth me," Annie told him.

"Your docile obedience pleaseth me well," the Beast said. "I knew you were intelligent when I first saw you. I knew you could be trained to my fancy." Then he lifted her from his lap and placed her upon the high board. "Spread yourself for me, Mistress Anne," he commanded her, and when she did he leaped upon the great oak table and freed his enormous penis, which sprang forth fully engorged.

A roar of anticipation rose up from the men in the hall at the sight before them on the high board. They came to crowd about

121

it, faces avid with their own lusts.

Annie's body was throbbing eagerly for the Beast's penis. She could scarcely wait to have him impale her with it. It seemed she had waited her whole life for this fierce lover. She held out her arms to him. "The Channel is now closed," came the hated voice.

No! No! Annie screamed silently. *Not yet! Damn it, not yet!* But she sensed her fantasy dissolving about her, and there was nothing she could do to stop it. It would be sixteen hours until she could get back to the Beast. Would her fantasy pick up where it had left off? Would he fuck her before his soldiers on the high board in his great hall? Tonight she had begun where she had ended last night, so surely it would be the same again. It had to be. She needed to be fucked.

She felt hot, and threw the coverlet off her fevered body. *Oh, God!* Why did it have to end the way it just had? Lust seemed to be consuming her. Getting up, she went into the bathroom and took a cool shower. Then, taking two aspirin, she got back into bed. It was quarter to five in the morning, and she needed to get a little rest. Soon enough Devyn would be coming to wake her. Annie closed her eyes.

CHAPTER FOUR

She felt feverish when Devyn came to awaken her. He noted it immediately. "You look as if you didn't sleep," he said, concern in his voice.

"I did and I didn't," she answered him. "Do I have to get up right now?"

"No, of course not," he said. "I'm going to go and get Ms. Buckley, Annie. You look drained, and we can't have our grand-prize winner getting sick on us." He hurried out, leaving her to fall back on her pillows.

Nora Buckley came immediately to see what was the matter. "Go and bring her breakfast here," she instructed Devyn. "She's not used to all this luxury and is probably exhausted now that her weariness is beginning to set in, poor woman." Nora entered Annie's bedroom, closing the door behind her. Sitting down on the bed, she reached out to feel Annie's forehead. It was damp, but not hot. "You look like you've been run over by a truck," Nora said candidly. "Now tell me why."

Annie flushed. "It's embarrassing," she said.

"Ah," Nora murmured, "it's your fantasy, isn't it?"

Annie nodded.

"What's it about?" Nora queried gently.

"You'll think I'm awful," Annie began. "I never had a fantasy before, and I never knew what I'd been repressing all these years." Then she went on to explain the fantasy she seemed to have created for herself.

When she had finished, Nora smiled slightly and said, "My goodness, you are a very bad girl, Annie Miller. I should have never thought it," she teased.

"I knew you'd think it was awful," Annie half sobbed.

"Oh, you poor dear," Nora said, patting her hand. "Not at all. Your fantasy is really quite mild compared to some of them. You just let yourself be sexually tortured too long. You needed to be fucked, and the Channel closed just as it was about to happen. It takes a while to get used to time within the Channel. Tonight you'll just pick up where you left off, and oh, my, what a delicious beginning. Tell me, what is your Beast like, Annie?"

"He's human, but part of his face is covered by a silk-and-leather mask. I think he is scarred. He's very tall. Big. His hair is dark. I haven't yet seen the color of his eyes. Nora, why did I create a fantasy that tortured me?" Annie asked the woman.

"I'm no expert," Nora Buckley said, "but I think you felt guilty about having a sexual fantasy. The realistic part of you knows you are a widow, and have been for several years, but the emotional part of you is still attached to your husband. However, he's dead, and you are very much alive. You have needs that should be fulfilled, but you also have five children, and you don't want to set a bad example. That's why the Channel is such a good thing, Annie. You can satisfy those needs privately. No one has to know."

Annie nodded. "I have to admit I am enjoying myself," she said softly.

There was a knock on the bedroom door, and Devyn came in with a breakfast tray. "Thought you could use this," he said cheerfully.

"Set it down on the table," Nora instructed him, "and then go and bring me Annie's schedule sheet for today." She turned to her companion. "I'll sit with you while you eat breakfast, and we'll talk some more." She took the clipboard Devyn handed her. "Are you up for a walk?" she asked, and Annie nodded. "And how about some time in the pool doing aquacise? The water is heated and just delicious. And a massage with Lars. I'll tell him you need a stress treatment. It will be an hour and a half or more. I think that should get you back on your feet." She handed the clipboard back to Devyn. "Set it up, and then wait for Annie in the living room. Close the door as you go out." And when the young man had left them, Nora turned back to Annie. "You know, you could take Devyn to bed if you wanted. Our personal assistants are trained to give their ladies sexual pleasure if they want it. The Spa is set up to give full service."

"He's a kid!" Annie said, just a little bit shocked.

"He's at his sexual peak," Nora said, "and I happen to know he has a very talented cock. It's perfectly all right to screw him if you want to between fantasies."

"I think I'll stick with the fantasy for now," Annie answered. And then she asked mischievously, "I wonder if Carole Kramer and Susie James have taken advantage of this full-service element of the Spa."

Nora laughed. "They were quick to figure it out, and yes, they did, although you did not hear it from me. Come on now. Get up and eat. You'll feel much better if you do, I promise you." She helped Annie from her bed.

Annie did feel better after she had eaten, although she wasn't certain whether it was the food or talking with Nora Buckley that had done it. She spent an hour outside in the August sunshine walking with Elise Van der Veer and Susie James. The young reporter from *Chic* turned out to be quite nice, and very amusing.

"This is really a plum assignment for me," she said. "I usually work out of the office, but my editor heard Carole Kramer was coming from *Pampered Woman,* and decided she wanted a younger take on the Spa for *Chic.*"

"How will you explain *all* the amenities?" Elise Van der Veer asked wickedly.

"Oh, we have code words for all kinds of stuff," Susie answered with a grin. "Our readers are pretty hip."

What the hell code word could you possibly have for personal assistants who will fuck on demand? Annie wondered.

She swam several laps in the Spa's lap pool, and then joined the rest of the guests for aquacise. The personal assistants exercised with them in the water. Annie couldn't help but notice that Devyn had great pecs and a cute ass. Afterward he escorted her to Lars. She lay on his massage table for close to two hours, and she had to admit that the aching in her nether regions was gone when he had finished with her. She had no idea what he had done or how he had accomplished this miracle, but he had. Annie thanked him, and Lars nodded his acknowledgment. After a long nap she joined the other guests for dinner, but she couldn't help glancing at her watch now and again. So were most of the other women.

"We're going to be showing that wonderful old Audrey Hepburn movie *Breakfast at Tiffany's* tonight in the lounge," Nora announced brightly as they were finishing a heavenly chocolate dessert made from egg whites, dark chocolate, and sweetener.

Only Carole Kramer and Elise Van der Veer seemed enthusiastic about the prospect.

"I adored the clothing of that era," Elise Van der Veer said. "So elegant, and so stylish. And Hepburn had a wonderful figure. Not like all these little anorexic girls today in the tacky clothing they seem to favor."

"I've never seen that movie," Carole Kramer noted.

"It's a classic," Elise Van der Veer remarked.

"Maybe I'll stay then," Susie James said.

But Annie and the other guests demurred, scattering to their own rooms as the tall clock in the central lobby struck eight p.m. She didn't even bother to undress or brush her teeth. Annie flung herself onto the bed, grabbing up the remote as she did, and pressed the open/close button, and then A. The roar of the soldiers in the hall sent a thrill of excitement through her. She was flat upon her back, her legs spread wide, and the Beast was standing over her, releasing his great cock from his breeches. He looked down at her, a cruel twist to his narrow lips as he considered his prey.

"Bring her legs back!" he said, and two soldiers jumped forward, pulling Annie's legs up and then back, revealing her sex to the men crowding about the high board.

Annie's heart was pounding against her ribs in anticipation. She watched as the Beast conjured from the air a long, thin feather with a narrow point. He was going to torture her first, and she instinctively knew he wanted her to protest. "No!" she cried to him. "Not the feather, my lord! Not the feather!"

The men in the hall howled with laugher at her cries. "Give it to her, my lord," they called. "Tickle her up and make her scream!"

The Beast knelt and, spreading her wider to reveal her throbbing clit, he ran the pointed feather down both sides of her nether lips several times. Then he touched the tiny tip of it to the center of her clitoris.

Annie bit her lip. That tiny point worrying at her sensitive flesh was pure torture. She cried out as he began to ply his weapon more vigorously. "Please, please!" she begged him. "No more, I pray you, my lord! No more!" She was going to have a clitoral climax, and it came quickly, sending a shudder of pleasure through her as her eyes closed.

A sharp pinch to her buttocks, however, sent her eyes flying open again. "You will look at me," the Beast said, and he teased at the opening of her vagina with the feather. "Come, Mistress Anne, you are almost ready. But a moment more." And the feather slid into her, twirling about and causing her juices to begin to flow. "Good! Good!" the Beast said approvingly as he moved himself forward. "Keep her legs up, men. I will deflower this virgin daughter of the merchant now."

"Plow her deeply, my lord," one of the men called out.

"Now, wench, you will acknowledge your master," he told her, bringing the head of his penis to the entry to her vagina and rubbing it against her. Leaning forward, he murmured softly so that only she could hear him, "Fight me and protest, Mistress Anne. Give my men a good show this night."

"No! No!" Annie screamed. "You shall not have me! I was to be your housekeeper, not your whore!" She struggled against the two men holding her legs up and back. "I shall go to the king! I shall!" Annie tried to claw him, but the position in which she was being restrained made it next to impossible.

"Your father gave you to me knowing full well my intent," the Beast told her. "Yield yourself to me, and cease your foolishness!"

"Never! *Never!*" Annie shrieked.

"Fuck her! Fuck her!" the soldiers in the hall began to chant.

The Beast pushed the head of his penis into her. "Now, wench, you will be well and truly fucked," he told her, and he thrust himself deep.

She was the merchant's virgin daughter, and he smashed past a tightly lodged hymen, sending a burst of burning pain through her. Annie screamed in genuine distress as a sigh went up from the men crowded about them. The Beast's great cock

131

buried itself to its hilt within her. She moaned as the agony subsided and a tingle of pleasure began to infuse her. And then he began to ride her. With each smooth stroke of his penis her desire rose higher. She could feel the life pulsing through the thick organ as it delved deeper and deeper. Annie's head thrashed back and forth. The two soldiers holding her legs wide grinned down at her, one licking his lips suggestively.

"Put her legs over my shoulders," the Beast growled, "and step back." He caught at the hands that attempted to hit him, holding her two wrists in a single big hand and forcing her arms above her head. "You're a born whore," he told her, sounding pleased. "Now I shall make you climax before all of these rough fellows, Mistress Anne, and then you will entertain a few more sturdy cocks before I permit you to rest."

"You cannot!" she gasped. *I can end this. I can!* But she did not.

"You are my possession," he reminded her, and then he found the tiny spot hidden deep within a woman that drove her to near madness. He worked it hard.

Suddenly Annie felt herself losing control. Fierce spasms began to rack her. Her eyes could not focus. The terrible pleasure washing over her was more than she had ever known. She moaned, and was close to giving in to it when she remembered that if she was to be safe within this fantasy she must tame the Beast. Concentrating, she contracted the muscles of her vagina, squeezing the great penis within her.

"Ah, bitch!" he groaned, surprised.

"You will come with me, my lord," she told him. "If you do not, I will not!"

He worked her all the harder, but Annie fought back, tightening her vagina about his huge member. She felt her strength wavering as the waves of hot delight washed over her, growing in potency with each passing second. This was a battle he meant to win, and having fought him well, Annie knew she must let him.

"Ah, God!" she cried out. "Oh! Oh! Ohhhhh!" Her body was racked with fierce tremors as he fucked her harder and harder. "No more, I beg you, my lord! Ohhhhh!" And she actually fainted away.

With a great groan the Beast came, pouring his lust into the woman beneath him. The men in the hall erupted with cheers for their lord. There were cries of "Well-done!"

Annie was revived as she lay upon the high board. Turning her head, she sought the Beast. He was sitting again in his high-backed chair. He smiled cruelly at her as he saw her conscious again.

"You did well, Mistress Anne, and so I will permit you the choice. Will you have two, or will you have three?"

"Only you, my lord," she whispered softly, crawling to the table's edge near him.

"Nay," he told her. "If you do not choose, I will. Have I not told you that you must obey me in whatever I ask of you? A large, airy room, a serving woman, and a bed are waiting for you once you have obeyed my command," he told her softly.

"Two, my lord," she answered him.

The beast nodded. "Kaspar and Rafe, you who held her legs for me. You may each have a taste of Mistress Anne, but you will do her as I command you."

"Yes, my lord!" the two soldiers said in unison.

"Kasper, have I not heard it said you have a taste for arse?"

The soldier grinned and nodded.

"Then you shall take her together. Rafe shall have her cunt and Kaspar her ass," the Beast told them. "Do it now, for the wench is wearied, but I would reward you."

The two soldiers pulled sturdy cocks from their breeches and, climbing onto the high board, pulled Annie between them. For a few moments they enjoyed themselves play-

134

ing with her breasts and her round bottom. Rafe pulled one of her legs over his torso and pushed his penis into her wet vagina. Kaspar drew her buttock cheeks apart and, pressing the head of his cock against her anal opening, pushed himself slowly and carefully into her.

Annie shrieked, for she had never before entertained a man there. She could feel his long cock throbbing as it lay still within her. His rough hands fondled her breasts, pinching the nipples and pulling at them. Rafe, however, pumped her vigorously, his mouth smashing against hers as he groaned and instructed her to his pleasure.

"That's it, wench! God, you're tight! And so wet and hot!"

Annie could feel both of their cocks, separated by but a single membrane, as they pleasured themselves in her body. Finally she squeezed them both as hard as she could, and they came together, groaning mightily.

"Nicely done, wench," the Beast said approvingly.

"May I speak, my lord?" she asked him, and when he nodded she said, "If I have pleased you, I am glad."

"I have high hopes for you, Mistress Anne," he told her. Then, pulling at the chain on her collar, he brought her down from the high board. "I will take you to your new prison," he told her, the odd smile touching the corner of his mouth.

Annie followed him from the great hall and up a flight of winding stairs within a large tower. At the top of the tower was a door that opened to reveal a small but comfortable chamber. Unfastening the chain from her collar, he said, "This chamber is yours now, Mistress Anne," and he pushed her inside. "Bathe and rest yourself. I will return eventually. Be ready to service me when I do." Then he closed the door behind her, and Annie heard him turning a key within the lock.

Annie looked about the room. It had two leaded, paned casement windows, between which was a small hearth with a blazing fire. There was an oak tub before the fire, and Annie immediately stepped into it and washed herself. The smell of the terrible lust of three men was soon erased by the scent of roses. Drying herself, Annie climbed into the large oak bed with the four twisted posts that held up a wooden canopy. The canopy held a panel of mirror, and, looking up, Annie could see herself quite plainly.

Flinging back the covers, she saw the body of the merchant's daughter. It was lush and it was ripe. She smiled at herself. The Channel was indeed a wonder. After over two years of widowhood she had just had sex with three vigorous lovers. She wouldn't get pregnant from any of the encounters, nor would she contract any diseases. And best of all, no one would ever know. The Beast was certainly the lustiest lover any woman could have. Oddly she forgave him his demanding nature. But what had caused him to need such mastery over a woman that he would share her with his soldiers? When she learned that — and she would, Annie thought — she would be able to tame the Beast.

The sound of the key turning in the lock caused her to feign sleep.

"Are you truly sleeping?" he asked her.

"Nay," Annie answered, opening her eyes.

"Good. I am of a mind to have you again this night, Mistress Anne," he told her, and, removing the long burgundy silk robe he was wearing, he revealed his nakedness.

"You are beautiful, my lord," Annie told him truthfully, and he was.

Tall and lean, he was well muscled, with broad shoulders and a chest that tapered into a narrow waist and hips. He turned to bar the door behind him, and she admired his hard buttocks, his long, furred legs, his thickly furred groin where rested his mighty cock. His chest too was furred, but lightly. "Men are not beautiful," he told her.

"You are," she said softly. "Will you always wear your mask, my lord?"

"You would not like what was beneath," he told her.

"You have been scarred badly, my lord," Annie guessed.

He nodded. "I would not frighten you, Mistress Anne."

"I am your possession, as you have told me quite firmly," Annie replied. "Would it make any difference to you if I were frightened?"

"Nay, it would not," he said coldly. "But a man must have his pride. I need no one's — no woman's — pity," the Beast told Annie almost bitterly.

"One day you will show me your face," Annie heard herself saying. "You will show it to me because you will love me."

He laughed harshly. "Wench," he said, "you fancy yourself, I can see. But you also amuse me. I will keep you with me for the interim, and not give you to my men for their enjoyment. They are very disappointed about that decision, for Rafe and Kaspar have highly praised you." Then he looked sharply at her. "You did not come for them." It was a statement, and not a question.

"Nay," Annie said, "I did not."

"Why?" he demanded to know.

"Because I have reserved my passion for you alone, my lord," she told him.

"A clever answer, wench."

"The truth, my lord," Annie responded quietly.

He climbed into the bed next to her and drew her into his embrace. He ran a finger over her lips. "Such a talented mouth," he said softly.

"If you permit me to handle you, my lord, it shall give you even greater pleasure," she promised him with a small smile.

"Indeed," he said. "You have my permission, Mistress Anne."

Pulling the covers back, Annie climbed onto his torso, her buttocks facing his head. Slithering down him, she caressed his big cock. She began to lick at its length, sliding her tongue up and down, down and up the pillar of flesh. Rolling his foreskin down, she took just the head of his member into the warm cave of her mouth. Her tongue encircled it slowly, and then she sucked him gently, feeling him burgeoning in her mouth. Annie smiled and, turning herself about, slid farther down to gather his furred balls in her hand. Bending, she licked them and then, taking them into her mouth, rolled them about with her tongue. He gave a loud groan. Releasing him, she found his penis was now at its full power, and he was very ready to have her, but Annie escaped his grasp and, pulling herself up, straddled his head, pushing her mons down as she commanded him, "You must lick and suck me, and when I am ready I will ride you."

"Bitch," he murmured against her labia, "you will be punished for your temerity." Then his mouth kissed her flesh, and he licked and sucked at her.

"Yes, my lord," Annie replied sweetly, and when she felt herself growing wet with his attentions she moved down once again, impaling herself on his hard length. Then she rode him until he was whimpering and his hands were crushing and bruising the tender flesh of her breasts. "You will come for me!" she told him.

"And you will come for me," he told her, rolling her onto her back as he pistoned her fiercely. "Did the slave think to master the master?" he demanded, pushing himself into her again and again.

"Harder, my lord! Deeper, my lord!" Annie cried to him. "I am near. So near!"

"As am I!" he answered her as he complied

with her demands. And then they cried out together as their bodies climaxed with their lusty passions.

He did not leave her then, and Annie fell asleep in his arms, content for the first time in months, and deliciously sated. She was at first confused and surprised when Devyn awakened her. She was in her own bed at the Spa. And she was still wearing the clothing she had worn the previous night. She knew he was pretending not to notice. "I fell asleep," she said sheepishly.

"You had a rough day yesterday," he said. "How about if I run you a bath?"

She nodded. "Make it rose scented today," she told him. She could smell the fragrance of rose all about her, she realized. The wall covering the flat-screen television was closed. She sought for the remote, and when she couldn't find it opened the night table drawer to find it there. Had she returned it there? She couldn't remember.

The next few days seemed to fly as she was treated to the various opportunities the Spa offered its clientele. She particularly liked the weight and strength training. Devyn was her instructor. The day he slipped boxing gloves on her hands and held up his own target cover mitts, she discovered just how angry she really was at Nat's death.

141

"I want you to hit as hard as you can at my hands, Annie. Think about something that really makes you angry or has made you angry. Something you haven't been able to let go of, or something you didn't dare express because of your kids. This is a cardio workout, but it's also meant to help you get past your anger."

She began to hit weakly at the targets he was holding up. Annie Miller was a strong woman. She didn't let anything get under her skin. She couldn't. She had to think of the children and their well-being.

"Not good enough," Devyn said. "Don't tell me you aren't angry about having been left a widow. And he sure as hell didn't leave you well fixed, did he? A bit selfish, I'd say. And why wasn't he watching where he was going that day? I mean, who steps into the path of one of those humongous red London buses?"

"That's not fair!" Annie said sharply, but she began to hit harder at the target mitt he was waving in front of her.

"He was probably looking at one of those hot London girls," Devyn taunted her, "and thinking how he'd like to get laid."

"You don't know Nat," Annie cried, striking more fiercely at him.

"Maybe you didn't know him. *Didn't* being the operative word, Annie. The man is dead. He left you with five kids and very little else." Devyn dodged the blow Annie blindly aimed at him. "Hey, keep your eyes on the targets!" he warned her.

Annie started to hit with all her strength at the mitts he was holding up. Her glove-covered fists flashed back and forth. She was angry. Oh, God, she was really angry! Nat was gone. Killed in a stupid accident that should never have happened. And she was so tired of struggling to keep what they had built going. Tired of having to listen to her dad tell her over and over again that he had warned Nat his insurance wouldn't be enough in the event of an accident. Tired of having to accept so many kindnesses from Lizzie, even if Lizzie did mean well. Tired of listening to her mother, who had every-thing and more, whine about her father's golf. But most of all she was tired of having to make compromises so that everyone around her would be happy. When did she get to be happy? Gasping with her exertion, Annie burst into tears.

Yanking off the target mitts, Devyn pulled her into his arms. "Geez, Annie, I'm sorry. I didn't mean to upset you," he said, hugging her.

"It . . . it wasn't you," Annie sobbed. "Not really."

"I should not have said those things. I mean, hell, I don't really know you or your situation. I just needed to get you going for the cardio workout."

Annie started to laugh through her tears. "Well," she told him, "you sure got me going, Devyn." *Good grief.* She was snuggled against his hard chest, and she had soaked his T-shirt. She pulled away. "I'm sorry to be such a baby, but you got me thinking, and you're right. I was angry, and I've never let it out. I've been killed being brave for everyone's sake but mine. But when you have kids you do that."

"You look awfully young to have five kids," he said.

"And one starting Princeton in a couple of weeks," she reminded him. Then she grinned. "Want to go another round, kid?" She held up the glove, and shuffled her feet.

"I think you've had all the cardio you need for today," he told her. "Look, I know you can't join the gym in Egret Pointe, but get yourself a pair of these gloves and target mitts, and work out with one of your kids. It's good for you."

"I've got a teenage daughter," Annie remarked. "She would be the one, I suspect.

It would probably be good for both of us."

He laughed and nodded. "Wish I could have done that with my dad," he said.

"You didn't get along with your dad?" Annie asked, curious, as he pulled the boxing gloves from her hands.

"My dad and I got on great. Maybe a little too great. We did a lot of things together, especially after my mom died. But in the end I guess he realized he had spoiled me too much. And he tried to correct the oversight. The rich really are different, Annie."

"You're rich?" She was surprised. Why was he working here if he was rich?

"My dad was, but I'm not. Hey, let's go have some fresh juice now."

They adjourned to the juice bar, which was set up on the stone terrace overlooking the bay. With the Grecian architecture all around them it almost didn't seem like Egret Pointe at all, Annie thought. "Apricot and celery, and maybe a little carrot," she told the juice maker.

"Carrot and apple for me," Devyn said.

They drank their juice, and then Devyn suggested they take a walk before she had to get ready for dinner.

"Why aren't you well-off?" Annie asked him. "Tell me more about your family."

They walked through the Spa's beautiful gardens. The air was a bit heavy with late-August humidity. Now and again a monarch butterfly flitted by, and there were large bumblebees hovering over the many flowers. Then they moved down to the beach.

"Well," he began, "my father's first wife committed suicide when my brother, really half brother, was eight. Less than a year later my dad married Mom. She had been his secretary. Six months later their *premature* son was born, weighing in at eight pounds even. That's me. At that point the gossip began, Mom said. She told me before she died that she had worked for Dad for four years, and it wasn't until Madeline died that they became involved. When she got pregnant he made the decision to marry her. They were really good friends. But the gossip didn't stop.

"My mother was very beautiful, and Madeline hadn't been. Everyone knew my father had married his first wife for her money and her connections. But he had always been good to her, and he had never embarrassed her. But all that went by the boards. All anyone could think of was that Dad had married nine months after Madeline died, and the secretary he married was pregnant when they married. Everyone assumed Dad had been carrying on with my mother while he was still married to Madeline. And then they began to say that the reason Madeline had committed suicide was because she had found out about dad, his secretary, and the pregnancy. No one considered the time line, that my birth had occurred fifteen months after Madeline had died."

"Your poor mother," Annie sympathized.

"My mother had a sense of humor about the whole situation," Devyn said. "She said if it had all happened like everyone was saying it had, she would have had a longer gestation period than an elephant."

"Your mother sounds like a really nice woman," Annie told him.

"She was. She said it didn't matter what anyone said or thought. Her conscience was clear. Unfortunately my older brother, Phillip, heard the rumors too. He was nine years older than me, and he'd never gotten over his mother's death. He's the one who found her hanging in the stables. He wanted someone to blame for Madeline's death, and he got that someone when he heard the rumors."

"What happened?" Annie asked. "No, wait. I shouldn't be asking you that."

"Nah, it's okay," Devyn said. "I was almost three when it happened. My parents had a dinner party, and our nanny brought Phillip and me down to say good night. I don't remember the incident, but my father said everyone made a big fuss over me, and said what a fine boy my brother was. Phillip then told everyone that I had something to say. Everyone looked to me, and Dad says I said, 'Mama is a whore.' There was this stunned silence, and then the nanny fainted dead away. Dad said it took nearly fifteen minutes to revive her. My father asked me who had told me to say that, and I answered, 'Philly teached me.' At that point my mother took me upstairs and put me to bed before returning to her guests. Phillip was sent to my father's library."

"The dinner party went on?" Annie asked, unable to restrain her curiosity.

"Of course. The Scotts are perfect WASPs. We ignore the elephant in the room," Devyn said wryly.

"What happened to your brother?" Annie queried. "And the poor nanny?"

"She retired home to England, and Dad gave her a reference on the chance she still wanted to work. He said she was a decent woman, but perhaps not as watchful as she should have been. As for Phillip, he was sent off to a military school two days later. I didn't see him after that night for many years. Dad wouldn't have him in the house. His school, St. Cuthbert's, named after the fighting bishop of Lindisfarne, had a summer camp too. Phillip went from school to camp for the next six years."

"What about his other vacations? Christmas? Easter?" Annie asked.

"He stayed at school," Devyn said. "Dad wouldn't even let him go home with friends over those times. My mother didn't like it at all. It was the only time she ever argued with my dad, but it came up every Christmas. She forgave Phillip. She said he was just a kid and didn't really understand what he had done. My father thought otherwise. He said Phillip was too smart for his own good, and damned well knew what he had done. You see, my mother was three months pregnant with her second child when this incident occurred. She miscarried a week later. Dad blamed Phillip for that, too. Especially when the doctors said my mother would be unable to have other kids."

"How sad for you all," Annie remarked. "What happened to your brother?"

"Well, after he graduated from St. Cuthbert's he went to Harvard. And during the summers he was in college, my father made him work in one of his businesses. One summer he worked packing waste in one of

Dad's wool mills in Scotland. He had to live with the foreman of the mill. He was paid what any waste packer would be paid, and half of that had to go to the foreman for his room and board. Whatever was left at the end of the summer was his to keep. He had to use it for his expenses at college, but my mother insisted that Dad buy him clothing once a year and pay for his books. The second summer, Phillip went to work in one of Dad's offices. His supervisor was so complimentary about his work that my father took an actual personal interest in my brother for the first time in years.

"First he ascertained that the supervisor wasn't just trying to kiss up to him. When he realized that Phillip was actually a chip off the old block, he began to treat him a little better. My mom died shortly after Phillip graduated from college. I was just fourteen. I hadn't seen my brother since that night when he had had me say, 'Mama is a whore,'" Devyn reminisced. "A couple of months after Mom died, Dad bought Phillip an apartment, and he'd come to dinner now and again."

"So you and your brother were reunited," Annie said. "That's good."

"Not really," Devyn told her. "You see, I was everything Phillip wasn't. He was cold, stiff, emotionless, and totally, seriously work-oriented. Dad always said he was more like his mother's family than the Scotts. The Scotts worked hard, but they liked a bit of fun. On my fifteenth birthday Dad bought me a very expensive call girl so I could learn firsthand what sex was all about. First he showed me what to do with the girl as I watched, and then he watched as I made my first foray. He said I was a natural. After that I went with my dad more often than not when he wanted to have sex.

"When I turned eighteen he arranged for a long weekend for me and my friends on his private island with a group of expensive prostitutes. We had a fabulous time. As long as I kept up my grades in school and got into a good college, he indulged and spoiled me as he always had. The indulgences just became more for mature audiences. Phillip knew about it all, and he was jealous. It didn't matter that Dad praised his business acumen. Phillip wanted Dad all to himself.

"When I graduated college I backpacked around Europe for two years, and then came home to learn my father's many businesses. But I didn't seem to be cut out for the business world. I really tried, but I kept screwing up. For the first time in my life my father grew impatient with me. He began to rely more on Phillip. When he died two years ago he left me a small inheritance in trust. Not enough to get into trouble, but just enough to be supported. The bulk of his wealth, the house, the island, it all went to Phillip. The first thing my brother did was kick me out of the house. Then he attempted to break the trust Dad had set up for me. When that failed he told me he didn't ever want to see me again."

"Oh, Devyn," Annie said. "I'm so sorry."

"Hey, he's the real bastard, not me," Devyn replied. "One of my dad's buddies took pity on me. He's a friend of Mr. Nicholas's, and he got me this gig here at the Spa. I like it, and I like what I do. I guess I've found my calling."

"How old are you?" Annie asked him.

"You asked me that once before," he said with a smile.

"I know, and you evaded me. How old?"

"I'm thirty-one," Devyn answered her.

"You can't be!" Annie exclaimed, surprised. "You look much too young."

"It's my baby face," he explained. "And what's worse, when I'm sixty, I'm going to look almost as bad. You can't get rid of baby faces, I'm told."

Annie laughed. "Men have all the luck, and they always look younger than the women around them. It just isn't fair! Did your dad have a baby face?"

"No, I look like my mom. She used to say it was her baby face that got Dad," he said with a smile of remembrance.

"What was your mom's name?" Annie inquired.

"Joan," he answered. "It was the simple name of a nice girl from a working-class family. Now, Phillip's mother had an elegant name, Madeline. It suited her, I guess. A rich man's daughter, his only child. But I'm talking too much — and about myself, which is worse," Devyn decided. "Tomorrow you go home, but not until you've had another manicure, pedicure, facial, and a final massage from Lars. I want you to enjoy the remainder of your stay, Annie."

"To be honest, I'm just really beginning to get used to all this luxury," Annie admitted. "I wish I could stay here forever."

"Hey, it wouldn't be so special if it were an everyday thing," Devyn told her.

"No, I don't suppose it would," Annie agreed. *And I do have my year's subscription to the Channel,* she thought to herself. *The Beast comes home with me.*

"It's almost time for dinner, and it's a farewell dinner tonight," Devyn told her. "All the special guests are leaving tomorrow. We open officially right after Labor Day."

They walked back up from the beach. The damp air smelled faintly salty, and above them the gulls soared, *skree*ing as they caught the whorls of the soft breeze. Annie had saved a pair of white silk slacks and a V-necked black tee for tonight's dinner. She smiled at herself in the mirror as she slipped a silver cuff decorated in great chunks of turquoise on her wrist. Behind her, Mr. Eugene fussed with her thick chestnut hair as he fashioned it in a style he called a French twist.

"Have I lost weight?" she asked Devyn. "My face looks a little thinner."

"According to your chart, you've dropped almost eight pounds this week," he told her. "Before you go home, you'll get a list of what you can and can't eat."

"I eat on the run at home. With five kids you can't really diet," Annie said.

"Sure you can," he told her. "Just keep away from the bread, the pasta, and the sugars. I'll bet your girls will love lots of salads and lean meats. You can add the hard carbs for the little guy. Remember, your older son will be gone. Other than Wills it's just you girls, Annie. You can do this!"

Devyn was so positive, Annie thought. He

made her feel good, like she could do anything. He made her feel as if she weren't just someone's mother. Well, hell, it was his job as her PA to make her feel good. She shouldn't read anything more into it than that, and tomorrow afternoon Cinderella would be back to her ashes.

Dinner was wonderful. The two reporters had departed after the weekend. Those remaining all sat at one table: Nora Buckley, Mrs. Van der Veer, Annie, and the two other specially asked guests, J. P. Woods, the head of a publishing company in the city, and a senator's wife from D.C. Annie had had virtually no contact with either woman. She found the publisher a little scary, even on short acquaintance; and the senator's wife turned out to be a lawyer whose schedule was so hectic Nora had allowed her to come during this preopening week. At dinner all she talked about was her desire to get back home, as she had to prepare for a very high-profile case.

Nora had invited the guests' personal assistants to join them at dinner. The inclusion of the four young men made the table livelier. Dinner began with shrimp cocktail. There was prime rib of beef, fresh corn, haricots verts, delicious plates of perfectly sliced ripe tomatoes, and for dessert sweet chunks of pineapple with individual bowls of dark chocolate for dipping, along with cups of pale tea. Tall green bottles of Pellegrino lined the table.

As the meal came to a close, Nora stood up and the conversation ceased. "I hope you have all enjoyed your week here at the Spa," she told them. "If you have any suggestions, I hope you will fill out the cards you'll find in your rooms before leaving us tomorrow afternoon. Mr. Nicholas wanted me to thank you all for agreeing to be our guinea pigs during this preopening. And we'd love to share the news that we're already booked a year in advance, and have a waiting list for cancellations. We're having a little piano concert following dinner. It's Van Long from the Belvoir Hotel in the city."

"Wonderful!" Elise Van der Veer said. "Franklin and I go at least once a week when he comes to play. How on earth did you manage to get him? He spends his summers in New Hampshire."

"He and Mr. Nicholas go back a long way," Nora murmured.

They adjourned to the open terrace to be entertained by the famed café pianist who played all the old standards — Cole Porter, Rodgers and Hammerstein, and the like. Mrs. Van der Veer and her PA got up to dance. Van Long smiled and waved to the dowager from his place at the piano. She waved back.

"Want to dance?" Devyn asked Annie.

She started to demur, but then it dawned on Annie that it was unlikely anyone was ever going to ask her to dance again. Well, maybe when her children got married one of her sons would do his duty. "Why not?" she asked, getting up.

To her surprise he was a wonderful dancer. He swept her into his arms and they glided across the floor. He twirled her. He dipped her, and soon Annie was laughing.

She was having fun! They rumbaed. They waltzed. And when they slow-danced he pulled her against him, and his lean, hard body felt wonderful.

"You feel good," he told her, echoing her own thoughts about him.

"You're too fresh," she said softly.

"Will you miss me, Annie?" he asked low.

"When I have time to," she told him. "Wills will be home tomorrow, and Nathaniel the day after, and then the girls. And school begins in a few days, and we've got some shopping to do. And there's parents' night for high school, middle school, and kindergarten this year. I just hope two aren't scheduled on the same night."

"What about Annie?" he asked her.

"Once I leave the Spa, Annie goes back into the closet and Mom comes out again," she answered him. "This has been an incredible week for me, Devyn. Until this week I was never away from family or friends. I never had any time for just me. I have loved every minute of it, and I'll always remember it."

"Somehow that just doesn't seem fair to me," he told her.

Annie laughed. "Whoever told you life was fair, kid?" she asked him as the music came to a close and everyone turned to clap for Van Long.

The remaining guests dispersed, escorted to their quarters by their PAs.

"I've got your schedule for tomorrow," Devyn said. "I'll wake you at eight a.m. You have breakfast, your final beauty treatments, and lunch, and the limo will be here at two p.m. to take you back home." He leaned forward slightly.

"Okay," Annie replied. "Good night, Devyn." And she quickly closed the door to her suite. She wasn't certain, but it had certainly appeared as if he were going to kiss her. *Wow!* That was certainly a cool end to the week. A forty-something mom of five being come on to by a cute thirty-one-year-old. She still wasn't certain she believed he was thirty-one. That baby face was very deceiving. Maybe he just felt he had to score with her at least once, because obviously most of the other personal assistants had been laid.

The Channel? Was she in the mood tonight? Maybe for a little while. She had never attempted to end her fantasy early, but she knew she needed her rest tonight. Still, it was unlikely she was going to be able to access the Channel for a while after she left. And from which television would she enter it? With four children at home she was going to have to be very careful. But her user's pamphlet had explained that if anyone came upon her while she was in the midst of a fantasy the television screen would show snow, as if she had lost the signal. *Still,* Annie thought, *I need to be discreet.*

She decided to pack so she wouldn't be bothered with it in the morning. Then she washed and got into her nightgown before climbing into bed, reaching for the remote as she did so. She pressed the open/close button, then A. The paneled wall opened slowly, revealing the darkened screen. Then, as the screen began to lighten, she felt herself sliding away.

"Ow! Oww! Owwww!" She found herself

159

over the Beast's knees.

"Next time when I tell you not to wear clothing to bed you will obey me, Mistress Anne," the Beast growled as his hand descended several more times upon her hapless buttocks. "Damn me, wench, you have a fine round bottom for spanking." His hand briefly fondled her flesh before continuing the punishment.

"But the night is cold!" she protested. "Owwww! Oh, you are cruel, my lord!"

"Aye, I am, but it is obvious you have still not yet fully accepted that I am your lord and master, Mistress Anne."

"My poor buttocks are burning, my lord!" she protested, and she wiggled suggestively against him.

"And they will burn a bit more before I am finished with you, my disobedient mistress," he told her, smacking her several more spanks. "Ah, now, there is the proper pink, wench." He abruptly stood up, pulling her with him, and flung her face-down upon the bed. "On your knees there, wench!" he ordered her fiercely.

"Ohh, you are a monster," Annie protested, and pretended to snivel, although she wasn't in the least harmed by the spanking. She had quite enjoyed it. Devyn had a cute little round butt. She wondered how he would take to a spanking.

"You are thinking of another man," the Beast said, to her surprise.

"Nay, I am not!" Annie cried. How the hell had he known her thoughts?

"Aye, you are, but it matters not. I am the one about to fuck you, and in this world you are mine and mine alone, unless I permit otherwise." He directed his long cock to lodge just within her vagina, and when he had he grasped her hips in his hands, thrust hard into her delicious body.

Annie cried out as his great length filled her. He remained perfectly still now that she had sheathed him. Annie waited. She grew nervous, for he did nothing more.

"My lord?" she queried him softly.

"Beg me for it, you duplicitous little bitch," he told her. *"Beg!"* His voice was dark, and harsh as his fingers dug into her flesh.

"Please, my lord! *Please!*" Annie said. God, she loved his games!

"Please, *what?*" he demanded.

"Please, my lord!" Annie repeated.

"Say the word, wench!"

"What word?" She played his game.

He laughed. "Say the word or I shall turn you over to my men. I'm certain they could make you say it."

161

"It is so naughty," Annie murmured.

"Say it!" His voice was a whip crack.

"Fuck me!" Annie cried. "Oh, please, my lord! Fuck me deep and fuck me hard! I need it! I need you! *Fuck me!*"

"Now there's a good and obedient lass," the Beast replied as he began to piston her with long strokes that grew faster and faster and faster until Annie was screaming with the pleasure he was giving her. And then he stopped suddenly.

"No!" she cried. "Not yet!"

"It does not please me that you come now, Mistress Anne," he told her. "You need a bit more discipline." He withdrew from her. "Remain as you are," he ordered her. Then, walking across the chamber, he took a leather tawse from a hook by the hearth. "Head down upon your folded arms," he ordered.

Annie quickly obeyed, for she knew what was to come. The tawse cracked as the leather met her buttocks. "Ohhh!" she half sobbed. He laid ten strokes upon her. Then, reinserting his penis into her vagina, he used her fiercely until they both came in a mutual burst of their hot juices. And Annie had to admit to herself that her climax was sharper for the delicious punishment he had administered to her.

He collapsed atop her, and after a few moments he arose, commanding her, "Go and fetch the basin so you may bathe our parts. I am not yet wearied of your company." He fell back upon the great bed.

And when Annie had obeyed his directive and climbed back into the bed to cuddle within the curve of his arm, she said, "Fantasy end," and she awoke within her bed in her suite. *Well,* she thought, *it does work. The next time I call up this fantasy it will be a more comfortable beginning.* She shifted to her side. Her butt definitely hurt, and her vagina was a bit sore from his ferocious passion. Relaxed, Annie fell asleep.

She awoke even before Devyn arrived. And the thought she had had the night before entered her head again as she waited for his wake-up call. Would Devyn take to a spanking? Maybe she would program the B button when she got home and find out. She felt her cheeks grow warm. God, what was the matter with her? He was a kid. *But he said he was thirty-one,* a voice in her head murmured. It was more than the age of consent. And he had a cute butt, and a pretty good package, she had noted when they were in the pool. My God, going without sex for two years had turned her into a horny middle-aged woman.

There was a light knock at the door, and Devyn entered the bedroom. He smiled. "You're awake. I guess you're excited to be going home today," he said.

"Yep," Annie agreed. "I sure am excited. What's for breakfast?"

CHAPTER FIVE

"I've asked your chauffeur to wait a few minutes," Nora Buckley said to Annie as she came down into the Spa's main lobby. "I'd like to speak with you. Have you time?"

Annie nodded, noting Mrs. Van der Veer slipping something into her personal assistant's hand as she bade him farewell and seeing the PA thanking her as the older woman gave his butt a squeeze. "Should Devyn be tipped?" she murmured to Nora.

"Ordinarily yes, but you're our prizewinner. He'll have a little something in his pay packet from the corporation at the end of the month for taking such good care of you. I can see that he did. You're glowing. You looked absolutely worn a week ago. Come into my office, Annie." She led the way through a small reception room and into a large, bright office decorated with fine seventeenth- and eighteenth-century antiques. The thick carpet was white. The

165

dainty settee was upholstered in a patterned cream-colored fabric. There was a single rosewood chair with a dark green velvet seat in front of a large mahogany desk. "Sit down," Nora invited. "Have you enjoyed your week?"

"Absolutely! If I had Elise Van der Veer's money I'd be here a week every month," Annie told Nora.

"How would you like to be here a couple of days a week all the time?" Nora asked with an amused smile.

"Huh?" The look on Annie's face was slightly comical.

"Mr. Nicholas liked the few suggestions that you made when you first arrived. Especially your idea of opening a small shop to sell Spa-related items. He wanted to offer you a job with the Channel Corporation, Annie."

"Me? A job here? Doing what?" Annie was astounded. "I don't have any business acumen. Working for my father for a brief year really doesn't qualify as serious experience, Nora. And I've got a family to look after."

"I didn't have any experience when my husband died, and I went to work," Nora said. "But the antique shop owner was willing to train me, and the corporation will train you as you work. We want you to run

166

the gift shop we plan to open just off the lobby. We'll pay you while we train you. You'll have full health care for you and your family. We'll open a retirement account for you. You'll work from eight thirty in the morning until two thirty every afternoon. So you'll be home to get the kids off in the morning, and there to take your little one off the bus."

"Five days a week, six hours a day? Even I know that's only part-time under the labor laws," Annie said. "Yet you're offering me benefits?"

"Mr. Nicholas believes you have great potential, Annie," Nora Buckley said. "He thinks you can move up in the organization. Eventually I'm going to hire an assistant manager, and after several years I will be moving on again to wherever the corporation wants me to go. You could easily end up running the Spa."

Annie swallowed hard. She was about to say she wasn't possibly smart enough to run the Spa, but then she thought, *Why not?* Yes, she'd done only menial stuff when she worked for her father, but she remembered how quickly she had learned his business. He had even said to her just before her wedding that if she wanted to keep on working for him he'd move her up in the ranks to agent. She had refused, of course, as she and Nat had wanted to start a family. But her brain hadn't atrophied yet. She could still learn. They were willing to teach her.

"And, of course, as one of our employees, you will have full use of the facilities of the Spa gratis whenever you want," Nora murmured.

"If I accepted your offer I couldn't start for a few weeks," Annie said. "Nathaniel is going off to college. Wills is starting kindergarten, and I have to get the girls set."

"How about September twenty-ninth?" Nora asked. "You should have everything in order by then."

"Can I think about it a few days?" Annie asked. She should take it. She really should take it. Why was she being so coy? She was going to take it.

"Of course," Nora said. "Let me know the day after Labor Day."

"Okay," Annie said.

"You haven't asked what we'll pay you yet," Nora remarked with a smile.

"No, I guess I haven't," Annie admitted. "I'm not used to this stuff."

"We'll start you at forty thousand," Nora replied.

"Dollars? Forty thousand dollars? Just to run a gift shop?" Annie was amazed.

"The cost of living around here isn't cheap," Nora noted. "To get good people we need to pay excellent salaries and benefits. Do you know what the personal assistants make? A hundred thousand in salary, and probably a couple thousand more in tips. If the spa is successful here, Mr. Nicholas is thinking of opening another in the Southwest."

"Wow!" Annie gasped.

"Wow, indeed." Nora laughed, standing and holding out her hand. "Good-bye, Annie Miller. Don't forget to call me in a few days. I hope you'll be joining us."

Annie shook Nora's hand. "I will," she said, and, turning, made her way back out to the lobby, where Devyn was waiting to see her off.

"Take care of yourself, Annie," he told her as he helped her into the white limo.

"You, too," she answered. "Maybe I'll see you again soon."

"I hope so!" he told her, smiling as he shut the car door.

Annie leaned back into the leather seat as her vehicle pulled away from the portico and followed the winding tree-lined road out to the highway. It had been an incredible week. And she knew in her heart that she was going to take the job that Nora

Buckley had offered her. It was a heaven-sent opportunity. Oh, she'd talk to her dad and to Lizzie about it, but she was going to take it.

Her sister, bless her, was helping to make certain that Nathaniel could go to Princeton. Amy, unless something changed radically, was unlikely to get into an Ivy school. The twins, now, were something else. But if she could advance within the Channel Corporation, Annie would be able to help them herself. And as for little Wills, who knew what he was going to turn out to be? The twins would be through with college before he even graduated high school. With a good job she had breathing room.

Nat would be very proud of her. And with that thought Annie realized that her mourning had finally come to an end. She was really ready to move on with her life, and the exciting thing was, she did have a life! She felt the car pull to a stop, and to her surprise her father was waiting for her with a smile. The chauffeur helped her out and set her bag on the front stoop. He accepted the generous gratuity that Bill Bradford handed him with a tip of his cap, and then he was gone.

"Daddy, what a nice surprise," Annie said as they went into the house. "No golf?"

"The club is having the summer tournament. I won't be ready for that until next year," he said. "So how was your week, baby girl?"

"Incredible! And wait until I tell you what happened! I've been offered a job up there, Daddy. A real job. I'm going to take it. I'm tired of having to watch every penny, and to rely on Lizzie. I know she does it willingly, but enough is enough."

"Good for you, baby girl," her father said. "But what about the kids?"

"My hours let me see them off in the a.m. and be home for Wills's bus in the afternoon," Annie said enthusiastically.

"Part-time," Bill Bradford noted.

"To start with, but Mrs. Buckley, the spa manager, says Mr. Nicholas thinks I've got potential, and there's room for advancement."

"Who's this Nicholas fellow?"

"CEO of the Channel Corporation," Annie said. "They're the people who opened the Spa. He's the nicest man, Daddy. About your age. Very courtly. Has just a slight British accent. And the Spa is gorgeous. I never realized such luxury existed. Well, I suppose I did, but I never expected to partake in it. I made friends with one of the other guests there — Elise Van der Veer. She's one cool old lady."

"That cool old lady is the head of Van der Veer Diamonds," Annie's father said. "Worth a couple of gazillion dollars. Well, baby girl, you were really hobnobbing with the rich and famous. Anyone else I might have heard about?" He grinned at her.

"No, just some press people who had been invited to write the place up, and one or two others, unknowns like me. The Spa doesn't open officially until next weekend."

"So what will you be doing there?" her father wanted to know.

"I'm going to be running the gift shop they're opening," Annie said. "I told them I'd never done anything like that, but they said they would teach me, and pay me while I learn. And they're giving the kids and me medical!"

"That's really generous," Bill Bradford mused. "Just women go there, right?"

"That's right. A spa for women only. And each guest is assigned a personal assistant who handles her schedule for the day, and makes certain her stay runs smoothly. It was really wonderful! Oh, and the facilities are all available to me as an employee of the Channel Corporation."

"Sounds like a perfect setup for you, honey. Now, listen, Nathaniel's plane is delayed until eight this evening. I'll go up to the airport and pick him up for you."

"Oh, Daddy, thank you! I'd invite you to dinner, except there's nothing in the house. I've got to go shopping," Annie said.

"Go shopping tomorrow," he told her. "We'll eat at the club tonight, baby girl."

Annie unpacked her bag while her father waited. They drove out to the Egret Pointe Country Club and sat out on the terrace having a drink while they waited for the dining room to open. The club bartender made the best daiquiris, and Annie loved them. She nursed one carefully. She had lost over eight pounds, and she wasn't about to pack them right back on. She ordered filet mignon and salad for dinner — no potato.

"But you love the club's baked stuffed potatoes," her father said.

"Potatoes are bad carbs," Annie told him. And so were daiquiris.

"You lose weight up at that spa?" he asked her.

"Yep, and I'm not gaining it back," Annie said.

"You've always looked fine to me," Bill Bradford told his eldest daughter.

"Thanks, Daddy, but no potato. I had a drink, remember?"

As they ate she learned that her mother

had fallen in love with Tuscany.

"Next August, she wants to rent the farm villa where they stayed, just for the two of us," Bill Bradford said. "I told her to go ahead. I haven't told her we're going to Arizona right after the New Year. I've bought a little condo on a golf course near Phoenix."

"Sight unseen?" Annie was surprised.

"Nah, I ran out there for a few days this week while you were up at the Spa. Some of the guys at the club told me about it. Your mother calls my cell phone rather than the house phone, 'cause she says she can never be sure where I am." He chuckled.

"Mom is going to be furious," Annie told him.

"I don't think so," he replied. "It's got a big clubhouse, and a population of old hens just like your mother. They go into the city for the ballet, concerts, museum trips. She'll have a heck of a lot more to entertain her next winter than here in Egret Pointe, and after a bit of initial grumbling, along with a reminder that we're going to Italy next August, she'll settle down, baby girl. Dessert?"

"Do you have any fresh fruit?" Annie asked their waiter.

"Yes, Mrs. Miller. Melon with berries.

Shall I bring you some?"

"Thank you, yes."

"And bring me a slab of that apple crumb pie," her father said. "With a nice scoop of vanilla ice cream, and coffee. The real stuff, not decaf."

"Yes, sir. Coffee, Mrs. Miller?"

"No. I'll just go with my water," Annie told him.

"You going to be dieting the rest of your life?" her father asked.

"No, but I am going to eat more sensibly, and the kids will, too. The twins were getting a little chunky, although I imagine a summer at camp has cured that, despite all the wonderful food I remember at Stoneledge Lake." Annie laughed. "Pancakes and corn and sloppy joes. I can't wait to see them. Their weekly letters weren't too forthcoming."

"Just like you and Lizzie." He chuckled.

They finished their meal, and he dropped her at home before heading for the nearby airport to pick up Nathaniel. Checking her larder, Annie found there really was no food to speak of, and so she called the local pizzeria for a cheese pie so her son would have something to eat when he arrived. And she did have the makings of a salad. The pizza came, and she put it in the oven to stay warm. A little after nine she heard her father's car pull into the driveway, and hurried to the door to greet her eldest son.

"Mom!" He picked her up and swung her about.

"I think you've grown!" Annie squealed.

"You couldn't have grown! I've got pizza, 'cause there was no food in the house. I just got back this afternoon myself. There's a layer of dust on everything. I haven't even gone to the vet for the beasts."

"Hey, sis!" Lizzie was standing in the door.

"I thought you were going back to the city," Annie said, and she hugged her sister.

"When we were late from Rome, I decided I'd take the puddle jumper with my nephew and go home tomorrow."

"Where's Mom?" Annie asked.

"In the car with Dad. Wave! He just told her about the condo in Arizona. She's still in shock." Lizzie giggled.

Annie waved at the car, and her father pulled out of her drive and drove off.

"Hey, kid, save some of that pizza for me!" Lizzie called to Nathaniel, who was already mongreling down a large slice. "We ate on the plane, but it was hours ago. I want to hear all about the Spa. Is it incredible? Is it wonderful?"

"All of the above, and more," Annie told

her sister.

"And are you now fully introduced to the Channel?" Lizzie asked softly with a sly grin.

"Not in front of the children." Annie giggled. "Wait until Nathaniel goes to bed and I'll tell you everything."

"You mean you, practical Annie, actually managed to dream up a fantasy? I think I am truly proud of you — unless, of course, it's a home-and-garden thing," Lizzie said, low.

"Even if the home builder wore nothing but his *tool* belt, and the gardener was in a breechcloth?" Annie teased Lizzie. Hmmm, that did have possibilities. Why hadn't she thought of it before?

Lizzie gasped softly. "Ohh, you did get the idea, sis, didn't you? Hey, kid, what did I say? Don't eat all the pizza!"

"I left you two pieces, *Zia Elisabetta,*" Nathaniel said, grinning. "Mom, thank you! Would you mind if I go to bed? I'm really beat, and I'm still on Italian time."

"Give me a kiss," Annie said, hugging him as he did so. "We'll talk tomorrow. Good night, sweetie."

"Tell me!" Lizzie demanded as they heard the bedroom door close upstairs.

"Let's go into the den, where I can close the door," Annie answered her.

177

And as soon as the two women were settled, Lizzie eating her pizza, Annie began to tell her younger sibling about the Spa.

"Was your PA cute?" Lizzie wanted to know.

"Great pecs, and the cutest butt," Annie replied.

Lizzie gasped. "You've stopped mourning!" she exclaimed.

Annie nodded. "Yes, I have. Nat loved life, and he would want me to go on with mine. Suddenly I find I can. Now, let me tell you about my fantasy. Remember my favorite fairy tale when we were kids, and Grandma used to read to us?"

Lizzie thought a moment, and then her mouth made an O. " 'Beauty and the Beast,' right? Omigod! But that's really such a sweet story," she decided in a disappointed tone.

Annie laughed. "Not with this Beast," she said. "He really is a beast." And then she went on to explain in detail the way the fantasy was playing out. She restrained her amusement as she watched first disbelief, then shock, and then absolute admiration come over her sister's face. "When I last left him I had just finished washing his dick and his balls as well as my own parts, because he had announced he wasn't through for

178

the night."

"It's actually twelve inches long?" Lizzie asked.

"I don't have a ruler, so I can't be certain, but he's bigger than Nat by far, and we did measure Nat once. He was eight inches. Beastie has a few inches on him, so I expect he is twelve inches," Annie said.

"I never thought to use a fairy tale," Lizzie responded thoughtfully. "Do you really think Sleeping Beauty slept alone for a hundred years?"

"Or who was Rapunzel really letting her hair down for?" Annie teased.

"Did you program a second fantasy yet, or were you having too much fun with the Beast?" Lizzie wanted to know.

"Haven't done a second fantasy yet. This first one is just about all I can handle," Annie said. But she was thinking of a second fantasy. One in which Devyn would play a major part. But could she do it if she was going to work up at the Spa? "Oh, I haven't told you the most exciting thing yet," she exclaimed. "I've been offered a job at the Spa." And then Annie went on to explain to her sister what had happened.

Lizzie listened carefully, and then she said, "You're going to take it, of course. What a coup for you. Sounds like this Mr. Nicholas likes you. I've heard a little about him. In an age of media overkill he seems to be pretty much a mystery. Almost a recluse. Yet now and again there's something said. And the Channel Corporation is one of the fastest-growing companies on the planet. Much of what they seem to be involved in is geared toward entertaining, pleasure, and I hear they are working on a fountain-of-youth pill that would let people live on indefinitely in good health. Very hush-hush. My firm has been trying to get their business forever. They don't seem to have anyone on retainer. I ought to give myself a long weekend at the Spa."

"Ms. Buckley says they're booked a year in advance," Annie told her sister.

"They always keep something open for important clients who call at the last minute. That's the way these places are," Lizzie said cynically.

"I am going to take the job," Annie said.

"Good girl!" her sister said approvingly. "And don't let Mom guilt you into changing your mind." She yawned. "I'm exhausted. Guest room bed made up?"

"Always for those last-minute important clients," Annie replied, smiling. "Lizzie, thank you so much for everything. Taking Nathaniel to Tuscany, sending the girls to camp, entering me in that contest, Princeton. No one could have a better sister."

"Hey, what's family for if we can't help each other?" Lizzie replied.

They went upstairs together and parted, each heading to her own room. Annie debated whether she would use the remote and the little television Nat had kept in the bedroom, but then she decided she was actually tired. A good night's sleep was in order.

Lizzie headed back to the city the following day. Nathaniel began to gather everything he felt he was going to need at Princeton. Wills arrived home from Disney World filled with tales of Cinderella's castle and pirates. And finally Annie drove the Dodge van up to the central meeting place to pick up her daughters from the camp bus.

"Any livestock in your luggage?" Annie asked suspiciously, and the twins laughed mischievously.

"Nah," Rose finally said. "They wouldn't let us bring home the salamanders."

"Or the chipmunk with the half tail," Lily added.

"Thank you, Stoneledge Lake Camp!" Annie said with a sigh. "Where's Amy?"

"Over there with her new BFF, Brittany," Lily said, a tiny hint of disapproval in her

181

young voice. "We'll see how good a BFF Brittany is when high school begins."

"Amy," Annie called. "Over here. Let's go!"

Her daughter turned an exasperated look on Annie. Turning, she whispered something to Brittany, hugged her friend, and hurried to join them. "You embarrassed me," she said in a surly tone as she got into the van and fastened her seat belt.

"I have other things to do than wait for you," Annie said sharply. "And when we get home, I have something to tell you all."

"How was the Spa?" Amy asked. "Brittany says it won't last long. They should be trying to get Lindsay and Paris."

"The Spa was wonderful, and trust me," Annie told her daughter, "the Spa will last. It's for rich grown-ups, and there seem to be plenty of them. They aren't interested in the likes of Paris and Lindsay. I was interviewed by reporters from *Pampered Woman* and *Chic.* They will be in the December issues."

"You look like you lost weight," one of the twins said.

"I did," Annie replied, pleased that someone had noticed besides her dad.

"You'll gain it back," Amy muttered.

Annie laughed. "Not this time, sweetie.

Oh, what the heck, I'll tell you my news now. I've been offered a job at the Spa, and I'm going to take it."

The twins squealed excitedly.

"Oh, Mom, that is so cool," Rose said.

"Can we have cell phones then?" Lily inquired.

"No, you cannot have cell phones," Annie replied. "They are much too expensive to maintain. The money is going to help us pay the bills every month easily. And maybe even provide for a trip to the mall now and again."

"What could you possibly do at a spa?" Amy asked her mother.

"I'm going to run the gift shop they're putting in," Annie said. "They will train me, and even though I'm only working thirty hours a week they are paying full benefits."

"Ohhh, how embarrassing!" Amy said dramatically, and she began to cry. "Are you trying to ruin my reputation in high school? I'm finally in the popular crowd. When it gets out that my mother works in a store no one will want to hang out with me."

"Oh, boo-hoo!" the twins teased their elder sister.

"Brittany has the IQ of a doorknocker," Rose said.

"No, a paper napkin," Lily put in. "Honestly, Amy, why do you want to hang out with someone like that? You've got a brain, and you're a terrific lacrosse player."

"You're too young to understand," Amy told her sisters loftily.

"It's okay for your mother to be a struggling widow, but not gainfully employed?" Annie said. "What kind of screwed-up logic is that?"

"Look, Mom, everyone in Egret Pointe admires you for being so brave and so dedicated to us, even though they know Daddy left you virtually penniless," Amy said. "But if you go to work, all that street credit goes by the boards. It's just not fair!"

"Please don't talk about fair," Annie said. "Sorry to spoil your life, but I start working on September twenty-ninth, and frankly I can hardly wait. And your father didn't leave us penniless, but he also didn't leave enough. However, he didn't expect to have his life ended at the age of forty-three by a big red bus. So shut up and live with it."

The next few days were a whirlwind of school preparations. Lizzie came out from the city to drive her nephew to Princeton. There was no way Annie could leave her four younger children, and she knew her eldest son didn't want to arrive at college with his siblings in tow. She made certain

184

he had everything he needed, including a new laptop from his grandparents, kissed him good-bye, and then cried after he was gone. The first of her hatchlings was leaving the nest. She wondered if she'd cry when Amy left, but right now she doubted it, Annie thought wryly.

School began for her other children. Wills went off to kindergarten without so much as a tear. Mrs. Gunderson and nursery school had prepared him well. Amy headed to Egret Pointe High School as a sophomore, and the twins were in seventh grade. Annie set up a schedule. Lunches had to be made and refrigerated the night before. School clothing had to be picked and laid out. The high school bus came at seven thirty in the morning, followed by the junior high bus at seven forty, and the kindergarten bus at eight fifteen.

"Why do you have to be so anal about everything?" Amy whined.

"Because I have to be prepared for September twenty-ninth, when work will start at eight thirty," Annie told her daughter.

"What if one of us gets sick?" Amy asked.

"Don't! At least not until after Christmas," Annie snapped. "How's Brittany?"

"She actually thinks it's cool you're working at the Spa," Amy answered. "She says her mother heard there are really cute guys working up there."

"So I haven't ruined your life after all," Annie murmured. "Darn! And I tried so hard. Well, maybe next time."

The twins giggled.

She had butterflies in her stomach the morning of September twenty-ninth as she got into her van and headed to the Spa. She had called Nora Buckley right after the girls got home from camp and told her she would accept the job. Nora had been warm and friendly, saying she'd see Annie on the twenty-ninth. She told her one of the PAs would show her where to park when she arrived. Annie felt a thrill of excitement to see Devyn awaiting her as she pulled up. He got into the van.

"Hey, Annie!" he greeted her. "Just go back down the circular driveway and hang a right when you get to the bottom," Devyn told her. "The employee parking lot is behind those hedges, and there's an entrance into the main building from there."

She followed his instructions.

"Right there in the second row," he directed her. "See. Your spot is marked with your name. A. Miller."

Annie pulled into the parking area designated with her name. "Wow," she said. "My own parking space."

He laughed. "Glad you're joining us," he told her. "Wait until you see the gift shop they've constructed for you. Oh, Ms. Buckley said come to her office and she'll fill you in on everything you need to know." He got out of the van and dashed around to open her door.

Getting out, Annie found herself face-to-face with him. "Thanks for showing me where to go," she said a bit breathlessly. What the hell was the matter with her? Her hormones were jumping all over the place. He was a kid. He was twelve years younger than she was. But, God, she really wanted to screw him!

Devyn smiled down into her blue eyes. "Glad to be of help," he said. "Come on." He grabbed her hand. "I'll show you how to get into the building, and to Ms. Buckley's office from there."

Get control of yourself, Annie! "Do you have a new client?" she asked.

"Yep, but she never opens an eye until ten a.m.," Devyn said. "She's a CFO of some big business, and actually I think she needs sleep more than anything else the Spa can offer her. Massage and reflexology every day. Nice woman." He opened the door, ushering her inside. "Okay, after we come in this way you turn right, and you'll see a door into the lobby. You know how to get to Ms. Buckley's office from there, right?"

"Yes," Annie told him.

"Then I'll leave you. Good luck!" And he went off in the opposite direction.

Annie exited into the lobby and hurried to Nora Buckley's office. It was just eight thirty, and she was pleased with her timing. She entered the outer office, where a secretary sat at a desk. "I'm Mrs. Miller," she said to the girl.

"Go right in," the secretary said. "Ms. Buckley is waiting for you."

Annie entered the spacious office. "Good morning, Ms. Buckley," she said.

"Nora," came the reply. "Good morning, Annie. Your timing is perfect. Come and sit down and I'll tell you everything that's happening. Coffee?"

"Thanks," Annie said, seating herself in the chair before the desk and accepting the mug Nora handed her. "I've brought all the papers you needed me to fill out," she said, giving her new employer a manila envelope. "I think I got everything right."

"I'm sure you did," Nora replied. "Now, here's where we stand." And she went on to tell Annie that the gift shop was practically ready to open by the upcoming weekend, and that it would be up to Annie to stock it before then. "We can get overnight delivery for everything," she said. "Any suggestions offhand?"

"I think we should sell the meringues the pastry chef makes. But they should have to be a special order," Annie said. "At least three days in advance of checkout. Four to a package, and the packaging should be both sturdy and elegant. We can also ship them for our guests."

"Cost?" Nora asked.

"Twenty dollars for four," Annie said, "plus shipping if we decide to take mail orders. I spoke to a lady I know who works in one of the shops in the village. She said to figure the cost of packaging in the price. Egg whites and sweetener won't be your major outlay. It will be the packaging, and because not all the guests who buy the meringues will ship, that should be extra. Too expensive?"

"No, not at all," Nora said. "I suspect it's just perfect. Every woman who goes to the bank gets twenties handed to her. And wealthy women fling twenties about like the rest of us do dollar bills. What else?"

"The Spa robes with the logo," Annie said. "They are delicious, and most guests will want to bring one home. The lotions and creams used here. I noticed they were packaged with the Spa logo. They should be sold, too. But Janka and the other facialists and the masseurs should recommend which ones are suitable for each guest. After two treatments the guest's PA should be given a list of what is suitable for the guest, and the guest given a copy of that list."

"It sounds to me like you've been giving this some serious thought," Nora said, fascinated to discover that Annie had a real knack for merchandising.

"Oh, I have!" Annie told her enthusiastically. "I'm not a runner, and I know you don't encourage it because of the damage it can do to knees, but walkers can use water bottles too. I think we should sell lightweight water bottles, again with the logo. And pedometers. Women new to even mild exercise want to know how far they've gone. It encourages them. And those yummy soaps in the bathroom. We have to have those. And I was thinking that maybe we could make a deal with Lacy Nothings, that elegant lingerie shop in the village, to stock a few items with us."

Nora smiled slowly, obviously very pleased. "Mr. Nicholas is going to be delighted by our first meeting. He does pride himself on choosing the right people to work for the corporation," she said. "I suspect you will go far with us, Annie." She stood up. "Let's go see the shop we've set up for you, and then you can get about your business. I'll get you a PA to work with you while you're setting everything up. Devyn's current guest is leaving late this afternoon. She wanted an extra day with us. Can you manage on your own today?"

"No problem," Annie said, smiling.

The shop was beautiful, and in perfect keeping with everything else. Set in a corner of the lobby, it had a wall of windows looking out over the Spa's gardens. It was painted white, with just the slightest touch of gold trim. Glass cases had already been installed to display the goods. In a small alcove there was a computer that Nora told her would contain her records. And behind the alcove was her little windowed office.

"I'm not very computer literate," Annie said nervously.

"No problem," Nora assured her. "Neither was I. Devyn can teach you."

There was a machine for credit and debit cards, and a computerized cash register for those people actually paying in cash. Everything was light and bright and in perfect harmony with the rest of the architecture. Annie stood looking around her, both excited and scared to death. Then Nora handed her a tiny cell phone.

"It's yours," she said. "All of our employees are given one."

"I can't afford a cell phone," Annie said softly.

"You don't have to," Nora replied. "It's one of your perks. We handle the bills. And one other thing. Like everyone here, you'll wear a uniform of sorts. Devyn can take you to be fitted later today after his guest leaves. Our uniform shop is right here. You'll get a couple of skirts, or trousers if you prefer, two blazers, some tees, and turtlenecks for when it gets colder. Uniforms keep everything professional."

"That's wonderful!" Annie told Nora. "I was wondering how I was going to make my little wardrobe look fresh after a week or two."

Nora left her, and, going into her new office, Annie found a list of suppliers on her desk. Picking up the phone, she began to make calls, telling everyone she would expect overnight delivery. One of the suppliers apologized that they had only two dozen robes in stock when Annie ordered a gross of them. She told them to ship what they had and get the rest to her by the end of next week.

A little before noon Devyn came in with a salad plate for her. "My CFO is leaving immediately after lunch," he said. "I'll be back as soon as she's gone. How are you doing?" He smiled down at her.

"A little frazzled, but I think I'm okay," Annie told him.

"Good girl! Now eat your lunch. You need your protein," he told her as he left.

Protein? Annie looked down at the plate. Chicken salad! Her favorite. How had he remembered? But she was glad that he had, and she was beginning to feel a little tired. Lizzie had warned her she would, but said it would pass once she was used to her new schedule.

Devyn returned to her office close to two p.m.

"Sorry to take so long," he said with a smile.

"Nora wanted me to be outfitted today," Annie said, "and I've got to jet in twenty minutes. The kindergarten bus will be coming, and they won't let Wills off unless I'm there to meet him."

"Come on then," Devyn said as Annie grabbed her bag. He quickly led her from her office, across the lobby, and through the door she'd entered this morning. Then down a hall he trotted, with Annie right behind him. "Here we are! Bonnie, I've got a customer for you. This is Annie Miller. She'll be running the gift shop. Nora wants her fixed up, and she's got to get home to meet the school bus."

Bonnie looked critically at Annie. "Size fourteen," she said. She was a big, tall woman with iron gray hair and a deceivingly young face.

"I think I might be a bit bigger," Annie practically whispered.

Bonnie shook her head. "Nope. You're a fourteen." She took a jacket off a rack behind her. "Try this on, honey."

Annie slipped into the dark green jacket. It fit her perfectly.

"What did I tell you?" Bonnie said with a smile. "I'm never wrong about my sizes. Take it off and I'll package it. Two, right? And skirts or pants? I think skirts for you right now. You've got a nice curvy figure. You want to show it off. I'll give you three. When it gets cold, if you want pants I'll give you a couple of pairs. You can get your turtleneck then, too. I'll give you a couple of tees right now." Bonnie gathered the required items and pulled a long plastic sleeve over the two jackets and the three khaki skirts. She put the white tees in a bag. "Here you go, Annie Miller. Welcome!"

"Thank you so much," Annie said, wondering if the skirts would go over her butt. She would try them on as soon as she got home.

Devyn led the way from the uniform room, taking her back to her car. "I'll be waiting for you when you get here tomorrow," he told her. "Nora says you need help learning the computer for the shop, and so she's assigned me as your PA for the interim. It'll be fun being with you again." He opened the van door she had already unlocked with her beeper as they walked to the car. Leaning in, he laid her new uniforms on the backseat of the van.

"I'll try to learn fast," she said. "I know not working with a guest costs you tips."

"Not to worry," he assured her, his blue eyes meeting hers. "Nora told me there would be more in my pay packet for this duty, but, Annie, I'd be glad to do it even if there weren't. It's fun being with you."

"Are you flirting with me, Devyn?" she asked, and then blushed for being so stupid. What was he going to think of her coming on to him like that? Annie slid into the driver's seat, feeling like an idiot.

"As a matter of fact I am," he told her. Then he shut the car door. "Drive carefully, Annie. I'll see you tomorrow." Then he turned away and headed back to the main building.

She watched him go, admiring that tight butt of his. God, what was she thinking? Annie chided herself as she started the car and headed for home. And what was he thinking? That he had discovered his own Mrs. Robinson? She pulled into her drive just ahead of the school bus, which was dropping Mark Iaonne off up the block. Seeing her getting out of her van, Mavis Iaonne waved brightly. Annie waved back. *I wonder if she gets the Channel,* she thought.

Lizzie called after the kids were all settled for the night. "So, how did the first day go?" she wanted to know.

"You were right. I'm pooped, but it was good. I'm glad I took the job. They've given me Devyn to help me get everything set up and learn how to operate the computer. He's flirting with me, Lizzie, and I want to flirt back."

"So?"

"So? Lizzie, I've got five kids! I'm going to be forty-four in December. He's thirty-one, if he really is."

"There are plenty of older women with younger lovers these days," Lizzie noted. "No one thinks anything about it. After all, older men take younger wives, girlfriends, and mistresses all the time. This is the twenty-first century, big sis."

"I think I need to visit the Beast, but I'm so afraid the kids will come in," Annie said. "How can I be certain my fantasy won't be on if they do?"

Lizzie reassured her sibling. "Look, go in after midnight and lock your bedroom door," she suggested. "Why not program the B button, using Devyn as your play-mate?"

"Not yet," Annie demurred. "What if the line between reality and fantasy blurred for me, Lizzie? How embarrassing would that be?"

"But you want him, don't you?" Lizzie persisted.

"Yes, I think I do," Annie admitted. "But, like you, I have a reputation to think of, sis. Can you imagine how mortified the girls would be if they found out I was screwing my personal assistant? He's only thirteen years older than Nathaniel."

"And only eleven years younger than you. I'll bet he could do it all night," Lizzie said, sounding envious. "I'll be meeting him soon," she said. "I booked the Columbus Day weekend at the Spa. If I could get the Channel Corporation as a client for the firm, it would be quite a coup. Even a private facility like the Spa should have a lawyer on retainer."

"You are shameless." Annie laughed. "I'm going to bed. Good night, Lizzie."

"Night, big sister," Lizzie responded, and hung up.

I am horny, Annie thought to herself. She hadn't been able to access the Channel since she had gotten home. Getting up, she went out into the upstairs hall and checked on the children, peeping into the three bedrooms where her son and daughters were. They were all sleeping soundly. She tiptoed back to her own bedroom and, taking her sister's suggestion, locked the door behind her. Opening the cabinet where the television was hidden, she climbed into bed and, pointing her remote at the screen, clicked the A button.

"I like it when you bathe my cock and balls," the Beast said. "You are gentle, Mistress Anne. I have never known gentleness from a woman."

"Was your mother not gentle with you?" Annie asked him.

"I had no mother," the Beast said harshly. "I killed her with my birth, and her death killed any affection my father might have held for me."

"My mother died when I was so young, I

cannot remember her," Mistress Anne, the merchant's daughter, told the Beast. "She birthed my sister too soon. They were buried together on the hillside behind our home. Surely your father was kind to you."

"All I remember of him were the beatings he gave me weekly. One was always for taking my mother's life. The others were for any small infraction I might have made that displeased him. You asked me if I wear a mask because I am scarred, and I told you aye. I did not tell you my father marked me when I was twenty. He had decided he wished to remarry. And he told me that if his new wife birthed him a son he would make that child his heir, if it did not kill its mother in the birthing.

"All my life he had punished me for something I did not do. Was it not he who planted the seed of life within my mother? I told him that it was he who had killed her with his unbridled lust and demand for a son. I taunted him with the knowledge that the woman he wished to wed had already succumbed to *my* lust, and taken *my* cock most willingly. I had had her virginity of her, and it had been sweet. He attacked me then, and in defending myself I killed him. But not before he had maimed me, screaming that my pretty face would never again lure a woman willingly into my bed."

"Ah, poor Beast," Annie said, and her hand stroked his face beneath the mask.

"I do not need your pity, wench!" the Beast snarled. "I am a fool for having told you my history. You shall be beaten for your temerity, and then I shall fuck you until you beg me for my mercy."

Annie caught at his arm before he could jump from the bed. "Why do you beat your women?" she asked him. "Did you learn nothing from your father's cruelty?"

He wrapped his hand in her chestnut hair and yanked her close. "Women need whipping to arouse their juices and their passions," he told her.

"Nay, I think it is you who gain the real pleasure from such actions," she accused. "Let me make love to you, my lord, and I will prove to you that you need no harshness to entice me into your arms."

Curiosity bloomed in the dark eyes behind the mask. "If you fail, it will go the harder with you," he warned her. "I will give you to my officers for an evening's entertainment, bold wench. Would you not rather take a strapping now, and be done with it?" the Beast said to her.

In answer to his question Annie loosened his hand from her hair and pushed him back against the pillows. "That magnificent cock of yours needs no inducement but my passions for you, my lord," she assured him. Bending, she kissed his mouth, running the pointed tip of her tongue along his lips until he opened them, his tongue fencing with hers as she caressed it with slow strokes. Her lips touched the leather-and-silk mask, kissing it. She gently pushed his head back and slowly licked his throat from its base to his chin. Then she nibbled gently back down the rough length of it.

She moved her body down slightly and sucked hard on his nipples while one of her hands encircled his taut belly again and again. Biting on his nipples, she elicited a small cry from him. With a smoky laugh Annie licked and nipped her way down his muscled torso. Then, before he realized her intent, she swiftly clapped the leather restraints fastened to the headboard about his wrists.

He gave a warning growl, but made no move to free himself.

Annie positioned herself with her bottom facing his head, but, restrained, he could not touch her. She tangled her fingers in the thick mat of black curls covering his groin and tugged gently upon them. Then, picking up his massive cock, which was already showing signs of his arousal, she licked its length several times before beginning to tease its Cyclops head with its single eye. Her tongue ran around beneath its rim. She sucked it as one would suck a tender morsel. When she began to take him more fully into her mouth he groaned. She sucked, gently at first, then harder and harder. The flesh within her mouth swelled and grew tight. It was beginning to throb.

Annie repositioned herself and crawled between his outstretched thighs. She nuzzled at his hairy balls, taking them into her mouth, rolling them about with her tongue until he was almost crying with the pleasurable pain she was inflicting upon him. When she was certain he was more than ready, Annie released him from his bonds, rolling onto her back and holding her arms out to him. "Come, my lord, and have your reward," she cooed at him.

He loomed over her. "Let us see how deep your tenderness goes when you see the truth of your passion, Mistress Anne," he said, tearing the mask from his face.

The scar was deep, and it had been administered with deliberate cruelty. It ran from the outer corner of his right eye, across his cheekbone, beneath his nostril, to the left corner of his mouth down to his jawbone.

Annie did not cry out, nor did she display any sign of the sorrow she felt at seeing the deformity. Instead she took his head between her two hands and, pulling it down to her, kissed him with every ounce of passion in her soul. "Have me, my lord," she whispered against his mouth. "I find you far more exciting in truth than with your mask." Her fingertips ran gently down the ridged scar.

With a roar he drove himself into her. Never had his lust risen so high, burned so brightly. "I will never let you go!" he told her. *"Never!"*

"Fuck me, my dearest lord," she cried out to him. "Fuck me!"

And he did. They came together the first time, his rich, thick cum so copious that it overflowed her vagina. But he did not withdraw from her, and he remained as hard as iron within her. Once again he began to piston her with long, hard strokes, howling like a crazed man with his climax. Now she came a second time a moment behind him, crying with the pleasure that weakened her. He rested briefly, still firm.

"I can bear no more," she whimpered.

"You have done this to me," he said gently against her ear. "Now you must see it through, Mistress Anne." And he kissed her tenderly as he began his third race. And finally he felt the peculiar stiffing that signaled his satisfaction. He shuddered hard several times, and came a third time with another cry.

As he did Annie climaxed a final time, passion washing over her in fierce waves. Her body arched up against his. She trembled as her insides quivered and quaked until she thought she would be torn apart. She cried out, half-fearful, but he held her tightly until the spasms racking her body subsided. He reached for his mask. "No," she said. "No more when you are just with me, my lord." And she drew his dark head back to her for a tender kiss. "Wear it if you will among your men, but not with me."

"Are you not fearful? Disgusted?" he asked her. "I am ugly now, where once I was considered the handsomest man in the kingdom."

"You are beautiful to me, my lord," Annie reassured him as he laid his head on her breasts. She stroked his dark hair gently.

"Mommy! Mommy!"

"End fantasy!" Annie said quickly, her head turning to look at her clock. It was almost four. Well, nothing lost. She climbed from her bed and, turning the key in the lock, opened the door. "Wills, what's the matter?" she asked her little son.

"My tummy hurts, Mommy," he said, his blue eyes looking up at her. "I think I'm going to throw up." And before she could move him, he did so on the carpet before her. *"Mommy!"*

Picking her son up, Annie raced to the bathroom down the hall as Wills began to vomit again, but at least this time into the toilet.

"Mom, what's the matter?" Rose was there.

"Your brother is sick. Stay with him while I clean up my bedroom doorway," Annie said with a sigh. The perfect end to a perfect evening, she thought wryly as she went to fetch a bucket, soap and water, and some rags. She checked back with Rose before she began her onerous task. Wills was still throwing up every few minutes. *What a disaster,* Annie thought as she cleaned up the mess. *I cannot stay home with a sick child on my second day of work. What am I going to do?*

Wills finally stopped throwing up, and she tucked him back into bed after bringing him a Pedialyte pop to suck on and ease any dehydration. "Thanks, Rosie," she said to her daughter.

"I heard something's already going around

the kindergarten," Rose volunteered.

"Wonderful," Annie replied. "Go back to bed, sweetie. It will be time to get up before you know it." Setting up the old baby monitor in Wills's room, she took the remote back to bed with her. There was just no help for it. She couldn't ask one of the twins to remain home tomorrow. They were too young. And Amy was going on a field trip to the city. It wasn't worth asking her to give that up. And if Wills had this bug, his best friend, Mark, would, too, so Mavis was out. She dozed, not hearing her alarm, only to be awakened by Amy before she left.

"I need money for the trip," her eldest daughter said. "What was all the noise last night? Is someone sick?"

"Wills."

"I cannot stay home!" Amy immediately cried.

"You don't have to," Annie said wearily. "Money is on my dressing table."

Amy grabbed it up, and was gone.

Annie reached for her cell phone and went to the directory, pushing the number marked, NORA/HOME. The phone rang twice, and then Nora's voice came on the line. "Nora, it's Annie. I am so sorry, so embarrassed, but I've got a sick five-year-old, and no sitter. If you want to fire me, I'll understand."

Nora Buckley laughed. "Get ready for work. I'll take care of it. The sitter will be there by eight, Annie. You couldn't expect that your son would get sick on your second day."

"I told them all no one could get sick until at least after Christmas," Annie joked weakly. "No one listens to me."

Nora laughed again. "The Channel Corporation doesn't just hire people, Annie. We hire the right people, and we back them up when they need it. You are the right person for the gift shop. Go have a cup of coffee and relax. It will all be taken care of, I promise you. See you later." And she rang off.

"Mom?" It was the twins.

"We could stay home today if you want," Lily said.

"No need. My boss is sending a sitter," Annie said, and she smiled. "Thank you, my twins, for offering. Now go get ready or you'll miss the bus."

The twins went off, and Nora checked on Wills. He was sleeping, but he was feverish. She hurried to get dressed and was ready when the sitter arrived. As the tall clock in the hall was striking eight o'clock the doorbell rang. Annie hurried to answer it.

Standing before her was a cheerful-looking woman in a dark green cape and hat.

"Good morning, Mrs. Miller. I'm Nanny Violet, here to take care of your wee laddie," the lady said in a crisp English accent.

"Come in," Annie said gratefully, and she smiled back at the woman.

CHAPTER SIX

"You poor thing, you look exhausted," Nanny Violet said sympathetically. "What's the wee laddie's name, dear?" She stepped over the threshold.

"William, but we call him Wills," Annie replied. "You can hang your belongings here in the hall closet."

"Oh, just like the lovely prince," Nanny Violet responded as she set her hat on the closet shelf and put her cape on a hanger.

"He woke me at four," Annie volunteered. "One of my daughters informs me that there is something going around the kindergarten. Oh, the bus! Excuse me a moment." She dashed back out the front door just as the school bus was pulling up. "Wills is sick," she told the driver. "Is there a bug in the kindergarten?"

The school bus driver, an older woman, nodded. "I'm half empty this morning," she said. "It's a bit early for it, but what can you do? Tell Wills Mrs. Baxter says to get well real soon. His friend Mark is ill, too." Then she closed the door and pulled away.

"Just as I thought," Annie said, coming back into the house to join Nanny Violet. "It's a bug. Half the kindergarten has it."

"And the other half will have it next week," Nanny Violet said. "Now show me the kitchen, dear, and then the wee laddie. You have to get to work." She bustled after Annie. She was a woman of indeterminate years, with a kindly face and lively brown eyes. Dressed in what could only be called sensible shoes, a gray tweed skirt, a white blouse with a round collar, and a gray wool cardigan, she exuded a cheerful grandmotherly air of confidence.

Annie showed her about the kitchen, which she was relieved was neat this morning. Amy never ate breakfast, and the twins had put their dishes in the dishwasher. Annie suspected the nanny wouldn't approve of a messy kitchen.

"You've five bairns, Ms. Buckley tells me," Nanny Violet said.

"The eldest boy is in college," Annie answered. "Tell me, how on earth did Nora find you so quickly? You really are a godsend."

"Why, the Channel Corporation owns,

among other companies, one that supplies professional and well-trained nannies to good families," Nanny Violet told Annie. "I was available because my last charge has just gone off to boarding school, and the family won't be needing me any longer. I was with them for twelve years, dear."

"You must miss them," Annie said.

"Yes and no," the nanny responded. "I was ready for a change."

"Mommy!" Wills came into the kitchen. "I'm hot, Mommy." He looked curiously at Nanny Violet.

"This is Nanny Violet, Wills," Annie said. "She's going to take care of you today while Mommy is at work."

"No!" His small face crumpled, and two large tears rolled down his cheeks. "I want you, Mommy! Don't go!" He clutched at her khaki uniform skirt.

The nanny knelt down and smiled a kindly smile. "Now, now, laddie, Mummy loves you, but she does have to be off to work. Do you know about Peter Pan?"

Wills nodded.

"Well, laddie, I've brought a lovely DVD of his story. Would you like to watch it with me, dear? And we'll have a bit of tea and toast while we watch. Do you know how to make toast, Wills?"

211

He nodded. "How do you know my name?"

"Your mummy told me," Nanny Violet said.

"A mummy is a scary thing in bandages," Wills told her. "My mommy isn't scary at all. And she doesn't wear bandages."

Annie burst out laughing. "Wills, in England children call their mothers Mummy instead of Mommy. Nanny Violet is English."

"Where's England?" Wills wanted to know. "Is it near Egret Pointe?"

"My goodness, no, laddie," Nanny Violet said. "But I can show you if you'd like."

Wills nodded. "And then we'll have tea and toast and watch *Peter Pan*," he said.

"Why, the day will simply fly," Nanny Violet replied. She turned to Annie. "He does have a temperature, dear. See how flushed he is? Where's your thermometer?"

Annie reached into her kitchen catchall drawer and pulled it out. "It's digital."

"You run along now," Nanny Violet said. "Wills and I will do swimmingly, won't we, laddie? Did you know there is a prince with your name? And one day he'll be a real king. What do you think about that?" She kept up a stream of lighthearted banter as they made their way to the door.

212

"Mind Nanny now," Annie said, kissing her son's tousled head.

"Okay, *Mummy*," Wills said with a mischievous grin.

She laughed and ran for her car. She was going to either just make it or be late, depending on Tuesday-morning traffic in Egret Pointe, which, despite the area's small-town status, could sometimes be dicey. There was no other car in her driveway or parked out in front of the house. How had Nanny Violet gotten there? Did she really care? The woman was a lifesaver. And straight out of central casting too. Annie chuckled to herself as she drove toward the Spa. She parked in her marked spot, glancing at her watch as she hurried into the building, heading directly for the gift shop. Devyn was waiting for her at its door.

"You made it," he said with a smile. "Ms. Buckley said you might be late. What happened?" He held up something. "Your key to the shop. I thought you'd want to open the door yourself."

"Thanks," Annie replied, taking it from him. "My little boy woke up sick. I called Nora, and she sent a nanny. It seems the Channel Corp. has a nanny service among its various holdings. Is there nothing for which they aren't prepared?" She fitted the key into the lock and opened the door.

"I don't think so," he answered as they went in, closing the door behind them.

On the floor were several large cartons.

Annie looked at the labels. "Looks like our day is already set. The stock is beginning to arrive. Overnight really means overnight, doesn't it?"

They spent the day unpacking. Devyn showed Annie how to set up a program to log the stock in and out as it was sold. Once she got the hang of it she found it surprisingly easy to manage. By noon they had most of the cartons emptied. Annie called to check on Wills. He was sleeping now, Nanny Violet told her. His temperature was one hundred and two, but he had managed to keep his tea and toast down.

"I might be a few minutes late arriving home," Annie said. "I have to stop in the village and speak with someone. Is that all right, or do you have to leave at two thirty? If you do I'll come right home and go back after the girls get home."

"No, no, dear," Nanny Violet's reassuring voice said. "Do what you must. I can stay until you get home."

"But what about your ride?" Annie queried, frankly curious to know how the nanny had managed to get to her house.

"Oh, no problem, dear. Just tell Ms. Buckley you'll be late, and she'll arrange it all," Nanny Violet said brightly.

Annie and Devyn took a quick lunch in the employee dining room. Nora was there.

"How's your little boy?" she asked Annie.

"Running a fever, but I think okay other than that. Nanny Violet is a miracle. I can't thank you enough. After a moment's hesitation, Wills took to her. I've asked her to stay a bit past two thirty because I have to stop at Lacy Nothings. I want to speak to Ashley Mulcahy about letting us showcase some of her items for our gift shop."

"Wonderful. When you get home just press three on your cell, and the car will come for her," Nora said. "I've arranged for her to be with you until your little boy goes back to school. Probably the rest of the week."

"I have died and gone to heaven," Annie said. "I never knew working could be so wonderful. I love the Channel Corp."

Nora smiled. "And Devyn is working out?"

"Yes, he's a huge help. I couldn't do this without him," Annie replied.

Devyn grinned.

"Good," Nora said.

Back in the shop's stockroom after their brief lunch, Devyn said, "Did you mean it?

215

I really am a help?" He was holding the ladder upon which she was standing while she set boxes of sea sponges, loofahs, and natural-bristle bath brushes on a top shelf. "And you can't do without me?"

She turned. "I wouldn't say it if I didn't mean it, Devyn." And then she lost her footing. "Oh!"

He caught her in his arms as she fell. They both looked startled at their close proximity. Then he put her down. "There you go," Devyn said.

"Thanks," Annie managed to gasp. "That was clumsy of me." Her heart was hammering, but whether from fright or desire she wasn't certain.

"That ladder can be tricky," he replied. He could feel his cock tightening in his pants, and he hoped she hadn't noticed.

"Well, I guess that should do it for the day then," Annie said, recovering first. "I should get going into the village if I'm going to catch Ashley at Lacy Nothings."

"Maybe I should go with you," he suggested. "I mean, the guests are going to be buying these negligees and stuff to please their men. Wouldn't a man's opinion be of value? I can follow you in my car so you wouldn't have to bring me back."

Annie thought about it a long moment,

and then she said, "Okay."

As she pulled out of her space and down the road she saw him following her in a slightly vintage Toyota, and smiled. The rich man's son drove a battered car in keeping with his impoverished status. In the village she pulled into a space in front of Lacy Nothings, and he parked a couple of spaces up. They entered the shop together.

Ashley Kimbrough Mulcahy came forward. "Hi, Mrs. Miller." She eyed Devyn, and Annie felt a jolt of jealousy.

"This is Devyn Scott, my personal assistant," Annie said, introducing him. "I'm working up at the Spa now. We're opening a gift shop — spa robes, high-end bath goodies, all the lotions and oils we use in our treatments. Would you be willing to put some of your stock in the shop? They're so beautiful and elegant. Just the kind of pretty things our guests can afford and would love."

Ashley thought for a long moment, then turned to her assistant, Nina. "What do you think?" she asked her.

"A few things, maybe one or two from the Venetian source. And one of our catalogs has to be put in with each purchase," Nina said.

"I'll sell you a dozen garments, your

217

choice, four times a year," Ashley said. "You'll purchase them from me at cost plus a forty percent markup. I will set the retail price. You'll make a small profit, but my stuff is really a come-on to get your guests into your gift shop. And my label remains in each garment. If you can live with those terms then we have a deal, Mrs. Miller."

"Take it," Devyn murmured softly.

"Very well," Annie said briskly in what she hoped was a no-nonsense voice.

"I'll want our deal legalized before I let you have anything," Ashley said.

"That's fair," Annie replied. "But I want something in the shop by the weekend. We have our official opening then."

"I'll call across the street to my lawyers," Ashley told her. "Tomorrow afternoon, same time, same place?"

"I think Annie would appreciate it if the agreement could be faxed up to the Spa tomorrow morning," Devyn put in. "Right, Annie?"

"Yes, of course. Ms. Buckley should really see anything before I sign it," Annie agreed. "And if everything is okay we can sign in Joe's office at two thirty tomorrow afternoon. He's my lawyer, too." She smiled. "I couldn't have survived without him and Rick after Nat died."

"Wonderful," Ashley said. "I'll see you tomorrow, then, at two thirty. And afterward you can come over and pick your stock, okay?"

"Perfect," Annie agreed.

They left the shop.

"I hope you didn't mind my chiming in like that," Devyn said to her.

"No. You were a lifesaver. I wouldn't have known whether it was a good deal or not," Annie told him. "I thought you said you were bad at business."

"It wasn't that I was bad at it; it was just that it didn't interest me at the time," he replied. "But I know a good deal from a not so good deal."

"Is this good?" she wondered.

"It's fair, and it's as good as you're going to get. Lacy Nothings is a very successful small business. We need them," he said.

"But if we could learn who some of their suppliers are . . ." Annie said thoughtfully as they walked to her car.

He laughed as he helped her into her van. "Why, Mrs. Miller, ma'am, I do believe there is a bit of the cutthroat in you. You might have a good future in business." He shut the car door. "See you tomorrow."

She could smell the faint aroma of his cologne. It was deliciously sexy, Annie thought as she headed home. Maybe she would program the B channel tonight. She had seen the most delicious little teddy in the window of Lacy Nothings when they had gone into the shop. It was a soft purple color, short, in practically transparent gossamer silk with lace inserts where the nipples would be, and with spaghetti straps. She couldn't afford it, of course, but she could wear it in a fantasy. Now that she had practically tamed her Beast, that fantasy was becoming a bit old. She wasn't quite ready to delete it, but she was ready for something new. A round bed with red silk sheets and lots of pillows. A mirrored ceiling. And Devyn Scott with a towel wrapped about him, entering the room where she would be lying in her purple teddy on the round bed waiting for him.

She almost missed the turn onto Parkway Drive, but caught herself in time. After pulling into the driveway she got out of the van and hurried into the house. There was the smell of baking brownies in the kitchen as she entered it. She heard voices from the den, and standing in the open doorway she saw Nanny Violet, Wills ensconced in her lap, both twins, and even the surly Amy seated on the floor as the nanny talked.

"And then his lordship said to me, 'Nanny

Violet —' " She stopped, looking up. "Oh, Mrs. Miller, welcome home." She gently shifted Wills into the chair as she stood up. "There's a nice beef stew on the back of the stove keeping warm. I've made dumplings, and there's a pan of brownies in the oven."

"You are wonderful!" Annie said. "Thank you so much, Nanny Violet."

"If you'll press the three on your cell, I'll be going," the nanny replied. "Eight tomorrow morning then, dear. Wills's fever is down to one hundred. It will probably rise a bit with evening, but the whoopsies seem to be over. I'd give him some soup and toast, though, for dinner. And as he's been a very good laddie today, a nice warm brownie if he eats it all up."

"I will, Nanny!" Wills promised.

"But what about the end of your story?" Amy wanted to know.

"Oh, I'll tell you all tomorrow," Nanny promised. She bustled into the hallway and, taking her hat and cape from the closet, put them on. Then, going to the door, she bade them good night with a smile and went out the front door.

Annie was surprised to see a small dark car waiting at the curb. Nanny Violet hurried toward it and got in. It sped off down the street into the midautumn gloaming, and Annie could have sworn it just disappeared. But of course it was a trick of the light. She turned back to her children. "I hope you didn't mind that I wasn't home when you got here, but I was delayed. I'm sorry."

"Hey," Amy said, "that nanny is really cool. Sort of an older Mary Poppins. Wait till I tell Brittany that we have a nanny. She will be *so* jealous."

"It's only temporary until Wills gets better," Annie said. "Probably the week."

"It's like *Nanny 911,*" Lily said.

"Only better, 'cause we're not brats," Rose added, "and we can have fun with her."

"Is everyone's homework done, or in the process of?" Annie asked her daughters.

The trio turned dutifully and headed upstairs.

"Dinner in an hour," Annie called, and then went into the kitchen, hearing the timer to remove the brownies from the oven. Looking into the den she saw that Wills had fallen asleep in the chair, and she left him there until they were ready to eat.

Her mother called just as she had gotten everyone down for the night. "What is this about you having a nanny looking after Wills?" Phyllis demanded. "I would have come over if you wanted me to, Annie."

"Thanks, Mom, I know you would have, but I didn't want to impose," Annie said, and waited for the outburst that was certain to come.

"Impose? Impose? I am your mother, the grandmother of those children," Phyllis began. "If you stayed home like you should, instead of depriving that poor sick mite of his mother in his time of crisis, there would be no need for me to come, or for you to have some stranger in the house. Is anything missing? Did you check?"

Annie sighed. "Mom," she said, "Nanny Violet was sent by my employers. She is a lovely Englishwoman, and Wills fell in love with her. So did the girls. When I got home dinner was on the back of the stove, and a pan of brownies was baking in my oven. The kids were all quiet. There was no rock music or television blaring. It was perfect. I wish I could have her all the time."

"And who is paying for this, I should like to know? Good help like that costs money, Annie," Phyllis said, as if her daughter were slow-witted.

"The corporation is paying for it," Annie told her mother. "They are incredible employers. I am really so lucky."

"Such generosity," Phyllis said. "It all sounds very odd to me."

"Lizzie's firm is attempting to gain them as a client," Annie murmured.

"They are?" her mother said.

Annie could almost see the wheels in Phyllis's head turning.

"Well, I suppose if Lizzie's people want to represent them, they must be on the up-and-up. Her firm is very conservative, you know."

"Yes, Mom, I know," Annie replied. "How's Dad?"

"Pulled a muscle out on the course today," Phyllis said sourly.

"Oh, I'm sorry. Give him a kiss for me, and tell him I hope he's better soon."

"Well, thank goodness it's going to rain tomorrow or he'd grumble all day about not being out on the course," Phyllis said.

"It's late, Mom, and I want to go to bed," Annie said.

"Yes, yes, you need your rest now that you're a working mother," Phyllis agreed. "Annie, I know I'm old-fashioned, but I really am proud of what you're doing."

"Thanks, Mom. Good night."

"Good night, dear," Phyllis responded.

Annie set down the phone. *Well, fancy that,* she thought. A compliment from Phyllis. It was a first. Locking up, she turned out all the lights and headed upstairs, taking the last brownie with her. She looked in on Wills, but though feverish he was sleeping, and that probably would last the night. She'd given him a Children's Motrin before tucking him in. The lights were already out in the girls' bedrooms. *Good.* She turned the key in the lock of her own bedroom door, washed, undressed, and got into her own bed. She looked at the B button, thinking of the round bed, the red silk sheets, the purple teddy. She remembered how she had felt in Devyn's arms this afternoon. The faint smell of his cologne. In reality she wouldn't dare to encourage him. If he rebuffed her it would be so embarrassing, and she would never be able to go back to work at the Spa again. But the B button offered her the chance of a new fantasy. One in which Devyn would be her lover. Annie pressed down on the letter B and immediately found herself sprawled against red-silk-covered pillows, wearing a purple teddy with lace inserts over her nipples.

The room was large, and there was a fire burning in a large hearth. And there were wide, tall windows. Intrigued, Annie slid off the bed and walked to them. She saw one was a door, and it opened onto a deck. Turning the handle on the door, she stepped outside into the night. Above her the black sky was dotted with stars. A moon was just beginning to peep over the horizon. A faint wind brought her the salty scent of the sea, and then she heard the waves lapping at the shoreline.

It was the beach house she had always dreamed about, Annie realized. It was set on a broad expanse of sand with the water at its edge. And coming out of the water was a man. He stopped to pick up something on the beach — a towel, she guessed as he wrapped it about his slender loins and moved toward her. Annie's heart began to hammer wildly. Was it Devyn? She wanted it to be Devyn. It had to be Devyn! Her nipples beneath the lace puckered, thrusting forward.

"Annie," he called her name, and then he was coming up onto the deck. His arm slipped around her, drawing her near. One hand began to knead a full, round breast as his mouth took hers in a hot kiss. "It took you long enough, Annie," he said against her lips.

"What do you mean?" She gasped softly. She could feel his cock through the towel, and he was already hard.

"To orchestrate this fantasy," Devyn said to her. "I like it. I like the sea, the beach, and oh, my, look at that delicious bed inside." He took her hand and led her back into the bedroom.

"This is a mistake," Annie murmured.

"No, it isn't. You've wanted to fuck me, and I sure as hell have wanted to fuck you ever since we set eyes on each other," Devyn said.

"You aren't the real Devyn," Annie protested. "The poor kid would be horrified if he knew I had the hots for him. It must be my age."

"No, I'm not the real Devyn. I'm the fantasy one, but it doesn't mean you and I can't have fun, does it?"

"He's almost twelve years younger than I am," Annie said. "I ought to be ashamed of myself."

Devyn laughed. "I know. You're a bad girl, Annie, but I'm a bad boy. And haven't you wanted to spank my butt? You think about it every time you look at me."

Annie blushed furiously. "How do you know —"

"Because I'm a part of you," he said. "You can spank me later, okay? Right now I want to put you on your back and do you."

Annie bit her lower lip nervously. Maybe this hadn't been such a good idea. If she did it with her fantasy Devyn, what was it going to be like every time she looked at the real Devyn? Would she want him as much? Or would the fantasy suffice?

Devyn dropped the towel covering his loins, and Annie's blue eyes dropped to his crotch. He was so well hung it should have been illegal. His dick was thick, and while it was not quite as long as the Beast's, there had to be nine or ten inches of prime meat hanging there. And it was all for her. Annie licked her lips slowly. She reached out and stroked his length. "That is so nice," she said softly as her fingers slid up and down him.

"Then what are we waiting for, Annie?" He backed her up to the round bed, pushing her down onto the red silk sheets. Kneeling down, he pushed the teddy up and spread her legs wide. His blond head leaned forward. She felt him opening her up. His tongue began to lick at her nether lips. "Umm, you taste so good, baby," he told her. His teeth nibbled at the insides of her creamy thighs. The tip of his tongue touched her clit. "Do you like this?" he asked as he began to fret the nubbin of flesh. The tongue worked her until she was squirming with her rising excitement. He nipped her clit, making her come with a moan. "Yeah, you like it," he told her as he stood up. His hands slipped beneath her buttocks, and, raising her on an angle, he pushed his hard cock into her wet, hot vagina. "But I'll bet you like this better," he said as his hands closed about her hips, and he began to fuck her with slow, rhythmic strokes of his penis.

"Yes!" she hissed at him. "Yes, I like this best, Devyn! Now prove to me that you were worth the wait. Fuck me hard, and fuck me deep. And don't you dare come until I've come at least twice, or I will have to spank your cute little butt until it burns."

"I'm going to make you scream," he promised her.

"Promises, promises, little boy," Annie taunted him.

His face grew dark with anger for a moment, but then his eyes narrowed as he concentrated on the task at hand. He had to find that wicked little spot that every woman possessed within her vagina. Find it and he would send her over the moon. The little bitch needed to be shown who was going to be the boss of this relationship. He probed her carefully, watching her face for any change in her pleasure quotient. And then he saw it as her face lit up with both wonder and delight.

"Oh, yes, there!" Annie cried.

He began to work it and work it and work it until she began to moan with the pleasure within her that kept building and building and building. Then she began to scream as it became so incredibly unbearable, yet so sweet, she didn't think she could survive another heavenly stroke of his thick cock. Her head began to spin. Stars exploded behind her closed eyes. She came with a sharp cry as her body arched with a shudder that left her half-conscious. He lowered her even as he pushed her farther back onto the bed, mounting her without withdrawing. "Open your eyes, Annie!" he said harshly. "Open your eyes and look at me as I fuck you until you come again, baby."

Annie forced her eyes open, although it took a fierce effort. Above her she saw their bodies in the mirrored ceiling over the bed. His thighs were on either side of her hips. His buttocks were contracting and releasing as he began again to delve into her. He ripped the purple teddy off of her, burying his face between her two round breasts for a moment. Then he sucked first on one nipple, which sent her vagina into small spasms, before biting on the other. She could see her hands running up and down his back, caressing the firm buttocks as he fucked her.

"Give me your tongue," he told her. Then he began to suck it in perfect time as his big, thick cock pleasured her.

Annie moaned into his mouth as he again touched that wicked little spot.

"Don't stop," she begged him. "Don't stop!"

"I could do this to you forever," he told her as he sent her spinning once more into time and space. "You shouldn't have waited so long, baby. You shouldn't have waited so long. I don't think I'm ever going to be able to get enough of you." He fucked her hard and deep again, and Annie screamed as they came together.

When she awoke in her own bed after the Channel had closed, she remembered he had fucked her several more times. Her vagina actually felt sore, and her thighs were sticky with cum. How could this be? And yet it was. She fell back asleep, and when she awoke with the beeping of her alarm she felt surprisingly refreshed. Showering quickly, she dressed in her Spa uniform, unlocked her bedroom door, checked on Wills, who was still sleeping, and hurried downstairs. The twins were already there, eating their granola and bananas. Amy was drinking some interesting-looking concoction.

"What is that?" she asked her eldest daughter.

"The twins made it for me," Amy said. "Pineapple, banana, a capsule of omega-three, a raw egg, and a little skim milk. I like it. I have energy all morning."

"I would worry, except the egg came from Baines Farm, and Grandma always made me an eggnog like that in the mornings, minus the omega-three, of course," Annie said.

Within minutes the girls were off to school, and Annie went back upstairs to check on her son. "How are you feeling?" she asked him.

"Where's Nanny?" he countered.

"She'll be here at eight, and it isn't eight yet, sweetie. Here." She put the digital thermometer in his mouth. When it beeped she saw that he still had a temperature.

"How much?" Wills asked her.

"One hundred and one, less than yesterday," Annie told him. "How's your tummy today, sweetie?"

"Okay, but my throat hurts," Wills told her.

"Open up and let me look," Annie told him, peering into her son's mouth. The back of his throat was bright scarlet. She sighed. "It's red. I'll tell Nanny to make you some Jell-O, Wills."

"Can I go back to sleep?" he asked her.

"Sure you can," Annie said. "I'll see you this afternoon. Nanny will be with you all day, and I'll tell her you still have a temperature and your throat is sore." He was asleep before she left the room.

The mantel clock in the front hall was striking eight when the sharp rapping of the doorknocker sounded, and Annie hurried to answer it. "Good morning, Nanny," she said, peering out and wondering where Nanny's ride had gone so quickly.

"Good morning, dear. How's the wee laddie?" Nanny Violet asked as she came in, hung up her cape, and set her hat on the closet shelf.

Annie told her.

"Well, don't you worry yourself at all, dearie. Nanny will be here to take care of the laddie until you get home."

"I'll be late again," Annie said. "I have to see a supplier this afternoon. I'm sorry."

"Not to worry, dear. Your children are delightful. Very mannerly in this day and age, I can tell you. It's lovely to be with them," Nanny Violet said.

Mannerly? Her daughters? Well, maybe the twins, but Amy? And yet Amy had been quite contented when Annie had gotten home yesterday, and didn't whine when told to do her homework. Nanny Violet was a miracle worker. "Then I'll be on my way," Annie replied. "Is there anything you need?"

"Nothing at all, dear," the nanny told her. "We'll be just fine."

Nora Buckley called her into her office as soon as Annie had arrived at the Spa. "This was faxed over from Pietro d'Angelo and Johnson a few minutes ago," she said. "It's an agreement between Lacy Nothings Corp. and the Channel Corp. I've read it over. It seems fine to me, Annie. Call them and tell them you'll be in to sign it this afternoon. When can we expect the stock?"

"As soon as I sign the agreement I'm going to the store to pick it out," Annie answered her. "I'll need a special glass display cabinet for it. I don't want too many hands pawing it. It will get shopworn, and it's too pricey to allow that to happen."

Nora smiled. "You are really a natural at merchandising, Annie. Mr. Nicholas is never wrong when he picks someone for the corporation."

"Don't let me dazzle you with my footwork." Annie laughed. "I'm really just feeling my way, but I will learn. I'm going to make the gift shop a moneymaking operation for the Spa. Just wait and see."

"How's your little boy?" Nora asked casually. "Did the nanny work out?"

"He's still sick, and Nanny Violet is wonderful!" Annie said enthusiastically. "I wish I could have her all the time. The kids already adore her, and I came home yesterday to dinner ready to go, and a pan of brownies in the oven."

"Gracious, she is a treasure," Nora said.

There were more boxes in the gift shop when Annie opened up. Devyn arrived, and for a few minutes Annie avoided looking at him. How could she, given her fantasy last night? But then she managed to gain control of herself. Devyn wouldn't know about her fantasy. He didn't know about the Channel. They unpacked together and put everything away. It went quicker today because they had arranged the shelves yesterday.

"If you don't object, I started making out the price tags last evening," Devyn said.

"That's wonderful, but don't you have a life after five p.m.?" Annie asked him.

"Sure," he said with a grin.

"Girlfriend?" she probed.

"Nah, not enough real time to hang out and find one," he admitted. "Besides, PAs are on call twenty-four/seven."

"But you're my PA, and I don't need you nights and weekends. You should go out and have some fun, Devyn," Annie told him.

"Are you dating anyone?" he asked boldly.

"Me?" Annie laughed. "Five kids, remember?"

"No one since your husband died?" he said.

"Nope," she answered him.

"Have dinner with me," Devyn said softly.

I didn't hear that correctly, Annie thought. "What?"

"Have dinner with me," he repeated.

Annie wasn't certain what to say.

"There's no rule here about employees going out together," he continued. "I checked it out."

"You're younger than I am," Annie finally managed to say.

"You're older than I am," he replied. "Can I help it if I like older women?"

"I can't leave my children alone in the evening," Annie protested weakly.

"Your daughters babysit, don't they? They could watch your little boy while we have a pleasant, early, and grown-up dinner," Devyn told her. "Just dinner. No strings. We could be home before dark," he teased her.

"The sun is setting earlier these days," she reminded him.

"But as long as the moon isn't full I don't grow shaggy hair and fangs," he said with a mischievous grin. "When was the last time you ate out someplace other than a fast-food joint with your kids?"

"Lizzie and I had lunch at the country club a while back." Annie defended herself. "The food at the club is very good."

"It's better at East Harbor Inn," he told her. "Come on, Annie, say yes. I haven't been out of the Spa for a meal since I got here. I don't want to eat alone."

"Then ask one of the guys who isn't working this week," Annie suggested.

"I'd rather sit across a table from an attractive and sexy woman," Devyn answered her. "What's the harm in two colleagues having a pleasant dinner together?"

The harm, Annie thought to herself, *is that I'm having a full-blown sexual fantasy about you, and I love it. It's my imagination gone wild. An illusion, except in the reality of the day my eyes keep going to your crotch.* And yet if she persisted in being so hung-up he was going to start to wonder why, and she really did like him. Her fantasy had nothing to do with the real Devyn, and it was the real Devyn who wanted to have dinner with her. It was flattering. This thirty-one-year-old sexy kid wanted to have dinner with her. About to be forty-four, mother of five. Yes, it was a good ego boost.

"Annie?"

She pulled out of her thoughts. "Not while

237

Wills is still sick," she said. "But next week would be nice. Wednesday night?"

"That would be great!" he replied with a grin.

He looked so pleased that Annie grinned back at him, shaking her head. "You'd think you just got a date with Miss Universe," she teased him. "Back to work, kid. I'm due at the lawyers' at two. Want to meet me at Lacy Nothings afterward to pick out the negligees? Give me that man's opinion?"

"Sure!" He was so enthusiastic.

She got to the lawyers' on the dot of two, and was ushered into Rick Johnson's office. "Got that contract for me to sign? Ms. Buckley up at the Spa says they're fine."

"Nora's an amazing gal," Rick said, laying three copies of the single-page contract out for her to sign. "Four years ago she was a homebody, and now she's working for a big corporation. And now you, too. Do you like it?"

"Very much," Annie said. "They're a terrific employer. Wills got sick, and they sent me a nanny! A lovely starchy Brit nanny to take care of him so I could do my job here and not have to worry about him. Imagine working for people like that! And it's only my first week." She signed the three copies. "There!"

He handed her one. "Give that one to Ms. Buckley for her files. Sounds like you've landed in a pot of jam, Annie," Rick said. "I'm glad. I know it hasn't been easy for you since Nat was killed. Kids okay?"

Annie nodded. "Nathaniel has settled in at Princeton. Amy's not being too awful yet. The twins haven't begun any petitions against animal cruelty in the schools to date. And Wills is getting over his bug. I'd say my life is on a pretty even keel right now." She bade the attorney good-bye and, leaving his office, hurried across the street to Lacy Nothings. Devyn was already there and charming Ashley Mulcahy's assistant, Nina. "We're good to go," Annie said. "Bring on the scanties!"

"Ashley thought you might like to look through what's on display, and in our stockroom. She apologizes for not being here, but she's a bit under the weather."

"Another baby?" Annie asked.

"I think so. She hasn't said anything yet, but she rarely gets sick except when she's expecting," Nina remarked.

"I like this one," Devyn said, pointing to the purple teddy with the lace inserts that Annie had imagined herself in last night. "It is so hot. Especially the lace, and it's soft, so it won't chafe the nipples."

Annie blushed furiously. "You really like it? You don't think it's too obvious?"

"I think it's sexy as the dickens," Devyn said.

Nina smiled. "It is, isn't it?"

They spent an hour picking out negligees and teddies. Annie decided against bras and bikini panties, since they were limited to only twelve selections. She wanted them to be the sorts of things a woman would pick up to take home to wear for her husband or her lover, or perhaps just for herself.

The Spa gift shop opened officially, and the weeks began to fly by. Annie suggested a day trip to the local harvest festival for interested guests. The fifteen women who went loved it, and came back enthusiastic, wanting to know if there would be any other day trips. Before Nora might answer, Annie spoke up.

"We do arrange trips now and again," she said, "but you've come to the Spa for pampering and relaxation."

"But it was fun," one wealthy matron said. "So country, but you're right. We don't want to take away from our pampering."

"Nicely done," Nora murmured.

"We can do the Historical Society when the natives get restless again." Annie chuckled. "I wouldn't have suggested such a thing, but this particular group of women was getting bored, and that's not good for our reputation. A little something different now and again can't hurt us. A picnic on the beach in summer, perhaps, or a clambake in August, with fresh corn and tomatoes. We should have carolers during the Christmas holidays. They don't have to sing hymns, but can sing holiday songs. Heaven only knows there are plenty of them."

"How clever of you to notice the boredom, and to come up with all these wonderful suggestions to alleviate it," Nora said. "I'll commend your ingenuity to Mr. Nicholas. You won't run the gift shop forever."

"But I love the gift shop," Annie told her. "Do you know we had to reorder all the soaps and lotions? And the loofahs and natural-bristle brushes! I've sold half of my stock from Lacy Nothings already."

"Mr. Nicholas is going to be very pleased with you, Annie," Nora responded.

And he was. The Channel Corporation's CEO came for his monthy visit and invited Annie into the private office that was set aside for him. It was not a large room, but it had great charm. The walls were paneled in dark wood. A bow window hung with dark crimson drapes looked out over the grounds. A fireplace burned brightly with a fire. A mahogany desk was set to one side of the window. Before the hearth a lovely Victorian settee was flanked by two upholstered oak chairs. There was an antique butler's tray set before the settee.

"Come in and sit by me, Annie," Mr. Nicholas said to her, beckoning. "Coffee?"

There was a silver tray on the table with a coffeepot, a creamer, a sugar bowl, and a plate of small breakfast pastries.

"Yes, thank you," Annie said.

His hands were so elegant, and the long fingers perfectly manicured, the nails pared and smooth. He poured her coffee, leaving just the right amount of space for cream. Handing her the pretty earthenware cup, he smiled. "Pastry, my dear? I'm afraid I have an unrepentant sweet tooth."

"Me too," Annie admitted, taking one from the plate he held out.

"I want you to know that Nora has simply raved about how well you have fitted into the Spa's staff. Everyone seems to like you. And the suggestions you've made to improve our little operation are quite excellent," Mr. Nicholas said. "I have made it a policy to always reward good work."

"Oh, sir, I've only been here two months," Annie said. "I've just been trying to help out. I don't deserve any extra praise."

242

"And modest as well as clever," Mr. Nicholas said in delighted tones. "My dear, it gives me great pleasure to reward my people, and I have the perfect reward for you. How would you like to have Nanny Violet live in and help you with your family? The holiday season will be very busy, and you may be required to stay later than you are used to staying."

"I can't afford Nanny Violet," Annie said.

"Oh, dear," Mr. Nicholas said. "It is obvious I did not make myself clear, Annie. The Channel Corporation will pay for Nanny Violet as long as you are in our employ, and it is to be hoped that will be for a very long time. That empty room off of the kitchen that you use for storage would make a fine bedroom for Nanny Violet."

How does he know about the storage room? Annie wondered. But then she put her curiosity from her. It had been so difficult dashing home to meet Wills's bus. And the girls couldn't be relied on constantly as babysitters. They had after-school sports and band, among other activities. The week Nanny Violet had been with them had been just perfect. "You would pay her salary?" Annie asked, feeling stupid as she did so.

Mr. Nicholas nodded. "And you will see she has the weekends off."

"Of course," Annie replied. She was stunned.

"Then it's settled," Mr. Nicholas told her brightly. "Now do drink your coffee, my dear. It's a special blend I made up myself."

"When could I have her?" Annie asked. "I need time to clean out the storeroom and make the room habitable."

"Just tell Nora when you need her, my dear. She'll take care of everything," Mr. Nicholas said. "How do you like your coffee?"

"It's delicious," Annie said. Nanny Violet was going to be *her* nanny! And once Annie had her settled she could take Devyn up on his dinner invitation. She had canceled twice now. She hadn't wanted the girls to know that she was going out to dinner with her PA. But once Nanny Violet was in residence she could call home and say she had to work late, and no one would be the wiser. "Thank you so much, Mr. Nicholas!"

He smiled benignly. "I always take care of my people," he said.

Annie couldn't wait to tell her children that Nanny Violet would be moving in with them shortly. They whooped enthusiastically when she did. They had all liked the British nanny, but Amy came right to the point.

"How can we afford it, Mom?"

She explained it to them.

"Wow! That Mr. Nicholas is some employer," Amy said. "I suppose this means you'll be working longer hours."

"Well, at least a full workday now," Annie said. "I won't have to leave in the early afternoon to come home for Wills."

And she told Devyn too. "If that dinner invitation is still available," Annie said, "I won't cancel this time. Just let me get the nanny settled." She hadn't run her Devyn fantasy again because it was just too difficult to work with him after a night of unbridled sex with the fantasy Devyn. She hadn't tired of the Beast yet, and tonight as she pressed the A button, she found herself strung up naked, back in his dungeon.

"Today, Mistress Anne," he said from behind her in his rough, smoky voice, "we shall see how well you have learned your lessons of obedience." The leather tawse cracked and made contact with her buttocks. "Excellent," he said approvingly when she did not cry out. "You will receive nine more strokes of my leather, and you may scream after the sixth blow. I will count for you so you can concentrate upon the biting and burning sensation of your tender flesh."

She wondered why it was that she had

programmed a punishment fantasy for herself, but it was certainly interesting. She bit her lip to keep from crying out as the fourth blow touched her buttocks. And then she noticed a young soldier standing in the shadows watching as the Beast whipped her. He was handsome, and he smiled at her. She heard the Beast intone eight, and Annie shrieked for him as he added the final two blows.

He said nothing at first when he had finished, instead winching her up and spreading her legs wide by shortening the shackles that bound her. "Is she ready, Klaus?" He directed his question to the young soldier.

Klaus stepped forward and cupped her mound. Then he shook his head. "Close, my lord. Perhaps a bit of tongue to help bring her on."

The Beast smiled wolfishly. "Do it, then," he commanded. Then his hand wrapped itself in Annie's thick chestnut hair, and he pulled her head back, looking down into her face. "You will not come, Mistress Anne. No matter how badly you desire it, you will not come because you come only for your lord. Do you understand me?"

"Yes, my lord," Annie gasped.

"Excellent," he said, and released her

head. But then his hands moved around to fondle and play with her full, round breasts.

As he did the soldier called Klaus began to tongue her. Her mons, she noted in her fantasy, was shaved, plump and pink. Klaus knelt beneath her, and his tongue began to explore her slowly and most carefully. He licked the edges of her nether lips. He ran his tongue up the shadowed slit several times. Then the marauding tongue pushed through those lips to find her clit, and he knew he had when she whimpered. The relentless tongue flicked back and forth over that tiny, sensitive nubbin of flesh.

Annie moaned. "My lord, my lord, I must come soon or I will die!" She gave a little shriek as the tongue dove deeper and found the opening to her vagina. The tongue worked around it before pushing itself into her a small way. "My lord, I beg of you, make him cease this torture!"

The Beast, who had been playing with her nipples, stopped. "Are her juices ready to come, Klaus?" he asked the soldier.

The young man raised his head. "Yes, my lord."

"You will be rewarded," the Beast told him. "Step away from her now."

The soldier rose to his feet and took his place again opposite Annie.

"Now, my pet, something new," the Beast told her. Coming about to face her, he held up a leather dildo. It was covered in small bumps. "Lubricant!" And the soldier held forth a deep bowl of oil into which the Beast dipped the dildo. "Remember, you cannot come," he warned her. Then he slowly inserted the dildo, rotating it so that she felt the tiny bumps irritating her vagina and setting it afire with lust. Annie cried out again. "I must come, my lord! *I must!*"

"Not yet, Mistress Anne. Not quite yet," he told her.

"No! No!" she sobbed.

"Will you show me disobedience again, wench?" he demanded as he thrust the dildo back and forth within her.

"You are cruel, my lord!" And suddenly, just as she was near her crisis, he withdrew the dildo, lowered her, and freed her.

"Hands against the wall, Mistress Anne, and spread yourself," he ordered her, his naked chest pressing against her naked back. Then he pushed himself slowly into her hot, wet vagina. "Remember, you will not come until I say you may," he growled. Then he drove himself hard and deep until she could no longer bear it. She began to spasm even as he came, and when he had filled her with his lust he snarled, "You were told not to come, Mistress Anne, until I gave you leave."

"But you came!" she sobbed.

"Disobedience is in your nature, I fear," the Beast said. "Klaus, you may have your reward now."

Annie felt the Beast step away from her, and the soldier took his place. Spreading the cheeks of her ass with two strong fingers, he directed his penis to her anus and began to push slowly, slowly into that channel. "Nooo!" she cried, but she felt her excitement overcoming her at this forbidden pleasure.

"Be silent, Mistress Anne," the Beast cautioned her, "and take his cock into your fundament obediently, as you are commanded to do."

Fully sheathed now, the guardsman reached for her breasts, crushing them in his big hands. He pulled the nipples and pinched them cruelly. Leaning forward, he nipped the back of her neck; then he began to whisper to her. "Do you feel my strong cock within your asshole, wench? You're tight as any virgin should be. Do you like being fucked this way? Aye, you do, for I feel you trembling with your excitement." He withdrew his penis slowly, and then thrust hard into her again.

Annie moaned.

"Squeeze me tightly, wench," the guardsman said, releasing her breasts from his grip. Then his hand slid between her legs, and he began to finger her clit until Annie could not stem the excitement rising within her heated body. He allowed her two small clitoral orgasms before whispering hotly in her ear, "Now, make me come, wench!"

Annie concentrated on tightening her rectal muscles until Klaus began to whimper like a child, and suddenly she felt him releasing his cum into her back channel. She gasped as he withdrew from her and fell to her knees. But the Beast was not yet finished with her.

"On your back, Mistress Anne," he ordered her, and when she obeyed him he covered her with his big body, and his huge cock drove into her heated body. "You will not come," he warned her again, "until I give you leave." He thrust hard and deep.

"No," Annie told him boldly. "It is you who will not come until I tell you! Ride me hard, my lord! I am not yet satisfied at all."

With a roar of fury the Beast fucked her until Annie was seeing stars and their bodies were covered in sweat. She heard the warning ping of the Channel about to close.

"Quickly, my lord!" she told him. "Now!

Now! Now!" And they both came in a frenzy of hot, sticky cum as Annie awoke in her own bed. She was panting, and exhausted with her evening. It had gone so quickly. But she was now satisfied, and at least when she saw Devyn tomorrow she wouldn't feel embarrassed. Maybe after their dinner she would play the B fantasy, and make it a perfect end to a perfect evening. She grinned to herself as she rolled over to go to sleep. She was addicted to the Channel, she knew. But she didn't care. And as for her late husband, well, the unbearable ache of missing Nat was finally subsiding. He had been one of the good guys, but he wasn't here anymore. The Beast and Devyn were. A woman had needs, and she now realized that those needs shouldn't be denied.

CHAPTER SEVEN

Nathaniel came home early from Princeton for Thanksgiving. "Wow!" he said as he stepped back from his mother, eyes admiring. "You've lost a little weight, and your hair is different. You look terrific, Mom! If this is what having a job does for you, I'm all for it." Then he hugged her and kissed her cheek.

Annie laughed. "I love it," she admitted.

He helped her clean out the storage room off the kitchen. When they had emptied it they discovered a small fireplace on one wall. It had been hidden by a barrier of boxes. Nathaniel opened the flue, lit a piece of paper, and grinned as the smoke went up the chimney. It was open and clear. The fireplace worked. They washed the two side-by-side windows that looked out on the woods in the empty lot on one side of the house. Nat had bought the lot several years after they moved into the house.

"Can't protect what you don't own," he had said.

They all painted the room a cheerful shade of jonquil yellow, with white trim, and added a floral border below the ceiling. They had found a heavy maple three-quarter-canopied bed when they had cleaned the room out. It had been in the house when they bought it. They set it up now, along with its bureau and nightstand. A simple ruffled white cotton canopy topped the bed, and matching ruffled white cotton Priscilla curtains framed the windows. Annie had enough disposable income now to purchase a mattress and box spring for the bed, along with some linens. A comfortable chair and ottoman in a deep yellow-and-cream stripe was positioned by the fireplace. Next to it was set a small round antique table with a lamp. The bed was made with fresh sheets, and the down quilt in its yellow-blue-and-white duvet was folded neatly at the foot of the bed. There were two large pillows propped against the headboard.

The room had no closet, but there had been a large, dusty armoire with a yellowed mirror set inside one of its doors. Cleaning it out, they painted the armoire yellow and white, and put in some hangers. The wide, dark floorboards of the room were covered with a large oval rag rug in light and dark shades of blue and creamy beige. They had found several old prints, pastoral and floral scenes probably as old as the house itself. They reframed and hung them. A lamp was added to the bedside table.

"Where is she going to wash and pee?" Nathaniel asked his mother.

Annie's face registered consternation. "Oh, lordy!" she said.

"The ooky bathroom," Amy reminded her mother. "The one we never used because it was so old and disgusting. Can we fix it up, too?"

The bathroom in question was directly across the little back hallway from what had been the storeroom. It had obviously once been the domain of whoever lived in what had become the storage room, now refurbished to be Nanny's room.

"I haven't looked in there in years," Annie admitted. "I'm not sure I even want to open the door. God only knows what's in there."

The twins jumped forward gleefully to open the door, but it was stuck. Nathaniel put his shoulder against it and shoved hard. There was a slight ripping sound, but the door creaked open slightly. Nathaniel pushed harder, and the door finally opened wide. They looked inside. There was an ancient toilet with an oak water box above it, a pedestal sink, and small claw-foot bathtub.

"Ewwww, it's disgusting," Amy said, wrinkling her nose.

"For once she's right," Rose responded, and Lily nodded in agreement.

"What do you think, Mom?" Nathaniel asked Annie.

Annie sighed, but then she said, "It's doable, but it's going to take some work."

"New toilet, absolutely," Nathaniel remarked. "That old water box looks like it could come down if you pulled the chain. And the plumbing may need a bit of a check. I'll call Mike Wheeler. He started working with his dad in high school."

"He didn't go to college?" Annie was surprised. They all went to college nowadays.

"Wasn't interested, and besides, he had a family business to go into," Nathaniel said. "And he likes being a plumber."

"Call him," Annie said.

The Wheelers, father and son, arrived shortly after Nathaniel called. Wheeler Senior was fascinated by the ancient toilet. "I'll trade you for a nice, new modern commode, and all the new fixtures you'll need for this room, Mrs. Miller," he said. "I have a collection of antique plumbing fixtures, but I don't have one like this."

"You got it!" Annie told him. *Less expense,* she thought happily.

The floor in the old bathroom was wood. They could refinish it, or get some vinyl tiles at the nearby Lowe's. They opted for the tiles. The Wheelers removed the sink, tub, and old toilet and redid the plumbing pipes. Annie and the girls repainted the room. They had enough border left over from the bedroom to put up. Nathaniel and Mike Wheeler laid the vinyl tiles. The new commode was installed, the tub and the sink restored to their proper places. Amy washed the little bathroom window and put up a shade.

Nanny would arrive the Sunday after Thanksgiving, and they were ready for her. Annie had been spared the trouble of cooking Thanksgiving dinner by her mother.

"With you working now," Phyllis said as they sat after the meal consuming pumpkin pie, "you really don't have time to do it properly, and with your father on the golf course all the time I do. I don't know why you didn't ask me to look after Wills."

"You're going on a three-week cruise to South America and the Caribbean right after Christmas, and then on to Arizona for the winter," Annie reminded her mother. "Besides, I'm not paying for it. The Channel Corporation is paying Nanny Violet."

"This Mr. Nicholas would appear to like you," Phyllis murmured. "He hasn't done or suggested anything inappropriate to you, has he?"

Annie burst out laughing. "Mr. Nicholas?" she said. "He's like a father figure to his employees. An old-fashioned guy who rewards diligence and hard work. Isn't that refreshing in this day and age, Mom? There is no way in hell that he could qualify as a skirt-chasing devil. I don't think he's trying to get in my pants by giving me a nanny."

"Anne Elizabeth Miller!" her mother exclaimed, red spots exploding on her cheeks. "Please remember I raised you to be a lady." Then, hearing a snicker, she turned on her other daughter. "And the same goes for you, Elizabeth Anne Bradford."

Nanny Violet arrived promptly at one p.m. Sunday afternoon. Wills and the girls greeted her joyfully, leading her to her newly refurbished room, showing her her own little private bathroom. Nanny Violet's eyes welled up with tears. "Why, it's a real home for me," she said in a quavering voice.

"Thank you so much."

Nathaniel set her bags down. "Come on, kids," he said. "Let's give Nanny a bit of time to unpack. Tea at four." And he ushered his siblings out. "I like her," he told his mother. "It's good to know there's someone reliable for the girls and Wills."

"You said you approved of my working," Annie replied.

"I do, Mom," her oldest child told her. "But the little ones need someone to be home for them. And you needed to find out who you were and what you can do. It can't have been a barrel of laughs in this day and age being referred to as Nat Miller's widow. Such a brave woman. You're more than Dad's widow, and only Wills is going to be here forever," he concluded with a grin.

"How did you get so wise?" Annie asked, ruffling his dark hair. "But I'm doing it all for you, Nathaniel. For the girls, for Wills. So Amy can have something new now and again when she sees it, and not just when it goes on sale, if it's even still there and in her size. So the twins can get those micro-scopes they have wanted so desperately for Christmas this year. So Wills can have the Disney Channel, and we can go out to dinner and a movie together instead of pinching our pennies so hard all the time. I got tired of having to think every time I opened my wallet. Every time I had to say no. I don't want to be brave anymore." But she didn't have to be now.

The village was decorated for Christmas now, and as was the custom the shop windows followed a single theme. This year's theme was "An Egret Pointe Christmas, Circa 1840." Annie took several groups of women from the Spa into the village to see the windows.

"Why, they're every bit as good as Fifth Avenue," at least one woman per trip was bound to remark.

Annie was staying later now at the Spa, but with Nanny Violet at home supervising the children, she didn't worry. Her life was suddenly perfect. After Christmas her parents disappeared to Arizona for the rest of the winter. Her father's golf fixation would be broken up with their January cruise.

Lizzie called her, excited, right after the first of the year to announce that she had snagged the Channel Corporation as a client for her firm. "My God, Annie, you have no idea how diverse they are," Lizzie exclaimed. "And Mr. Nicholas runs it all. He's got his finger on everything. He's amazing! A little unnerving with those coal black eyes of his, but a brilliant guy nonetheless. The senior partners were going to put one of themselves in charge, but Mr. Nicholas said no. He said I was the one who sold him on the firm, and so I was to be his personal lawyer, his main contact. There were a couple of noses out of joint, I have to tell you."

"That's wonderful!" Annie congratulated her sister.

"Downside here, however: I won't be able to get out to Egret Pointe this winter. Mr. Nicholas wants me to travel to all the corporate divisions, meet his people in charge so I'm familiar with everything. It's really a good idea, and you know how I hate being unprepared, so I'm going to do it. Will you be all right with Mom and Dad away?"

"I'm fine," Annie assured her. "I've got my wonderful Nanny Violet, remember?" *And I've got my job,* Annie thought to herself. *I've never been happier.*

There was new stock coming into the shop for the Valentine holiday. Annie was up on the rolling ladder putting away scented loofahs one afternoon when she lost her balance and fell into the waiting arms of her PA. She gave a small shriek of surprise as his arms closed about her.

"Gotcha!" Devyn said, smiling at her.

"I don't know what happened," Annie said. God, it felt good to be in his arms.

He set her down, her back to the shelves. His lean body was pressing into her soft curves. His mouth found hers, and he kissed her hard, his tongue plunging between her lips, fencing with hers. "Ummm, you taste good," he told her.

"Devyn, I don't think —" Annie began, her heart beating rapidly.

"No, don't think," he said softly against her mouth. A hand slid up beneath her skirt as he nuzzled her neck. "Don't think at all, Annie." His fingers stroked the soft inside of her thighs. His hand cupped her mons.

This was wrong, she thought, but her body was rapidly responding to his touch.

Pinning her against the shelving of the stockroom with his hard body, he slipped his other hand beneath her turtleneck and reached around to unlatch her bra. Then he began to fondle her round breasts.

"Devyn!" she murmured. His hand felt so good there.

"Yes, Annie?" he answered her.

"This is . . . oh . . . very inappropriate behavior," she finally managed to get out.

"I'm going to fuck you," he murmured against her mouth. "Fuck you hard and fuck

261

you deep, Annie, just like I've wanted to do since the first day I laid eyes on you."

"I don't think —" she attempted to protest.

"I told you, Annie, don't think." He removed his hand from her breast and unzipped his fly. "One day when I do that, I'm going to have you go down on your knees and suck me off, but not today. Just watching your cute little ass up on that ladder has made me as hard as a rock. Wanna see?" He stepped back just slightly.

She didn't want to look, but she did. To her surprise he was just as big as his fantasy counterpart. "What do you want me to say?" she asked him. "Oh, wow!"

He laughed softly. "Save the wows for later," he told her. The hand beneath her skirt ripped her panties off, tossing them aside. His hands slipped quickly beneath her butt, and before she could catch her breath, he had her impaled on his cock.

Annie gasped. "You've had practice at this," she murmured as her legs instinctively wrapped themselves about his torso.

"Shut up," he told her, and he kissed her again even as he began to fuck her.

Oh, God, he felt good inside of her. Annie threw her head back between two wide shelves, and his mouth raced down her straining throat. He was going to make her come, and come fast, the devil. "Do it! Do it!" she heard herself moaning to him.

He fucked her harder and deeper until her head was spinning with the pure pleasure that he was giving her. It was wrong! *Why is it wrong?* the voice in her head demanded to know. *I'm married! You're a widow! He's younger than I am. He's hot!*

"Come on, Annie," he crooned to her. "Give it to me, baby. Come for me!"

And she did, in strong spasms that rocked her to her core. But he was still hard inside her. "What's the matter?" she whispered to him.

He laughed low. "You're going to have two, Annie." And he began again to fuck her with slow, deep strokes of his hard cock. "Didn't your husband ever give you two in a row?" He nipped at her neck, and then began to lick it.

Could she come again this quickly outside of the Channel? Annie wondered. "Someone could come in," she protested weakly.

"The door is closed," he said, "and we'll hear if they do." He never broke his rhythm as he talked. "We're going to be doing this a lot from now on. I've been waiting for you to get the picture, but you haven't. Got it now, Annie?"

"You've got an ego as big as all outdoors," she answered him.

"To match my big dick," he replied. "God, you feel good! I want you in bed, where I can enjoy every inch of you." He began to move at a faster pace.

"Well, turnabout is fair play," Annie said mischievously, "and I'm certainly enjoying every inch of you, even if this is inappropriate behavior."

"Tell me to fuck you," he whispered in her ear.

"Why?" she teased him.

"Because I want to hear you say it," he answered her.

She could have played with him for a few minutes more, but every moment they spent like this increased the danger of being caught. And she wasn't about to lose her job over a casual screw in the storage room. "Fuck me, Devyn," she purred to him. "Fuck me hard and deep. Make me come again." *What am I saying?* Annie wondered as he complied with her request. She had never in her life been this bold and bad. Not even close. But suddenly it felt right, and she wanted it. And then he found her G-spot. Annie screamed softly, and within moments she was climaxing again, but this time he came with her, groaning as his hot cum spurted into her tingling, spasming vagina.

When it was over he let her down. "God, that was good!" he said, and, pulling her close, he kissed her hard. "Mad at me?" he asked almost sheepishly.

"Next time wear a condom," she told him.

"I'm clean," he assured her. "They test us after every guest has gone just to be certain. What about you?"

"I haven't had sex since Nat died," Annie admitted, "and we were monogamous with each other."

"Then we won't need condoms," he said.

"No condom, no nooner," Annie said firmly. Bending over, she picked up her panties. They were virtually destroyed. *Note to self: Keep change of underwear here.* "And next time, caveman, don't rip my clothes. I'm going to have a damned cold ass by the time I get home tonight."

"I could give you a little spanking and warm it up," he offered.

"You are just full of yourself, aren't you?" Annie told him.

"Tell me you wanted what happened as much as I did," he said.

Annie sighed. "Yes, I did, but I would never have taken the initiative," she admitted. "You're way younger than I am. We work together. There are so many reasons why this should not have happened, Devyn." *Not to mention the fact that I'm screwing you in a fantasy.*

"Forget the age thing. It doesn't matter to me. You've got the ass and tits of a twenty-five-year-old. I can't wait to get you in bed, see you naked, lick your body from head to toes. I want to eat you, and have you eat me. I can't get to sleep at night thinking about all the things I want to do to you, for you, Annie."

"I don't know how we're going to make that happen," Annie told him practically.

"You've got a nanny," he said. "Can't you take a weekend somewhere with me?"

"Nanny Violet gets the weekends off. She's gone on Saturday morning when I get up, and she returns Sunday evening at six p.m. precisely," Annie said, turning her back to him. "Hook me up again."

His hands slid around to cup her breasts. "Umm, so nice," he whispered, giving her nipples a little pinch. Then he fastened her bra for her. "I'll think of something. In the meantime, we always have the storage room."

Annie smoothed her skirt and tucked her turtleneck in. "We could have been caught," she said. "One of us has to be the grown-up."

"I liked the danger in that," Devyn replied. "But I think I have an idea. We could use one of the unoccupied rooms for a little tryst. Or my cubicle. You could *work* late one evening, couldn't you? The nanny's there twenty-four/seven during the week."

"Gracious, what an eager little boy you are," Annie said softly. "Wants to see his presents before he should. You're the one who needs to be spanked, Devyn." She turned around so that the tips of her breasts were just touching his chest. "Want me to spank you, little boy?" It was as if she were possessed, Annie considered as she flirted with him. Why was she behaving so suggestively? So . . . so . . . wantonly? What was the matter with her, for heaven's sake?

"Well, well." He chuckled. "Underneath that prim-and-proper widow with kids is a bad girl. What fun we are going to have together, Annie Miller."

The shop's bell tinkled, and a voice called, "Anyone here?"

Without another word Annie exited the storage room. "Sorry, I've been putting away stock," she said to the spa guest who had entered. "How can I help you?"

■ ■ ■ ■

It snowed in late February, and Annie contacted a local farmer so she could rent his old-fashioned sleigh and horses. The spa guests were offered sleigh rides through the snowy countryside. A portable ice rink was set up over the outdoor pool. Both two-blade and single-blade skates were available. A sauna hut was erected so guests could steam, then run out into the snow briefly, then back to the sauna. The Spa was booked to capacity.

One afternoon Nora Buckley called Annie to her office. "Sit," she said, indicating a couch in front of her fireplace. She handed Annie a cup of Apple Spice tea, and held out a plate of chocolate biscotti. "Hardly spa fare, I'll admit," she remarked with a smile.

"But yummy," Annie answered, taking one.

"I want you to train someone to run the shop," Nora said without any preamble.

"Aren't you satisfied with my work?" Annie said, surprised by the request.

"Extremely so, but your talents are being wasted there," Nora replied. "I want you, and Mr. Nicholas wants you, to become the

Spa's assistant manager. You've actually been doing much of what an assistant manager would do since the first of the year. And we've never hired one before. With the success of the Spa we need one."

"I don't know anything about managing a spa," Annie protested.

"You didn't really know anything about stocking and managing a shop, but you learned, didn't you? The gift shop has turned a profit since the moment it opened, Annie. That's highly unusual, you know."

"We've got a built-in clientele," Annie said. "Women with money to spend, and I've stocked only quality merchandise. It isn't exactly rocket science."

Nora laughed. "No, it isn't. But you've shown great ingenuity and imagination, Annie. You're intelligent, and you're personable. You know how to work with people. I heard how you defused that publishing CEO when the teddy she wanted from Lacy Nothings was sold out before she could purchase it. J. P. Woods is a highly volatile woman."

"I had met her casually when I spent my week here," Annie explained. "I just told her I would special-order the teddy and send it to her home. Then I told her to please not tell anyone I was doing it because

I would have to take it from my spring stock, as we were only allowed to have a dozen garments each season. She loved feeling extra-special, and that I was going out of my way for her."

"That's just what I mean, Annie. You know how to compromise," Nora responded.

"I'm raising five kids," Annie said wryly. "You want to learn compromise? Have five kids. Best tutorial I've ever had."

"You can hire locally." Nora picked up the original thread of their conversation. "The ad will appear in the local paper tomorrow, and I've given the shop's direct line as the contact number."

"What happens to Devyn?" Annie asked.

"Do you want to keep him as your personal assistant?" Nora inquired casually.

"Yes, I think so," Annie said. "We work well together."

"Tell him he'll have to wear the Spa blazer then," Nora said. "You can wear your own clothes if you prefer."

"I'll stick with my uniform for now," Annie said. Besides, she didn't have any clothes that would be suitable.

"One other thing," Nora told her. "You'll be getting a hefty salary increase as the Spa's assistant manager. How does one hundred twenty thousand a year sound? And, of course, you'll keep all your benefits."

Annie's jaw dropped. "No way!" she exclaimed, and then she blushed at having responded with such a colloquialism.

"Way!" Nora Buckley said, laughing. "You are going to more than earn it."

Annie couldn't believe her good fortune. She would have been content to remain the gift shop's manager forever. Assistant manager of The Spa at Egret Pointe. It sounded so important, although she knew it really wasn't in the grand scheme of things. She was actually going to be able to afford some new clothes. She could pay for camp this summer for the girls. She called her sister and shared her news.

"Wow!" Lizzie said. "That's incredible, Annie!"

"Come out and help me shop for some appropriate clothes," Annie replied. "Come out and help me celebrate. I'm scared and excited all in one."

"I can't this weekend," Lizzie replied. "The Channel Corp. is turning out to be a great deal of work. I've spent most of the winter learning all their companies. It's fascinating. They seem to specialize in giving people what they want. Their companies are mostly geared to service."

"I can't shop without you," Annie protested. "I'm so out of touch with what's hot, what's not, what's appropriate, and all that stuff. You live in the city. You know, and you simply have to help me, Lizzie!"

"It would be easier if you came into town," Lizzie said.

"Nanny takes the weekends off," Annie said.

"Look, ask her to give up her Saturday, and tell her she can have Monday instead. Tell her why, and she'll understand, if what you say about her is true. Mavis Iaonne can take Wills off the bus one day, can't she? And then the girls will be home."

"I'll see what I can arrange," Annie said to her sister.

"Stay here Friday night," Devyn said when she told him.

"What?"

"Stay at the Spa. The nanny will be at home with your kids. You can hitch a ride on the Spa chopper into the city Saturday morning. They've got an early pickup and a late return. That way you don't have to drive it."

"And how do I get back if I don't drive?" Annie asked him.

"Same way," he replied. "Then we'll have

dinner before you go home, okay? Ask Ms. Buckley. I'll bet she says it's okay."

Annie asked. Hesitantly.

"Of course," Nora replied. "Smart idea. Tell the front desk you want one of the staff rooms Friday night."

The local paper came out Thursday with the Spa's help-wanted ad. Annie had half a dozen calls immediately. She spoke with Nanny Violet, who was perfectly happy to give up her Saturday.

"No need to bother with Mrs. Iaonne, dear," she told Annie. "One day off will be perfect for me this week. I'll just take Sunday."

"I'll try to get back at a reasonable hour on Saturday so you can leave then," Annie promised.

"Thank you, dear," Nanny Violet said.

"Amy's curfew on Saturday night is midnight, and don't let her tell you otherwise," Annie warned the nanny.

"Amy won't be going out this weekend, dear," Nanny Violet said. "She has a term paper due and wants to work on it. She had such good grades last term, she wants to keep it up and get into a good college."

"What about her BFF, Brittany?" Annie wondered aloud.

"Oh, Amy doesn't see a great deal of

Brittany these days," Nanny Violet said.

"Brittany's one of the most popular girls in school." Annie was surprised. She sought out her oldest daughter. "Nanny says you don't hang out with Brittany a whole lot anymore. I thought she was your BFF. What gives?"

"Oh, we're still friends," Amy said, "but Brittany isn't serious about school."

"And since when have you been?" Annie wanted to know.

"Look, Mom, I'm a sophomore now. Nathaniel says that if I expect to get into a decent college I have to settle down. And Nanny says that Brittany may be a fun girl, but she's really no better than she ought to be. Nanny says a girl's reputation is very important, and she doesn't want to be tarred by another person's bad habits. She says colleges look at your MySpace and Facebook Web sites. Nanny says they're just as important as good grades and extracurricular stuff. Some of the things Nanny says are so funny — and old-fashioned, but I do trust her. And as Nanny says, it can't hurt to err on the side of caution," Amy finished.

Amazing, Annie thought. And wonderful as well. Nanny Violet had worked a miracle with her eldest daughter. The twins hadn't gotten into trouble once this year over their

274

environmental and animal-loving stances, which Annie now realized was probably due to the nanny's good influence, and her knack for directing them in a more appropriate direction. And Wills's table manners were suddenly better than any of theirs. Her children were safe and well cared-for. She could concentrate on her career and the new responsibilities that were hers as of March first.

She stayed overnight at the Spa before going into town. She had a pleasant room in one of the new wings that had been added when the mansion was renovated. She noted, however, that there was no flat-screen television to access the Channel. But Devyn had joined her uninvited, and he had brought a friend. It had been a couple of weeks since their encounter in the storage room. She had made certain not to be caught alone there with him again. She needed time to think. The reality of having a lover was dangerous in her mind, and now here he was with another PA, called Connor. They both had towels wrapped about their waists.

"Who let you in?" Annie wanted to know.

"We got the extra key card," Devyn said. "I thought maybe you would like to play with me and Connor."

"There's that ego again," Annie said. "Biggest thing about you, Devyn."

"Connor's is just as big," he told her, slipping an arm about her waist. "I know you've never had two men before, but it would be fun for you. Something different." His arm tightened about her. "Come on, Annie, you know you're curious."

While he talked to her Connor had come up to stand before her. He unzipped her skirt and slid it off. Devyn lifted her out of the garment, which had fallen to the floor. Moving behind her, he pulled her blazer off and yanked her turtleneck over her head. Then, undoing her bra, he tossed it aside, his hand closing over a breast. Connor grasped her other breast and began licking at the nipple. After a moment or two he took it into his mouth, biting down gently, and then sucking strongly on it while Devyn fondled the breast in his keeping, pinching and pulling at the nipple.

Annie leaned back against Devyn with a sigh. She had just been quickly and very efficiently stripped naked except for her panties. She had two men playing with her breasts. Devyn's other hand was kneading her butt. Connor's other hand was pushing past the elastic band on her panties and cupping her mons. She sighed again. It was too delicious, and totally naughty. No. It was wicked, and she was thoroughly enjoying it. Reaching behind her, Annie first pulled Devyn's towel off and then, reaching in front of her, drew Connor's off. Gazing down, she saw he was indeed well hung.

In response he loosened his hold on her breast and, kneeling in front of her, pulled her panties down completely, and off. His big hands slid up the sides of her legs and thighs, reaching around to squeeze her buttocks. Devyn now held her before him, his hands capturing both of her breasts and playing with them. He kissed the edges of her face and licked the shell of one ear, breathing hotly into it suggestively.

Connor's tongue now began to explore her. He licked the soft insides of her thighs first, making her murmur softly. Then his tongue slid along her slit. He nibbled on the edges of her labia. Then his tongue pushed through her nether lips to find her clit, and when he did he began to worry it with teasing touches. When Annie began to move restlessly he sucked on her clit, and she squealed. He alternated sucking and flicking his tongue back and forth over her clit. Annie could feel her juices coming.

Connor lifted his dark head up. "She's wet now, man. Can we fuck? She is so damned hot. Let me do her first."

"Go ahead," Devyn responded. "Annie's going to do something for me, too."

They half carried, half dragged her onto the bed. Connor was on her quickly, rolling a condom over his big dick. She didn't protest. He thrust himself eagerly into her with an almost sobbing sound, and then he began to piston her hard.

Devyn moved behind Annie and, straddling her head, said, "Open your mouth, baby. I told you next time you were going to suck me off." He rubbed his thick penis along her lips. "Open wide for me, Annie," he told her, and when she did he pushed his cock between her lips, groaning as her mouth closed and she began to suck him.

Annie couldn't believe what was happening to her, and she was letting it happen. It wasn't even in the Channel. It was here and now and very real. She was being fucked into submission by a kid who she damned well knew was close to twenty years her junior, and sucking on another man's big dick with vigor. She drew Devyn deeper into her throat and sucked him harder.

"Annie, Annie," he practically whimpered. "I'm going to come."

She loosened her hold on his cock. "Don't you dare until you've fucked me, Devyn! If you do I'm going to spank you for being a bad boy," she threatened.

"I can't help it! You are so warm and wet and sexy." He pushed his penis back into her mouth. When she gave it a quick tug he came, his thick cum sliding easily down her throat. Annie sucked him hard until she had drawn every bit of juice from him. Devyn fell back on the pillows, temporarily sated.

Annie turned her attentions to Connor. "Make me come," she commanded him. "You can do more for me than just grunt and sweat."

He grinned down at her, and with unerring aim found her G spot. When Annie gasped he began to work it until she was dizzy with the pleasure she was getting from him. When she had had enough she tightened herself about his penis until he was squealing like a girl. Together they came in a burst of orgiastic fury that left them both weak as their shared climax drained away.

"You boys are lots of fun," Annie told them as she sat up to view her young lovers with their now limp cocks lying flaccidly against their thighs. She swung her legs over the edge of the bed. "Devyn, get over here now! You are about to get your cute butt spanked for coming when I told you not to come. I wanted another fuck, and you will give it to me or else!"

He crawled over to her and lay across her lap obediently. Connor grinned.

"You," Annie said. "Go home now. You've had all you're going to have tonight. If you say a word about what happened here I'll deny it, and I'll fire you. I can do that as of March first, Connor. I'm the new assistant manager. Did Devyn tell you that?"

"No, ma'am," Connor said politely as he quickly pulled on his clothes, which were folded neatly on a chair. "I won't say a word, but, ma'am, you are one hell of a fuck."

"Why, thank you, sweetie. Now give me a kiss and beat it," Annie said, holding up her lips to him. He kissed her mouth softly, his blue eyes meeting hers. *My God,* Annie thought, seeing the look in those eyes. *He's fascinated by me.* She watched as Connor beat a hasty retreat. She heard Devyn snicker, lying over her lap. "When was the last time you were spanked?" she asked him.

"Not since I was five," he told her softly. "Will you spank me hard, Annie?"

"Yes, I will, for two reasons. For coming when I told you not to come, and for springing Connor on me before you asked," Annie said.

"You would have said no, and the truth is,

you enjoyed having two men," Devyn replied. "Maybe next time I'll bring two others. You've got three orifices, after all."

Annie's hand came down on his round butt, and he yelped.

"Ouch! That hurt," he said.

She began to rain blows on his squirming buttocks until they were crimson. He really might have escaped her, but he made no effort to do so. Finally her hand was sore, and she ceased whacking him. "Get up now, you bad thing, and tell me you're sorry," Annie said. She shifted him from her lap.

Devyn scrambled to his feet. "I've got a better way of saying thank-you," he said, revealing his cock, newly revived by her blows and ready to fuck her.

"Ohh, yes!" Annie half moaned as she climbed into the center of the bed and spread herself open for him. "Fuck me, Devyn, and you know just how I like it. Hard and deep until I am screaming."

"My way this time, Annie," he told her. "Hands and knees, head down on your arms, and your butt high. This time I'm the dominant."

Annie didn't argue with him. She wanted that big cock inside of her, making her cry with pleasure. Rolling onto her belly, she assumed the position he'd ordered, and waited for him to impale her. Instead Devyn stroked her buttocks slowly, gently, suggestively. He reached beneath her to play with her clit, making it tingle with rising desire, but he did not satisfy her. "Devyn!" she complained, and then she gasped as he penetrated her vagina in a fierce, swift move. His hand closed over the back of her neck, holding her steady as he fucked her deeper and deeper. She could feel the orgasm beginning to build.

"Ohh, yes, Devyn!" she encouraged him. "Do it to me! *Do it!*" And he did. Annie came in a crashing climax that rendered her almost, but not quite, unconscious. She screamed with enjoyment, relishing every jerk of his dick as he spilled his cum.

Damn, she thought. He hadn't worn a condom again, and she didn't need to get, as they said in Victorian novels, in a family way, and without a husband. Five kids were more than enough. "I'm going to kill you if I get pregnant," she told him.

"Aren't you on the pill?" he asked her.

"I'm a widow," Annie said in an exasperated tone. "I haven't had sex since my husband went to London and then didn't come home."

"Whoops," he said softly. And he leaned over to kiss her.

Annie pushed him away. "Listen to me, boyo. Five kids are enough. They are at last all in school. I've got a budding career. If you louse up my life with your overactive libido . . ." She stopped. "I'll have to get my doctor to give me a prescription for the morning-after pill, and then everyone in Egret Pointe will know I'm having sex. Terrific. Dr. Sam won't talk, but the pharmacist gossips."

"Fill it in the city," Devyn suggested.

Annie nodded. "Now beat it," she said. "I need my sleep."

"Annie?"

"What?"

"I think I'm falling in love with you," Devyn said.

"Don't!" she snapped. And suddenly she realized she meant it. She didn't want another permanent man in her life. Nat had been her greatest love, and she would always love him. The memories she had of them, of their life together, were wonderful. She had a family. At her age she wanted a man for companionship and for sex. But she also wanted to be dropped off at her door afterward and left alone.

Reaching out, she stroked her lover's face. "You're adorable, and you are a great lay," Annie told him, her tone softer. "But that's all I want, Devyn. I don't want a permanent man. At least, not at this stage of my life. Maybe never again. I had a wonderful husband, and if Nat had been alive, this — none of it — would have happened.

"I'd be home tonight with my husband and our children. We'd be playing board games, because we usually did on Friday nights. I wouldn't be a working woman. I took this job so my little boy could have the Disney Channel added to our cable. So that my twins could have the microscopes they wanted. So my oldest girl could have the latest fashions, and not feel left out in school. Nat's insurance wasn't enough, and I've just been getting by, Devyn. My sister is making up the gap between Nathaniel's scholarship and Princeton's fees. Maybe in another year I can do that for my son. I don't like being dependent, but I've swallowed my pride for almost three years now, and taken whatever was offered to me for my kids. I have to do right by my kids. Nat would want me to do it. But if a handsome man wants to bed me now and again, I won't object. After all, there has to be something in all of this for me."

"I can't help how I feel about you," he told her. "But I do understand, Annie."

"I'm your first older woman," she answered him with a small smile. "You've just got a crush on me, sweetie, and that's flattering. Now put your clothes on and go away."

When he had gone Annie got up and showered. She reeked of wild sex. Two men. It had been exciting, and it had been fun. Connor certainly had a skillful penis. She wondered if she was brave enough to find a way to screw him again. She would have to think about that. She didn't want Devyn thinking he had an exclusive thing with her, and after all, it had been Devyn who had added Connor into the equation. She was amazed with herself. How could she think like this?

She and Nat had had a perfectly nice sex life. *Nice?* Yes, nice. So she didn't always have an orgasm. He thought she did, and it made them both happy. But it hadn't been exciting, or wild, or deviant. It had been nice, and she could have been happy the rest of her life not knowing exciting, wild, and deviant. But not now. No, not now. And given her "Beauty and the Beast" fantasy, her subconscious had obviously been very stifled until Annie Miller met the Channel. There was no turning back, and frankly she didn't want to turn back. But maybe she had better keep her fantasies as fantasy. No need to get a reputation as a red-hot mama among the PAs. Especially now that she was about to become the Spa's assistant manager.

Devyn brought her breakfast, and she told him no more multiple partners, explaining why. He nodded, agreeing it had been foolish.

"And tell Connor he is to keep his mouth shut," Annie said.

Again Devyn nodded. He escorted her to the chopper. "Do you want me to come with you?" he asked her hopefully.

"No, you can have the day off," Annie told him. "I'll see you Monday."

"Dinner tonight?"

"I'll see you Monday," she repeated.

The trip to the city was so much faster than driving in, and they were landing at the heliport on the river before she knew it.

"I go back at five p.m., Ms. Miller," the pilot said.

"I'll be here," Annie told him, and turned at a touch on her arm.

"I'm your driver, Ms. Miller," the uniformed man said, smiling. "Hey, Bill," he said to the pilot. "Nice weather for a trip. You taking anyone back?"

"Yeah," the chopper pilot said. "Ten a.m."

"What time do you want Ms. Miller back?"

"Five p.m.," the chopper pilot replied.

"I didn't know I had a driver," Annie said with a smile as they walked to the black Lincoln Town Car and got in.

"Yes, ma'am. Mr. Nicholas likes his people taken care of," the driver said.

"Do you know where I'm going?" Annie asked.

"Yes, ma'am. And I'll be with you all day. My name is Frank."

The car pulled out of the heliport and into the city streets. It was Saturday, and the roadway wasn't particularly crowded. Lizzie was waiting for them outside of her apartment building. Frank pulled up in front of it, and the doorman opened the car door, allowing Lizzie to get in. The two sisters kissed.

"Hi, Frank!" Lizzie said.

"Ms. Bradford," the driver said.

"You know him?" Annie asked, surprised.

"Frank is always there to bring me home the nights I work late," Lizzie said.

"Which is almost every night." Frank chuckled as he pulled away from the curb. "Where to, ladies?"

It was just nine a.m., and they spent the next four hours shopping. Lizzie had an unerring fashion sense. "When you're in a service business, how you look is important," she explained. "You want classic clothing that can be refreshed over the next few seasons, with good accessories and jewelry so it all looks different. No trendy stuff," she cautioned.

"I wouldn't know trendy from untrendy," Annie said with a smile.

"You look different," Lizzie remarked. Then her blue eyes grew wide, and she dropped her voice. "You're getting screwed, and not just in the Channel!" she gasped.

Annie flushed.

"Who is he? Tell your sister," she said, grinning.

"Shut up, Lizzie," Annie muttered.

"It has to be someone at the Spa, because the only places you go are there and home," Lizzie murmured low. "And your household is all women but for a five-year-old boy, so it's someone at the Spa." She grew thoughtful, and then she said, "It's your PA, you naughty girl. Is he good? Well, of course he is or you wouldn't look so content."

"I need shoes," Annie said.

"We'll go to Ferragamo," Lizzie responded, grinning. "You're going to tell me, you know. I could always get stuff like this out of you."

"At lunch," Annie said. "Not in the car."

"Okay," Lizzie replied. "And I'm going to want every last detail."

They finally stopped for lunch at one of the lovely old-fashioned small restaurants that catered to women shopping. They ordered soup, salad, and bread-and-butter sandwiches. As they ate Annie told her younger sister about Devyn seducing her in the shop's stockroom, and about Devyn bringing Connor last night. Lizzie ate slowly, and listened.

"When did you become so adventurous?" she asked Annie when her sister had finished her recitation. "I would never have thought you of all people could be so naughty. Two guys at once! I'll have to try it."

"This wasn't the Channel, Lizzie. This was for real," Annie said thoughtfully.

"I know," Lizzie answered her sister, "but I can't get involved for real."

"And I shouldn't," Annie responded. "It really wouldn't do for the assistant manager of The Spa at Egret Pointe to be known as the open road for boys, would it? I've only been with Devyn twice, and I think I'll put our relationship back on a proper track. The Channel is a safer place to go for wild sex."

Lizzie nodded. "I think you're right, sis," she agreed. "Mr. Nicholas seems to prefer his enterprises to maintain a low profile. And he seems to like you. Don't disappoint him, Annie." Finishing her lunch, she ordered dessert for herself and her sister.

"Hey, I'm watching my weight," Annie said.

"You look great," Lizzie replied. "Everything we bought today was a size twelve. You were a sixteen, last I looked."

Annie sent her purchases home to Egret Pointe so that when Frank dropped her back at the heliport and she climbed aboard the Spa's chopper she had nothing with her. Lizzie had come with her, and she waved to Annie from the tarmac where she stood. Annie waved back. It had been a wonderful day, and with this promotion she had a lot of wonderful days ahead of her. The chopper rose up and banked over the river. Then it headed north and east toward Egret Pointe. The sun was beginning to set, and the sky was awash with color. Annie leaned back, admiring the view. She had a marvelous new life, and she was enjoying it to the fullest.

CHAPTER EIGHT

It was late May, and Nathaniel was home briefly from Princeton before taking up a summer internship he had gotten. "You look great, but you look a little stressed, too," he told his mother as they shared a few moments over cups of coffee on the back porch of the house. "This promotion isn't too much for you, is it?"

"No, I love it," she told him. "I think I want a woman for a PA instead of a man, and I'm not certain how to broach the subject with Nora Buckley."

"What's wrong with the guy?"

"Nothing really. He's nice, but I sometimes get the feeling he thinks he's in charge and not me. I've tried speaking to him about it, and he apologizes, but nothing changes. I don't want him fired. I just want to work with someone else."

Nathaniel was silent for a moment, and then he said, "The guy coming on to you,

Ma?" When she blushed he chuckled.

"Really, Nathaniel! Devyn is much younger than I am," Annie replied.

"A lot of guys like older women," her son responded quietly.

"It is flattering," Annie admitted, "but uncomfortable now that I've got an executive position. I'm perfectly capable of doing my job. I certainly don't need to be protected, or have Nora Buckley and Mr. Nicholas think I can't cope."

"You don't have a choice, then," Nathaniel said. "You'll have to speak with Ms. Buckley and have this Devyn reassigned. Don't hesitate, Mom, or this guy will make you look bad. Until recently I haven't seen you smile since Dad died. It's nice to see you happy again, and I know Dad would be glad of it."

"I can't believe I'm widowed three years now," Annie remarked.

"You still miss him?"

"I do," Annie said.

"Ever think of remarrying?" her oldest son inquired.

Annie shook her head. "Nope. Nat was the love of my life, and there is no replacing him, Nathaniel."

"What about sex?"

"Excuse me?" She pierced him with a

292

sharp look.

"Sorry," he replied, flushing. "Just curious, Mom."

"That's something even a college-age son shouldn't quiz his mother about," Annie said with a small smile. She stood up. "I've got to get to work."

"It's just after eight o'clock in the morning," he noted.

"I like to get there early," Annie said. "Being assistant manager of the Spa isn't just sitting about and being charming. I review all the applications, fix the reservations, monitor the personal assistants, check and approve the daily menus, order supplies. The staff come to me with any problems, Nathaniel, from the pool thermostat not working properly to deer getting into the salad garden. And I circulate among the guests making certain that they are happy and have everything that they need. It's a long day."

"The girls say you work late a lot of nights now, Mom," Nathaniel remarked.

"I do, but Nanny Violet is here for them," Annie said, and she glanced at her watch. "I really have to fly, darling. Enjoy your day. I'll see you this evening."

"Have a good one, Mom," her son called after her.

"You have to sign the camp applications," Nanny Violet told her as Annie came back into the kitchen. "They're due up at Stoneledge next week."

"Give them to me," Annie said. "Amy wants to be a CIT?"

"Yes," Nanny Violet replied. "There is a separate application for her. The twins are on a single page." She handed the papers to Annie, who barely glanced at them before placing her signature at the bottom of the pages where required. "Thanks so much for doing this," she told her nanny. "Do we need a check?"

"Just sign here," Nanny Violet responded, pushing the household checkbook toward her. "The deposit is fifteen hundred, and I'll mark it down in the register."

"Thanks, Nanny, you're a lifesaver," Annie said as she scrawled her signature. "I shouldn't be late tonight."

"I'll do a nice roast beef, then," the nanny replied. "Have a good day, Mrs. Miller."

Annie hurried out. She hadn't seen Amy this a.m. Her school bus had already come and gone. The junior high kids were waiting, and the bus rounded the corner as she got into her little red Miata. Her promotion had netted her a company car. She backed out of the drive and waved to the twins as she sped by just ahead of the school bus. They waved back. It was a beautiful morning, but she was feeling a little nervous as she reached the Spa. Nathaniel was right. She had to speak to Nora about replacing Devyn. She headed directly for the spa manager's office.

Nora was already there, and smiled as Annie stuck her head in. "Good morning!"

"Do you have a minute?" Annie asked her nervously.

"Sure, come on in and close the door," Nora answered. "What's up?"

"I want to replace Devyn," Annie said. She had to get it out in a rush or she wouldn't say it at all. "I want a female PA."

Nora nodded. "I know there's been a little flirtation between you," she said.

Annie flushed. "That's not the reason." She neither confirmed nor denied Nora's statement. "He's sweet. And he's a great PA, but not for me anymore. He tries to do my job for me, and I am entirely capable of doing it for myself. Frankly he's beginning to annoy the shit out of me, Nora."

Nora laughed out loud. "Good for you," she said. "If there is anything I dislike, it's being hovered over and told what to do by a man. You'd never know I used to be a meek little homemaker who looked to my big, strong man for guidance. But I got over it when Jeff tried to divorce me, and take everything besides."

"Working here has been a revelation and a lifesaver," Annie said. "I love it, and Devyn is spoiling it by second-guessing every decision I make."

"And using sex to control you," Nora remarked. "You should really keep him in the Channel."

"I intend to from now on," Annie replied. "Look, I don't want to get him in trouble, Nora. I just want him to let me do my job."

"Understood," Nora responded. "I will speak to Mr. Nicholas about him. I think Devyn is moving past being a PA, and I suspect Mr. Nicholas has other plans for him."

"Thank you!" Annie said.

"Don't say anything to him right now," Nora told Annie. "We'll take care of the problem for you."

"That's wonderful," Annie said. And then she asked softly, "How did you know I had a Devyn in the Channel, Nora?"

Nora laughed again. "If he were my PA I certainly would. Lucky guess, I suppose. But when reality intrudes on fantasy it can cause problems, can't it?"

"Agreed," Annie replied, nodding her head.

Devyn hadn't been happy since Annie had gotten her promotion. She had been avoiding sex with him, and he wasn't used to being told no. "I could fuck that pretty thing you hired for the gift shop," he told her irritably that morning when she pushed him away. "She's been giving me the eye since the second week she came."

"Go ahead," Annie said cruelly.

"What the hell has gotten into you?" he wanted to know.

"I told you when I got this promotion that that part of our relationship was likely to end, Devyn. I cannot, will not, be known as the woman who screws her PA. My reputation among the staff has got to be a good one. If I don't have their respect I can't work with them. Now, where are those new applications for a Spa visit that I'm going to need to approve today?"

"You are turning into such a bitch," he complained.

"I warned you not to have feelings for me, Devyn," Annie said coldly.

Angrily, he backed her up against her desk. "I've always wanted to do it on a desk," he said to her.

"Frankly I've never thought about it," Annie said, "but you seem to think about sex all the time, sweetie."

He pressed himself against her, and she could feel his hard-on. "I want to do it to you now," he said softly.

"I don't," Annie told him. "But if you are a very good boy and don't annoy me, maybe I'll let you do it later." She pushed him away. "The papers," she said.

Annie managed to keep him so busy the rest of the day that there was no time for a romantic interlude. She was gone by the time he got back to the office, after she sent him on an errand at ten minutes to five o'clock.

Devyn cursed softly and found his way to the gift shop to flirt with the new shop-keeper. It wasn't long before he had her in the storage room against a wall fucking the daylights out of her. She was a screamer, and he hoped to God no one had heard her. But he did feel better afterward. Her name was Nancy, and she had taken the edge off of his lust.

Over the next few weeks Devyn would visit the gift shop whenever Annie would refuse his overtures, which was all the time now. Nancy was as lustful as he was, and he was frankly beginning to enjoy doing her every day. Annie would smile when he would make some excuse to go to the gift shop. He had no feelings for Nancy, as he did for Annie, but she was a complaisant screw, and until he could figure out how to get into Annie's pants again, Nancy would do nicely.

Mr. Nicholas paid a visit to the Spa in mid-June. Annie and Devyn were called into the lovely office that was kept for him. Nora was with him. "Annie, my dear," he greeted her with a warm smile. "How are you? Nora tells me you are doing very well. I knew my faith in you would be justified. Sit down, both of you."

"Tea?" Nora was seated before the mahogany butler's tray. "It's green." When Annie nodded she poured some from the porcelain teapot into a delicate cup, and passed the saucer to Annie with a smile.

"Devyn, my boy," Mr. Nicholas said in his cultured voice, "I am afraid that I have some rather dreadful news to bring you. Your brother, Phillip, was killed in a plane crash early this morning. It seems he was piloting his own plane back from his Nantucket cottage after a long weekend. The pilot of a commercial jet saw the plane several thousand feet below him. It just exploded in midair. He radioed it in immediately, and the coast guard went out, but the aircraft was in pieces. All the bodies, your brother, his wife, his two sons, were recovered. You are now the head of Scott Industries, my boy. I should congratulate you but for the circumstances."

Devyn looked astounded, but then he said, "Phillip wouldn't have left the business to me."

"He didn't, but your father did, my boy," Mr. Nicholas informed Devyn. "Your father's will stated that if anything happened to Phillip, the family business would go to you. Your brother wasn't just trying to break the trust your father set up for you; he was trying to have that part of your father's will declared invalid."

"My God," Devyn said softly.

"I believe your father hoped that you and Phillip would reconcile, and that as you matured, your older brother would teach you, and share the responsibilities of Scott Industries with you."

"Fat chance," Devyn remarked. "Phillip hated my guts from the moment I was born. And now the business is mine? I have no idea what the hell I'm going to do with it. What a mess this is."

"Not at all, my boy," Mr. Nicholas said soothingly. "Charlie Kramer, one of the company's three vice presidents, is a personal friend of mine. He's going to help you find your sea legs. I assure you that you can depend upon his expertise and his total loyalty to you. You're going to do very well, I promise you. I think at this point we can all agree that you are past being a handsome young personal assistant at an exclusive spa." He chuckled, and then grew serious again. "This is what your father wanted for you, my boy. Sadly he didn't live long enough to see you mature into the fine man you are today. You will do Scott Industries proud. Now run along and begin your packing. A limo will be here shortly to take you home. You'll have a funeral to prepare. I hope you do not mind, but I have had a statement issued to the press in your name."

Devyn nodded, still stunned by this sudden turn of events. Then, with a nod to Mr. Nicholas, he turned and left the room.

The CEO of the Channel Corporation turned to Annie, whose tea was untouched as she sat shocked by what she had just heard. "And now, my dear, I believe you will need a new personal assistant, won't you? Nora tells me you would like to hire a female. Do you have someone in mind?" He smiled, but she noticed that the smile did not touch his black eyes. "A local girl, perhaps?"

"Y-yes," Annie replied. "I thought someone young with good skills, who would be willing to learn, and content to keep her place."

Mr. Nicholas chuckled. "Of course," he agreed. "Devyn, I take it, did not keep his place. Well, then, he certainly is ready to take over his family's company, isn't he? This accident came at rather the right time, didn't it?"

Annie felt a shiver race down her spine. "It's a terrible tragedy," she said softly.

"Not for Devyn," Mr. Nicholas responded. "If you lost your family it would be a great tragedy, but Phillip was nothing to Devyn. A half brother who hated him. A woman, and two children he had never even met? They meant nothing to him. Oh, he will plan and attend the funeral, exhibiting just the right amount of proper familial sorrow, but it will be because he loved and respected his own father. Nothing more. You will want to make your good-byes, of course, Annie, my dear. You have my permission to hire whomever you want. Nancy has turned out quite nicely, so I believe we can trust your judgment in the matter of a personal assistant."

She was being dismissed. Annie stood up. "Thank you, sir," she said.

When she had gone, Nora said, "I think she is beginning to understand."

Mr. Nicholas nodded with a faint smile. "Perhaps," he responded.

"You could lose her," Nora murmured.

Mr. Nicholas laughed. "No. I do not believe I will lose her. But, then, there is always that chance. Still, she is a woman who loves her family and sees the advantages that working for the corporation has given her, has given them. And Nanny Violet makes it quite easy for her to soothe her conscience. And then there are her visits to the Channel to be considered."

"What have they got to do with anything?" Nora asked him. "They're a fantasy."

"Annie is not a woman who grew up fantasizing," Mr. Nicholas said. "And so she programmed her favorite fairy tale as her first fantasy, casting herself as the heroine. Imagine her surprise to learn the pleasures of sexual punishment. An interesting fantasy for a practical woman, and not one she consciously considered. But she still felt guilty for her subconscious needs, for her *betrayal* of her deceased husband. Annie prided herself on being a faithful wife and a good mother." He chuckled again. "But then, of course, her guilt began to ease. Her visits to the Beast are sporadic now, although she has not deleted it, for she still feels the need to be punished now and again for being a very bad girl with Devyn, both in and out of the Channel."

"I prefer to forget you are able to access our fantasies," Nora said with a delicate shudder. "But why am I surprised you are a voyeur? You prey on human weakness."

"I no longer bother with your fantasies, dear Nora. They are quite boring, for you are basically monogamous with your Kyle. Had you not owed me for my kindness to you in that matter of your late husband, perhaps I should not have had you," he said to her.

"Possibly not," Nora agreed with a smile. "But then again . . ."

"Ah, Nora, I knew I was right when I chose you," Mr. Nicholas replied. "Your mind is so deliciously devious and has the capacity to be wonderfully evil. I will not keep you here at the Spa for much longer. I have already chosen your replacement."

"Annie Miller," Nora said.

"Indeed, yes, but not quite yet, my dear," Mr. Nicholas told her.

"I am yours to command," Nora responded.

He nodded. "Yes, my dear, you are," he said with an arch smile.

Annie had left Mr. Nicholas's office and gone to the front desk. "Where is Devyn's room?" she asked the young man on duty.

He told her, smiling slightly, surprised that she didn't already know. All the guys knew Dev was balling her on a regular basis. Hadn't Connor said so? And Connor knew all the gossip. How he did his job so well and still had time to ferret it out was a mystery.

Annie hurried upstairs to the staff quarters. She entered Devyn's room to find him liplocked in an embrace with Nancy. "I came to say good-bye," she told him, amused.

He grinned mischievously. "Wanna have a threesome? We haven't too much time before the limo comes, but we can do it."

Annie laughed. "Why am I not shocked?" she wondered aloud as she pulled her panties off. "But only if I get to be on top. You can have Nancy's pussy, can't he, dear?"

"Mrs. Miller," the young woman said, blushing, "I don't know what you think, but —"

"Sweetie, he's been fucking you for the last month. Daily, I'm told, so don't bother denying it. If you're wearing panties get them off."

Annie moved next to Devyn, and his arm wrapped about her, his hand reaching up to knead her breast while, turning his head, he kissed Nancy again. The younger woman turned into him, unzipping his trousers, reaching in to fondle his cock and balls. Annie began to tongue his ear suggestively. In short order Devyn was hard. Pulling the two women with him, he fell back on the bed. Nancy squirmed about, going down on him as Annie kissed him, her tongue playing with his. Finally he pulled his head from hers.

"Nancy, I want a taste of pussy," he told her. "Get over here now!"

The younger woman crawled up the bed and positioned herself over Devyn's head, pressing down lightly so he could access her cunt with his skillful tongue. As she did, Annie mounted his cock, purring as she took him all in, and then began to ride him, slowly at first, but with increasing rapidity and vigor as the moments passed. Soon the two women and the man were moaning with the pleasure they were both giving and receiving. Devyn licked and teased at Nancy's cunt, nipping at her clit with his teeth to bring her on. When he was near to coming and felt that Annie was, too, he pushed two fingers into Nancy's vagina, moving them quickly back and forth so that the trio climaxed practically together with a simultaneous cry. Then they fell back onto the bed.

Annie sighed. "God, that was good," she said to him.

"It's a hell of a way to say good-bye." Devyn chuckled. "I wish I had thought to do this before now."

"You only get to do it once," Annie told him. "And, Nancy, this never happened. If you breathe a word to anyone, including nosy Connor, you'll be out of a job."

"Gotcha, Mrs. Miller," Nancy said as she got up and pulled down her skirt. "I've said what I had to to Dev. I'll leave you two." Picking up her staff blazer, she hurried out of the room.

Annie swung her legs over the edge of the bed, but he pulled her back into his arms, his hand sliding into her dress to grab a breast. "Devyn!" she scolded him.

"One more time," he said, giving her a little boy face.

"No time, sweetie," she told him, pulling his hand out of her dress, easing out of his grip, and standing up. "The limo will be waiting for you by now, and Mr. Nicholas is still in house. Pack your dick away and get going." She smoothed the skirt of her dress.

"God, you are one cold bitch," he said as he followed her instructions and stood up to face her. "You used to be so warm and sweet, Annie. What's happened to you?"

"Devyn, come on now. You got what you wanted from me. You seduced your boss and introduced her to the wonders of fun sex. Whatever was between us was never going to go anywhere. I'm forty-four. You're thirty-two. We had fun, but that's all it was. I've had a husband. A wonderful husband. I don't want another, and a lover would only complicate my life for me. I've got a career now. I've got a family who depend upon me, Devyn. My family will always come first with me."

"So it's wham, bam, thank you, ma'am," he said bitterly.

"Oh, Devyn," Annie answered, reaching up to stroke his face. "I loved every minute of us, of what we had. But it's over now. Don't be angry. You'll understand when you have a family to care for, sweetie. Remember your mom and dad, how they loved each other, and how happy and safe they made you feel. Find a nice girl, fall in love, be happy. And make her happy. And give your kids all the love and security that you can.

That's what I'm doing. It's all for my kids. You'll understand someday." She smiled at him. "I'll see you downstairs." And then she hurried from his room.

Downstairs she found that the limousine had just pulled up in front of the front entrance to the Spa. Mr. Nicholas and Nora Buckley came from his office. The staff elevator opened and Devyn exited, carrying a dark green duffel. He walked toward them.

"Well, my boy, now the adventure begins for you. The car will take you directly to your home. Charlie Kramer will be waiting for you. I will be attending the funeral. You will be judged at first by the company you keep, Devyn. It will not harm you for the people who count to see I am in your corner, dear boy."

"Thank you, sir," Devyn replied gravely. Then he turned to the two women. "Goodbye, Ms. Buckley, Mrs. Miller."

"We are so sorry for your loss," Nora said.

"Thank you," he responded. Then he turned and got into the waiting limousine.

They watched as it pulled off, and then, turning as one, they reentered the lobby.

"I shall be on my way," Mr. Nicholas said. "It was good to see you both. Keep up the excellent work, Annie." Then he turned and went back through the entrance, where a second car was now waiting.

"An amazing man," Annie said. "He seems to know us better than we know ourselves," she noted.

"Yes, he does, doesn't he?" Nora Buckley replied softly.

June was almost over now. Annie had watched on the television news the small piece about the funeral of Phillip Scott, his wife and two sons. It had been such a horrific tragedy the media couldn't resist covering it. Especially as it was well known that Phillip and his half brother had been estranged. There had at first been a hint that perhaps the deaths weren't accidental, but an investigation by the FAA proved otherwise.

Devyn had looked suitably mournful as he had entered the church for the funeral. He had spoken briefly to a network reporter at the cemetery. "My brother and I were not friends, but neither were we enemies. To lose him before we might reconcile our differences is a great tragedy for me. I shall endeavor to carry on with Scott Industries in the manner I know our father would have wanted me to. Thank you." And he had gotten into the waiting limousine, accompanied by another man.

He'll survive, Annie thought to herself, just as she was going to survive. She had been right not to get herself emotionally involved with Devyn.

Annie had a new personal assistant she was now training. She had gone to the high school guidance counselor and asked for a list of girls who were not attending college but would be graduating with secretarial skills. There were three, and she interviewed them. Then she consulted her oldest daughter.

"What do you want to know, Mom?" Amy inquired.

"Gossip, reputations, that kind of stuff. Who'll be serious about the job," Annie replied. "I don't want some fashion-conscious, boy-crazy assistant."

"Then you don't want Brandy Peters," Amy said. "She's a northeast valley girl."

"What about the other two?" Annie wanted to know.

"Carol Anderson is ambitious. I think the Spa would just be a stepping-stone for her," Amy responded thoughtfully. "You want someone who'll do the job, can think for herself, will keep her place, but will stay, right, Mom?"

"Right!" Annie agreed.

"Then it has to be Mary Finch," Amy

said. "She's smart enough to go to college, but there's no money. She's stuck in Egret Pointe. Her dad's disabled. Her mom is a clerk in a mall store at the county seat, and she has a little brother. He's in eighth grade. She has to stay home, and she has to work."

Mary Finch. Yes, she had stood out by virtue of not standing out, Annie thought. Brandy and Carol had both been dressed for success. Mary had been wearing a dark cotton skirt and a white blouse. She had a pretty face, but not too pretty. Annie fingered through the three résumés. Mary had the best grades of the three. "Then it's Mary Finch," she said to Amy.

The high school guidance counselor told Mary Finch she had been chosen.

"Me?" Mary looked surprised. "I thought for sure it would be Carol or Brandy."

"Well, it's you," the guidance counselor said. "You're to go up to the Spa after school today, and Mrs. Miller will finalize the details. You'll be expected to fill out all the employee forms so that the Monday after graduation you'll be ready to start work."

"Oh, God!" Mary Finch started to cry. "How am I going to get there? I haven't got a car. The best job in town, and I can't get to it. What am I going to do?"

"I'll call Mrs. Miller right now," the guidance counselor said, frowning. But when she got off the phone she was smiling. "I'll take you up this afternoon," she told the girl. "It seems you get a company car to use, since you're working for the Spa's assistant manager. You do have your license, don't you?"

"Yes, ma'am." Mary Finch nodded. "I get a car? My own car?" And she started to cry again. "It really is the best job in town." She sniffled.

"And you are provided with uniforms, too, so you won't have to worry about clothes every day," the guidance counselor told the girl. "Skirts, blazers, blouses, even a pair of black leather pumps. You are really a lucky girl, Mary, but you deserve it."

That afternoon the guidance counselor drove Mary up to the Spa, where she met with Annie. Her duties were explained. She picked up her uniforms, filled out all the employment forms she needed to, and was given the key to a little Toyota Corolla.

"It's not new," Annie told her, "but it's been gently used. And here's your company gas card, Mary. Use the car for work only, please."

"Yes, ma'am," Mary said, and Annie didn't correct her.

"Your title is administrative assistant to the assistant manager," Annie said. She held out a piece of paper. "This is your salary, benefits included, and there will be periodic raises as you merit them."

Mary looked at the paper and her mouth fell open. She quickly closed it.

"If you have any difficulties you are to come to me," Annie said. "The Channel Corporation wants its employees one hundred percent happy, Mary. A word of warning: Don't take any of the personal assistants seriously. They are picked for their charm and their good looks. They know it, and a nice girl like yourself could be taken advantage of, so be advised that they're a naughty bunch." She smiled. "But that doesn't mean you can't flirt back. Just don't buy into their lines. Beware of the PA called Connor. He's a terrible gossip, and more often than not he gets the wrong end of the stick."

"I'm not taken in by boys," Mary said softly. "I can't get in trouble, and I have to set a good example for my little brother."

"Good girl!" Annie said approvingly.

"Thank you so much for giving me this chance, Mrs. Miller," Mary Finch gushed.

"You were the best candidate, Mary," Annie told her. "Now, I'll see you the Monday after graduation."

And indeed Mary had arrived that morning at eight thirty, although she wasn't due until nine a.m. She was dressed in her tan skirt, white blouse, and dark green spa blazer. Her sandy blond hair had been cut in a short, fashionable bob, and she wore only a smear of pink lipstick. On the lapel of her blazer was a little polished brass name tag that read, MARY FINCH, and below her name, ADMISTRATIVE ASSISTANT. Putting her small purse into the bottom drawer of her desk, Mary set everything up the way she wanted it, and smiled brightly when Annie arrived at eight forty. "Good morning, Mrs. Miller."

Mary was perfect, Annie thought as the weeks went by. And she didn't mind working late either. Right now Annie was working late several nights a week. Nathaniel had gone off to his summer internship. Amy and the twins were off to Stoneledge Lake for eight weeks. Her parents had rented a condo at a beach resort with a golf course and insisted on taking Wills with them. Nanny Violet had gone off to visit her sister in England. Annie was alone for the summer, and she was enjoying her freedom. She had been assistant manager of the Spa for almost four months now. Every day she

315

learned more and more about the running of the enterprise. With Mary Finch by her side, her workdays had taken on a smooth rhythm.

She had deleted her beach fantasy with Devyn, replacing it with another beach fantasy with two handsome men, Luka and Max. Sometimes she invited one of them into her bed, and at other times she would bring them both. She very much enjoyed having two men pleasure her. She had not deleted her first fantasy of Beauty and the Beast. For some reason she did not understand, she seemed to need the Beast and his leather tawse.

It was raining tonight as she pressed the A button, finding herself a nanosecond later being prepared for punishment.

She was naked and bent over a thickly padded bar. Her legs had been spread and were shackled to the bottom of the legs of the bar. Her arms were outstretched and fastened to the top part of the bar's legs.

"You are a perfect picture of submission, Mistress Anne," the Beast's rough voice growled at her. "Your bottom is perfect in both its size and its shape. A lovely peach." He ran a hand over her flesh. "And like silk to my touch. Today it shall be tawsed with twenty strokes of the leather. Then your pretty ass will be burnished to a fine glow with a small bundle of aspen switches. And afterward you will be fucked first by me, and then you will remain the night here in my dungeon, a treat for any of my men who choose to use you. You have a great and lustful appetite for cock, Mistress Anne. Tonight you shall have your fill. Come the morning I will whip you again, and the last prick you shall take will be mine once again."

"My lord, what have I done to displease you so?" Annie asked him.

"Why, Mistress Anne, you are quite pleasing to me in your obedience as a rule, but you have kept yourself from me for some days now, remaining in your tower while I languished for your cunt. And surely by now that eager maw of yours is ready to be plowed vigorously by more than one man. I know your tastes well, my dear," he murmured, bending to lick the whorl of her ear. "Beneath your meekness is a lascivious wench with the rollicking heart of a pure wanton." Reaching down, he pinched one of her nipples, and when she shivered he laughed.

She felt him step away from her, and knew he was picking up the broad leather strap. "Am I to be kept bent over like this all night?" she asked him.

"Nay," he said. "You will be bound to yon bed to keep you readily available. Look, my pet, I have a new tawse for you tonight." He held it out, and she saw the end of the broad length of the tawse was now split into several narrow fingers of leather, and each strip was knotted several times. "See?" He allowed her to look quickly at it, and then he removed it from her sight.

Annie tensed, waiting for the first blow. Being punished like this always aroused her to a fever pitch, but of late she had needed more blows. Tonight, however, was different. When the first blow was laid on her she felt the slender ribbons with their knots sting. She squealed, and he laughed delightedly as he counted out the other blows. Several of those fingers burrowed between her thighs and stung at her mons. She actually squirmed to eacape them. When the last blow had fallen he set to work on her helpless buttocks with the bunch of switches. Her sensitive flesh was quickly burning, and her arousal was high. "Fuck me, my lord," she pleaded with him. "Fuck me!"

"But a few strokes more, Mistress Anne," he told her as he whipped her with the switches. "You are quite able to take a bit more of this delight."

"No! No!" Annie cried as the switches

rained down upon her buttocks. "I must have your cock! I must!"

"And so you shall, my beauty," he said. His hands gripped her hips, and slowly, slowly, he inserted his great penis into her vagina. When he was fully sheathed he purred at her, "Now, Mistress Anne, you shall be well fucked, hard and deep until you can bear no more, for my lusty nature is boiling, having been denied your cunt for so long."

He began to ream her, and once he had found the perfect rhythm he released his hold upon her hips, bent low over her, and, reaching about, grasped her breasts. He squeezed them, he teased at the nipples with his rough thumbs, he pinched and pulled at the nipples while she squealed and moved in time with him. Dissatisfied, however, he called out, "Rafe and Ziven, to your master!"

Annie watched as two guardsmen emerged from the shadows, where they had been standing watching their master and her.

"Each of you attend to a breast," the Beast commanded them. "She needs more, and I must attend better to her wet cunt."

The two guardsmen positioned themselves so they might have access to her full breasts. Their hands closed about each one, and they began to suck upon her. Their eager mouths produced a throbbing within her as they drew strongly. One of them bit her nipple, and she screamed softly, which encouraged the other guardsman to do the same. And all the while, as their fingers kneaded and squeezed her flesh, the Beast pounded into her harder and deeper than he had ever done before, Annie thought. And then she felt the moment of her crisis approaching. Her vagina began to spasm as he fucked her to climax, howling as his own juices burst forth.

The Beast fell away from her onto the straw of the dungeon cell. As he did one of the guardsmen was quickly behind her, thrusting himself into her as the second guardsman pushed his swollen prick into her mouth. "That's it, lads," the Beast encouraged them. "Mistress Anne is a lusty bitch, and will take all you have to give her, won't you, my beauty?"

And Annie sucked on the cock in her mouth while moving her buttocks in time with the guardsman plundering her vagina. Her blue eyes met the dark eyes of the Beast in perfect understanding, and he smiled a slow smile at her as the trio came.

When the three men had finished with her they bathed her private parts with warm water from a small basin, and then bound her to a small bed before leaving her. After a brief interlude two young guardsmen entered the dungeon cell. They unfastened her bonds and climbed into the bed with her. They stroked her breasts and licked at her cunt before they took turns fucking her. When they had finished they bathed her parts again, and departed after binding her to the bedposts once more. Another man entered after a span of time had passed. Unlocking her bonds, he put her facedown over the edge of the bed and pushed his cock into her forbidden channel. Holding her down with a hand on her neck, he grunted softly, and after a stroke or two of his swollen dick he exploded his juices within her. Then, chaining her back up, he departed.

Four guardsmen entered now. One of them was very young. "He's a virgin," the grizzled older guardman said. "You must be his first woman. We'll get you good and ready. Then you must suck him to a stand and take him." Then he unfastened her shackles, and two of them joined her in the bed. The old guardsman spoke.

"Normally a man respects another's woman, but the master has given us his woman as a treat this night. You are most fortunate, lad. See what fine tits she has. You get to feel her up, and suck on those big rosy nipples."

The two men in bed with her demonstrated as the boy looked on with excited eyes. He would need little priming, Annie considered.

"And their cunnies can also be given a lick and a suck," the narrator continued. "Show the lad how, Viktor."

And the soldier called Viktor dove between her open legs to lick and suck upon her as the old guardsman explained about the sensitivity of her clit. Annie squealed as Viktor sucked it, and he gave her a small clitoral orgasm. She could see over his head that the young guardsman had a decided bulge in his breeches now. The narrator saw it, too.

"Time to give the lad a bit of a lesson, eh, my lady?" He reached down to help her from the bed as the other two guardsmen jumped up. "You know what to do."

Annie smiled at the younger man. Then, falling to her knees before him, she unlaced his breeches and pulled out his cock. It was small, but had distinct possibilities. She took him into her mouth and began to suck upon him. Her partner groaned as the old guardsman spoke again.

"Now, lad, shortly you will have a great desire to release your juices, but do not. Another time, aye, but tonight you want to know what it is to fuck a woman. Be careful with him, my lady. When they're green they're undisciplined."

Annie nodded as she brought the young man to a good stiff stand; then she released him, drawing him back with her to the bed. They fell upon it, and under his companions' guidance the male virgin found the opening to her vagina and eagerly rammed himself into her. Annie laughed at the look of wonder that suffused his face. She wrapped her legs about his torso and said, "Now, darling, thrust it back and forth. Go deep and hard. You cannot harm me." Then, taking his head in her hands, she kissed him, pushing her tongue into his mouth.

The young man atop her moaned, pulling his head away from her, his eyes glazed with his need and his lust. He pistoned her with vigor as his mates cheered him on. Annie squeezed his hot prick with her vaginal muscles, and his eyes practically rolled back in his head. He screamed as he came, collapsing atop her with a whimper. The others cheered, but then the old guardsman pulled the younger one from her.

Annie saw the gleam in his brown eyes as

he did so, looking down lustfully on her lush body. With a smile she beckoned him to mount her. "Come now, and finish what the lad started, if you can," she teased him.

The senior guardsman unlaced his breeches and pulled out an engorged cock of most sufficient size. "Will this do you, my lady?" he said as he climbed atop her to thrust deep. "I know how to satisfy a wench, and in time the lad will, too. But for now your kindness and generosity should be rewarded." And he fucked her until they both reached a delicious climax as Annie heard the ping of the closing bell.

What a pity. The Beast had not had time to return and pleasure himself once more. But Annie knew that when she next visited him her fantasy would pick up exactly where this one had left off. The older guardsman would be fucking her to that lovely peak. And then the Beast would return to have his way with her. And she knew he would strap her again, for he seemed to enjoy it, and if the truth be known, so did she. Rolling over, Annie fell asleep.

It had been a very vigorous night, and she was fortunate that it was Saturday, and she would not have to arise early for work. This was Nora Buckley's weekend to remain on duty at the Spa. One of them always had to be available there for emergencies. Nora, of course, had her apartment. And Annie now had a small studio apartment for herself for those weekends when she watched over the Spa. She loved the elegant bed-sitter with its small galley kitchen and luxurious bath. And she loved all the amenities that came with her employment.

"You can get any of the treatments offered here, and they're free to you as an employee of the Spa," Annie told Mary Finch. "They do seaweed wraps, facials, manicures, pedicures, salt scrubs, massages."

"Oh, I don't think so," Mary said nervously.

"You've never done anything like that, have you?" Annie probed. "Hey, I didn't know about most of this stuff either until I won that contest and then came to work here. The head of the corporation, Mr. Nicholas, likes his employees to be happy and relaxed. He's very kind."

"Does he live here, too?" Mary Finch wanted to know.

"No, but he does have an office. It's kept locked when he isn't visiting us," Annie explained. "He comes now and again to see how everything is going. Nora Buckley is an executive in his corporation. She says he'll move her on to another project once he's satisfied that the Spa is getting along nicely. Try a manicure, Mary," Annie tempted her. "We'll go together, okay? Set up appointments for us with Mei and Pei."

Reluctantly Mary Finch obeyed Annie's instructions. And at the appointed time she followed her boss downstairs to the elegant treatment rooms. Mei and Pei greeted the two women cheerfully, sat them down, and set to work. When Mary's hands had been manicured Mei asked her, "Polish?"

"Oh, no," Mary said. "I don't wear polish. I don't want to draw the wrong sort of attention to myself."

"Clear polish won't make you a harlot," Mei said in practical tones. "Let me show you, Mary Finch. You don't like, we take off." Then she proceeded to cover Mary's nails with clear polish. When she had finished she said, "See? No bad girl. Good girl. Mrs. Miller, now, she a bad girl." And the manicurist cackled.

Pei and Annie laughed, too.

"Just because I like bright red polish now is no cause to say I'm bad," Annie said.

"You miss Devyn? Connor say he bet you miss Devyn," Mei said slyly.

"Connor would lose, then," Annie replied coolly. "I don't miss Devyn, and you should know better than to listen to Connor's gossip. He's worse than an old lady."

"He screwing this week's old lady," Mei remarked.

"Oh, my!" Mary Finch turned bright red.

"Mei!" Both Annie and Pei spoke in unison.

"Well, that's what he say," Mei said.

"Pay no attention, Mary," Annie told her assistant. "How do you like the clear polish? I think it's quite nice."

Mary nodded. "Me, too. My mom always says I'm too cautious."

"Well, next time we're doing pedicures," Annie told her with a grin. "All this luxury is ours for the taking. It's a shame not to avail ourselves of it."

"I suppose," Mary Finch said softly, glancing at her hands and smiling shyly.

"Wait till she get her first massage," Mei said, laughing at Mary's surprised face.

CHAPTER NINE

The summer had raced by, and before Annie knew it autumn was looming on the horizon. The girls were home from camp, and it seemed to her that Rose and Lily had grown at least a foot while they were away. Their coltishness was morphing from the preteen years into their teen years as they celebrated their thirteenth birthday two days after arriving home. They had all had a wonderful summer. Amy, who had turned seventeen in June before they left, had matured even more. She had loved being a counselor in training.

"I'm going to be an AC next summer, Mom. The camp director said they are very much looking forward to having me back. His parents ran the camp when you and Aunt Lizzie were there. He says you two were a little wild."

Annie laughed. "I don't ever remember being even a little wild. It must have been

Lizzie he was thinking about."

"I think I might like being a teacher," Amy said.

"Now, there's a fine and noble profession," Nanny Violet responded. "My sister was a teacher for many years."

"How was your visit with her?" Annie wanted to know.

"Fine, dear, just fine. Margaret has a sweet little cottage on the edge of a village near the town of Hereford. We had a lovely time chatting, gardening, and going to all the summer events. I hope to retire there one day myself," Nanny Violet said. "Now, when is my laddie coming home from the beach?"

Wills arrived just after Labor Day with his grandparents.

"I don't know how you do it," Phyllis Bradford remarked to Nanny Violet. "My hat is off to you. He's a wild little Indian, and I am utterly exhausted looking after him for so many weeks, with Annie's father doing nothing to help except taking him out on the golf course now and again."

"You could have brought him home anytime, Mom," Annie murmured.

"I'm learning to play golf," Wills announced proudly. "Grandpa is getting me my own set of clubs. He says golf is good for a man."

Phyllis Bradford rolled her eyes. "He's made a convert," she said.

"And Grandpa says I can come play with him this winter in Arizona during the school break," Wills continued.

"Only if you have good school grades," Nanny Violet told him. "Golfing with your grandfather is a special treat, and not given out to boys who don't study properly."

"You've lost weight again," Phyllis noted. "You're working too hard, Annie."

"But I love what I do, Mom," Annie replied. "Nora Buckley is giving me more and more responsibility. She says if she got sick or couldn't be there, I would have to know everything there is to know about managing the Spa, because I would be the one in charge, and she's right. It's true we're a small spa, but all of our fifty rooms are booked almost year-round. And the guests' comfort is our first priority."

"Listen to you," Phyllis said admiringly. "You've only been there a year, and already you sound so professional. I always knew that Lizzie would be someone special, but I never considered that you'd be anything more than a good wife and mother."

"Thanks, Mom!" Annie smiled at the backhanded compliment. There would have been a time when she would have resented her mother's words, but not now. Annie felt sure of herself now. She knew that she was more than just Nat's widow and the mother of five. She was a woman who was in charge. Except, of course, in the Beast's castle, and she smiled a secret little smile.

Nathaniel returned home briefly before going back to Princeton. He had spent a summer interning with an environmental group. "I've decided I'm going to go to law school when I've finished my undergraduate studies," he said at a Sunday family dinner.

His grandparents smiled and looked proud.

"Yale or Harvard for you," Lizzie said. "I'll help."

"Lizzie!" Annie protested.

"Look," her younger sister said, "we want him coming out debt-free, and you've got the others to think about. Thanks to Nanny, Amy has shaped up, and will go to a good college when she finishes high school. Two years from now she'll be gone."

"Gee, thanks, Auntie," Amy said wryly.

"And we've always known the twins were smart."

"I want to go to veterinarian school," Rose said.

"I want to go into animal research," Lily

331

told them.

"And who knows what Wills will turn into when he grows up?" Lizzie said.

"I want to be a spaceman," Wills piped up, not wanting to be left out.

"See?" Lizzie said. "You're going to have your hands full, sis."

"We'll talk about it," Annie said.

"What kind of law?" Lizzie asked her elder nephew. "Have you decided yet?"

"Environmental law," he told her.

"Not a hell of a lot of money in that, Nathaniel," Lizzie said. "Intern with my firm next summer, and see what we have to offer."

"You do litigation," he replied. "I don't want to do litigation."

"We do other things, too," Lizzie said. "The Channel Corporation is my client, and I do all kinds of work for them. It's fascinating. Intern with us. It will look very good on your application to law school."

"It's a good opportunity, buddy," his grandfather put in quietly.

"Okay, I'll think about it," Nathaniel said. "But interning with your high-profile, high-powered firm will be like interning for the devil, as far as I'm concerned."

Lizzie laughed. "I guess it does look that way, doesn't it?" she replied. "Big shops like ours are always feared by the little guys."

In November Nora Buckley told Annie that Mr. Nicholas was so pleased with the way the Spa was performing that he had asked Nora to go to California to check out locations for a second spa. "He wants a small town with the charm of Egret Pointe, rather than someplace trendy, like Monterey or Napa," Nora said. "I'll probably have to look in the mountains in the northern part of the state. There has to be some cute little villagey spot where we can find another perfect site."

"You'll need easy access to transportation," Annie remarked. "Or I suppose you could offer transportation to the clients. Make that the only way to get there. It would appear to be even more exclusive if you did that," she mused.

"That is a wonderful idea!" Nora replied enthusiastically. "Oh, by the way, you'll be in charge while I'm away, Annie."

Annie took a deep breath and exhaled.

Nora laughed. "Well, who else did you think was going to manage this place while I'm gone, sweetie? You're ready. Both Mr. Nicholas and I think you're ready."

"Oh, God," Annie said. "I hope you're right. What if I screw up, Nora?"

"You won't," Nora said. "You know you're going to be taking over here a lot more now that the corporation has decided to expand these spas. Mr. Nicholas is talking Europe, as well as an island in the South Pacific, and Central America, probably Costa Rica. Because I have the experience from the planning stage to operations I'm going to be the one he's sending out to choose the sites and oversee everything, the way I did here."

"What you're saying is that I could end up being the manager here if I do a good job," Annie replied slowly, thoughtfully.

"That's right," Nora Buckley told her.

Annie closed her eyes briefly. This was incredible, and she knew she could do it.

"You'll get a small bump in salary while I'm away, but if it becomes permanent your salary will double, Annie," Nora said. "That's certainly going to take care of college for your kids, isn't it? And I hear Nathaniel is aiming for law school when he graduates."

Annie opened her eyes. "Who told you that?" she asked.

"I was speaking with your sister on a legal matter last week, and she mentioned it," Nora responded. "He should consider Duke. My daughter graduated from there.

But, of course, it's all expensive, isn't it? Where is Amy going to college?"

"She's just a junior," Annie said.

"Still, you'll have to start thinking about it this year," Nora told her. "I've been through all of this myself with my two, so I know."

"The twins are four years behind Amy," Annie remarked. "Still, Amy will graduate, and they'll be headed off. At least I'll have a three-year break between them and my youngest."

"Unless, of course, your twins do grad school," Nora murmured.

"I guess I'd better get your job then when you go off for Mr. Nicholas," Annie replied with a small grin. "I'm obviously going to need every penny I can get."

Nora laughed. "I guess you are," she agreed.

"I couldn't have done anything for my children if I hadn't come to work at the Spa," Annie said. "Everything I do, it's all for the kids. That's what Nat used to say to me. 'It's all for you and the kids, baby.' I'm glad I could pick up where he left off, Nora, and it's all thanks to you, and to Mr. Nicholas. What a nice man he is in a world that isn't so nice. There should be more people like Mr. Nicholas."

"You'd be surprised to learn that there

really are, Annie," Nora told her. "He just does what he does with style, elegance, and finesse. Don't be fooled. He's a hard businessman, but he's also smart enough to know that happy employees are more productive employees."

"Well, I think he's wonderful!" Annie said enthusiastically.

"I'll be leaving next week," Nora told Annie. "I probably won't be back until late December, six weeks or so."

With Nora gone Annie assumed full control of the Spa's operations. It wasn't long before the employees began to scent a change in the wind.

"They say you'll be taking over for good soon," Connor buttonholed her one day in the staff elevator. "Is it true?"

"You must know more than I do," Annie replied.

He pushed the stop button, and the elevator came to a halt. "I've been thinking about you, Mrs. Miller. Thinking about what fun we had that day. Want to have some fun again?" He pushed her back against the wall of the elevator cabin and rubbed himself against her. "Ever do it in here with Devyn?"

Annie reached out to push the start button, but he caught her wrist, squeezing it tightly. "Let go," she said through gritted teeth.

"Come on, baby, let me do you here. Don't tell me you don't want to, don't need it. I know everything that goes on in this place, and you haven't done it with anyone else since Devyn left. I'll fuck you real good, baby." He reached out to stroke her full breast.

"You are within a nanosecond of losing your job, Connor," Annie said in an icy, level tone. Then she kneed him hard, and when he fell back, gasping, she restarted the elevator. When the doors opened on the lower treatment floor she stepped out, turning to say to him, "If you ever accost me again, baby face, you will be gone in the next minute. And why aren't you with your guest?" Leaning back into the elevator, Annie pressed the lobby floor button, withdrawing her arm as the doors closed on the white-faced Connor. Then, turning, she walked sedately down the hall. She was due to have a massage.

"I was just about to call up to your office," Lars said. "I thought you forgot."

"I never forget my dates with you," Annie told him with a small smile.

"What happened?" he asked.

"Who said anything happened?" she replied, stepping into the dressing room and stripping down to her bikini panties. She exited, clutching a towel about herself, and climbed up onto his comfortable massage table, handing him the towel as she did so.

"Your color's a little high," Lars noted, "and you look mad despite the smile."

"Connor," was all Annie said.

"You telling me that little shit had the nerve to come on to you? You know, he's told everyone who'll listen that he had a threesome with you and Devyn once." Lars poured some coconut oil into his hands, rubbing them together before reaching out to begin his massage of her back.

"He did," Annie said. "He was with us for about ten or fifteen minutes, and then we sent him packing. I could be his mother. But I guess he can't get past it, and wants to take over where Devyn left off. I stopped with Devyn when I got this promotion, you know. Except for a little farewell party Nancy and I gave him the day he left." Lars was her confidant, and she knew he was a man who kept his mouth shut.

"I could probably take care of him for you," Lars said as his fingers kneaded her tight shoulders.

"Thanks, but I took care of him rather nicely, if I do say so myself." Annie chuckled. "He'll be limping about for a while, and I hope his guest doesn't expect any special services from him today. I don't think he'll be able to get it up for a while."

"You kneed him?" Lars burst out laughing. "Good for you, Annie!"

When the masseur had finished her back Annie turned over. "Do something special today," she said. "I'm pissed, and maybe I'm even a little horny."

"Gotcha," Lars replied. He started with her shoulders again, working his way down to her breasts. His big hands gently kneaded them, his fingers brushing lightly over the nipples at first, pulling them out, pinching them firmly. "You've got such great tits for a woman your age. Hell, for any woman," he told her. Then he moved on down her torso to work the soft flesh. When he reached her mons he massaged it, and then his fingers pushed through the twin folds of her labia, seeking out her clit. He played with it as Annie murmured, giving her a small climax. Then his two thick fingers pushed into her vagina, massaging its walls.

"Do it," Annie said softly, and he finger-fucked her to orgasm. "God, that is so good." She sighed. "You give the best massage, Lars."

"Would I be out of line if I said I'd really

like to do you someday?" he asked her as he licked her juices off his fingers.

"Probably not," Annie answered him. "But not today. Today I've got to go back up to my office and go over the list of guests scheduled to arrive this weekend. The publisher lady is coming again. She really loves this place. By the way, how many of your clients do you give this *special* treatment to?"

He smiled at her. "It's by request only. Let's finish you up," Lars said as he began to work on her legs and feet without answering her question.

"Let me see what you've got," Annie teased him wickedly.

With a grin he unzipped his fly and pulled out a half-hard penis. "What do you think? Good enough for you?" His gray eyes were serious.

"Oh, that is very nice," Annie complimented him. She ran her fingertips down his length. The tip of her tongue touched her top lip suggestively. "I do believe it will do quite nicely. Now put it away before I'm tempted further, Lars. Another time and another place. But it will only be a fuck. You do understand that? I want nothing more of you than a hard and talented dick."

He nodded. "I like a woman who enjoys

her sex, but doesn't want to get involved. I don't want to get involved either."

"Maybe when I stay over some night you can come to my apartment and give me a massage," Annie murmured softly.

"I'd like that," he said, "as long as I don't have to stay the night."

"God, no!" she agreed. "A little pleasure and you're gone."

Annie returned to her office feeling considerably more relaxed after her massage.

"Mr. Nicholas called," Mary Finch said. "He would like to set up an appointment with you right after the New Year."

"Call his assistant back, and tell her it can be at his convenience," Annie said.

"Right away, Mrs. Miller," Mary answered.

"Mary, how would you like to be the administrative assistant to the manager of the Spa?" Annie asked her.

"Oh, no, Mrs. Miller. I'd prefer to stay with you," the girl replied.

"There is a chance Ms. Buckley will be moving on, and I'll be taking over," Annie told her assistant. "But it's our little secret, okay?"

Mary Finch gave a little squeal. "Ohh, I'd like that that!" she said excitedly.

"It will mean a pay raise," Annie told her.

"You'll like that, too." She laughed.

Thanksgiving came, and Annie was relieved that her mother was preparing the feast once again. She just didn't have the time to do it, but her daughters insisted on bringing a green bean casserole, which they prepared beneath the eye of Nanny Violet.

"I know you prefer fresh green beans," the little Englishwoman said to Phyllis Bradford. "I've taught the girls to French cut the beans properly, and we've made our own French-fried onions. It will be quite tasty, Mrs. Bradford."

"You're a wonder," Phyllis said. She was no longer jealous or resentful of her children's nanny. Indeed, the woman made it possible for Annie to have the small success she was having with her new career.

There was no time to Christmas shop, but Annie gave Nanny Violet a list of gifts to get. The nanny would use the new credit card Annie had gotten for household expenses. And Nanny would wrap all the presents, and secrete them away so the children wouldn't find them until Christmas morning beneath the tree. Nanny Violet took Wills and his sisters out to buy the Christmas tree the weekend before Christmas. Annie had to remain at the Spa to host the staff Christmas party and pass out the yearly bonuses to everyone. Nora Buckley had not yet returned.

The dining room waitresses, the kitchen staff, the gardeners, the personal assistants, the staff from the treatment floor, Nancy from the gift shop, and all the auxiliary staff ate, drank, swapped stories, laughed, and danced. Lars came up to Annie and murmured in her ear so that only she could hear him. She smiled and nodded as he moved away from her to ask Pei to dance. As the party began to wind down Annie realized she hadn't seen Mary Finch; nor had the girl gotten her bonus. She went into her office and, finding the door locked, knocked upon it, calling as she did, "Whoever is in my office, please open the door.

"Mary, what's happened?" Annie asked as the door slowly opened.

Mary's sandy blond hair was unruly, and she was crying.

"Mary, tell me! What has happened?" Annie sat down next to the girl, who was huddled in a corner of her office couch.

"I . . . I . . . I told him no, but he wouldn't listen," Mary sobbed.

"Whom did you tell no?" Annie wanted to know. But she already had an idea of who had attempted to assault her young assistant.

"C-Connor!" Mary burst out. "He grabbed me. I managed to push him off balance, and lock myself in your office. He said I had been looking at him, that I was a tease."

Annie was furious. An incident like this could give the spa a very nasty bit of publicity. "Did you ever speak with him, Mary? I mean before today."

"No!" Mary said vehemently. "I would just see him in the lobby or in the staff dining room, but I never spoke to him. And he never spoke to me, Mrs. Miller. Oh, what am I going to tell my parents?"

"We're just lucky you weren't hurt," Annie said. "I'm going to fire Connor right now. Your parents would be very upset if they learned what happened. They would probably make you quit working for me. Do you want them to do that, Mary?"

"No! I love working for you here at the Spa!" Mary said vehemently. "I don't think I ever want to have sex now." She began to cry again.

"I'm going to call your mother," Annie said. "Be quiet now." She picked up her phone and dialed the Finch residence. "Mrs. Finch? Hi, it's Annie Miller up at the Spa. Look, the staff party is running a bit late. I could really use Mary to stay and help me batten down the hatches when it's all over. I'm going to keep her over tonight, if that's all right with you. She's never stayed here, of course, and she's really excited about it." Annie laughed lightly. "She is such a wonderful assistant, I thought I would give her a little extra Christmas treat in addition to her bonus. I must tell you that you've raised a lovely daughter." Annie listened, smiling. "Fine, I'll tell her. She'll see you tomorrow after work. Merry Christmas to you and the family now. Good-bye." Annie put the phone back in its cradle. "There," she said.

"Thank you, Mrs. Miller." Mary sniffled.

There was a short knock on the door to her office, and Lars stepped into the room. Mary shrank back against Annie. "What happened?" he asked quickly.

"Find Connor," Annie said. "Be discreet. Bring him here."

"Oh, Mrs. Miller, I couldn't face him. He was horrible." She began to cry.

"Shit!" Lars swore. "What did that asshole do to her?"

"Tried to attack and force seduction, but failed. Mary managed to lock herself in my private office, and he had to give up. I want to take her upstairs to my apartment," Annie told him. "Find the little bastard, and

345

don't kill him before I get my chance." She stood, drawing Mary Finch up with her. "Come on, sweetie." And Annie hurried her out of her office to the staff elevator. The lobby was silent. There would be no guests now until the day after Christmas, and most of the staff had dispersed, or gone home if they lived nearby. "You stay here," Annie told Mary Finch when she had gotten the girl to the new apartment. As manager she had been given a large quarters. "I will be back soon. You're safe here. I'll lock the door behind me, and no one else has the key card."

"Okay," Mary said softly as she looked around the beautiful space into which she had been deposited. "I'll be all right now."

Annie hurried out, returning to her office, sat down at her desk, and, pulling out the company checkbook, wrote a check. Several minutes later Lars came in with Connor, whom he held by the scruff of his neck. Connor looked decidedly nervous. "Did you think you could attempt to assault my assistant and get away with it?" she asked the younger man.

"Hey," he blustered, "she's been asking for it with that innocent act she puts on."

"She's a virgin, and you've traumatized her. You're fired." She pulled the check from

346

the book and handed it to him. "Two weeks' severance. Lars will escort you to the door. We'll send you your belongings if you'll tell us where."

"What about my bonus?" Connor demanded to know.

"I'm giving it to Mary Finch as compensation. Get out!"

"I'll go to the press about this place," Connor threatened.

"What could you possibly tell them?" Annie said innocently. "We'd take you down with us.

"Take care of removing Connor, Lars; then return to me. I'm going to see if I can calm Mary down. It may take a little while, but then I'll be ready for a *massage*. It's been a long day." She watched as, with a grim smile, Lars hustled Connor out of her office.

Taking Connor to his car, Lars said, "We'll send you your stuff, asshole. Get going before I decide I want to beat the crap out of you." Then, returning to the spa, he walked through the quiet lobby to the kitchens. He was hungry, and he knew Annie would need a little more time to calm that nice Mary Finch. He'd bring a tray upstairs with him when he had finished eating. He was looking forward to fucking Annie. She was quite a woman, he thought with a smile.

Annie knocked at the door of her apartment and identified herself before she inserted the key card into the lock. She found Mary Finch sitting quietly. "How do you feel now?" she asked the girl.

"Better," Mary said. "Thanks for letting me stay tonight. I don't think I could face my folks after what happened. I know my parents. They would say it was all my fault, and I must have led the guy on. But I didn't, Mrs. Miller! Honest, I didn't!"

"I know you didn't, Mary," Annie said quietly. "Connor has been troublesome for some time now. I've had two complaints from guests about his aggressiveness. I've had to fend him off a couple of times. I warned him one more infraction and he'd be fired. He has been. And he won't bother you again, I promise you."

"I don't know a whole lot about sex except what they taught in health education in high school," Mary admitted. "My mom has always said that when I needed to know she'd tell me. They didn't let me date either, except with a group of friends. My dad said going out alone with a boy could just lead to trouble sooner or later. I must really sound like an idiot to you, especially in this day and age. Do you talk to your daughters about sex?"

"Amy yes, but so far the twins haven't been too interested," Annie said. "They'll ask when they are. Rose and Lily aren't shy. And I expect Amy will say something to them if they want information, and, of course, their friends. They'll ask me when they want to ask. Some parents are shy about discussing sex with their kids, Mary, but sometimes it's better to suffer a little embarrassment so your kids don't suffer worse."

Mary nodded in agreement. The two women spoke together for some time. Mary asked questions, and Annie answered them. And when a knock came upon the door of the apartment Annie got up, answering it, and let Lars come in. He was carrying a heavily laden tray.

"I thought you ladies might like something to eat," he said cheerfully.

"I am hungry," Mary admitted, eyeing the tray.

"You go first," Annie said. "I have to discuss something with Lars." She took the big masseur aside. "Connor is taken care of now?" she asked him.

Lars said quietly, "I personally escorted him."

"Good! I'll call Mr. Nicholas about the situation, if you're willing to sit with Mary for a little bit." She smiled up at him.

"You want to call off our *date?*" he asked. "I'd understand."

"No," Annie said. "We're going to show little Mary that sex can be fun, exciting, and tender. I don't want the memory of what Connor tried to do to spoil it for her. She said that after what he attempted she never wants to have sex. That's just not right, Lars."

He smiled slowly. "You, lady, are a very interesting woman," he noted.

Annie smiled. "Am I?" she said coyly. Then she picked up her cell and punched in the number one. "Go," she told him. "Mr. Nicholas, it's Annie Miller." She didn't wish him a merry Christmas. Nora Buckley had said he didn't celebrate Christmas, and actually had a strong dislike for the holiday. "I'm afraid we had a bit of a situation with one of the PAs. He made an attempt to assault my young assistant. Yes, Connor. I've fired him, and taken care of everything else." She listened for a short time. Then Annie said, "Why, thank you, Mr. Nicholas. I'm glad you're pleased with my decisions in the matter. I'll look forward to seeing you January second. Yes, sir, the bookings for next week are excellent. We're full up. Yes, sir. Good-bye now." Annie closed her cell, smiling.

"The big boss okay with everything?" Lars asked casually when Annie returned.

"Yes, he is," Annie replied. She reached for a sandwich half and began to eat.

"Lars says he made these sandwiches himself," Mary said with a small giggle. "My dad doesn't even know how to boil water. Roast beef on buttered white bread, and the crusts cut off. Aren't they good, Mrs. Miller?"

"They certainly are, Mary," Annie agreed, reaching for another sandwich half.

They ate all the sandwiches Lars had brought, and drank a glass of wine each. Then they devoured the tiny mincemeat minitarts he had included. Finally they sat talking for a time, and, seeing that Mary was now calm again, Annie decided to put into effect the rather naughty plan that had formed in her head earlier. She was quite surprised at herself, but then, she thought, she wanted to help Mary get past her trauma.

"Feeling better now?" she asked her assistant.

Mary nodded.

"I thought you were very brave tonight,

considering what happened," Annie said. "Do you think you could be brave some more for me, Mary?"

Slowly the girl nodded again. "What do you want me to do, Mrs. Miller?"

"Nothing awful." Annie laughed lightly. "But your experience with Connor has given you the wrong idea about sex. I don't want you missing out on something wonderful because of that prick, Mary. Lars and I have become, um, good friends. We would like to demonstrate to you that sex between two consenting adults isn't terrible or awful at all. It's really lots of fun, and quite delicious."

"What would I have to do?" Mary asked, nervous now. She gulped down some more of the wine Lars had discreetly added to her glass.

"Nothing at all but watch us," Annie told the girl.

"Watch you?" The look on Mary's face told them she didn't know whether to be afraid or shocked. "Watch you have sex?"

"Watch us make love," Annie corrected her gently.

"I wouldn't have to do anything myself?" Mary queried again.

"Nope. Not unless you want to, of course, but I really think you should just watch us tonight, Mary. You can ask questions afterward if you want," Annie said.

"If you don't want to watch," Lars told the girl, "you don't have to, Mary. You can go to the guest room, and we can take this into Annie's bedroom. But when that little turd Connor tried to force you, he scared you. That's not our purpose. Annie and I just want you to know that making love is really great." He pulled off the tight black T-shirt he was wearing, revealing a smooth, well-muscled chest and a torso of washboard abs. Then, standing, he pushed down his pale gray sweatpants, stepped out of them, and kicked them aside. He was wearing nothing now but silky-looking black briefs that outlined his tight, round butt and barely contained his large wad. Walking over to the big bed in the room, he turned, holding out a hand. "Annie?"

Mary Finch's eyes were huge in her face, and she couldn't keep them from the bulge in Lars' briefs. Her breathing quickened, and she licked her lips.

Annie watched the girl surreptitiously as she unzipped her dress and stepped out of it. Beneath she wore a lacy bra and matching bikini panties. She stripped them off and, walking over to Lars, knelt down, pulling his briefs off. Taking his cock into her mouth, she began to suck on him slowly, with obvious relish as her fingers reached beneath to tickle his balls.

Mary watched Annie and Lars, wide-eyed.

His eyes had been closed with the pleasure Annie was giving him. He opened them now and said, "You see? I'm not making her do it. She wants to do it, because lovers like to please each other." His hand reached out to touch Annie's head gently.

"Sucking cock is an intimate thing. It should only be done between people who like and respect each other," Lars said. His fingers dug into Annie's head, signaling her that he wanted her to stop, and she did. Pulling her up, he kissed her deeply. Then he said, "Come on over here, Mary, so you can see better what's going on."

"If you want to lie on the bed with us, it's okay," Annie put in as she got up to lead them into her bedroom.

Mary followed, and while she stood near the bed she made no attempt to join them, but she did move a little closer as Lars began playing with Annie's breasts. She was shocked by their nakedness, yet she was also fascinated by it as well. She had often imagined what it would be like to be naked with a lover. Connor's attempted assault of her earlier had frightened her. But these two people were obviously enjoying themselves very much, as evidenced by Annie's face as Lars bent and suckled on her plump breast. "Is that nice?" she asked shyly. She had let a few boys in high school fumble with her breasts, but she had never let them touch her bare flesh. They had all said she was a prude.

"Ummm, yes, very nice," Annie said. "It's an arousal technique, and a very successful one, too, I might add."

"I enjoy it, too," Lars said, turning about. "Annie's tits are quite a turn-on."

Mary Finch's eyes grew big again at the sight of his penis.

Seeing where her gaze had settled, he smiled at her, his eyes twinkling.

Mary blushed, but then she asked him, "Are you considered big?"

"Bigger than some, not as big as others," Lars admitted with a small smile. "Haven't you ever seen a penis before, honey?"

"In books," Mary said. "But not for real until tonight. You look very big to me."

"I'm not even fully aroused yet," he told her. He looked over at Mary Finch, wondering if she would remain, would eventually join them. "You okay? Want to stay? It's going to get interesting now." He had never really paid a great deal of attention to her before, but now that he was beginning to know her, Lars decided that Mary was adorable. It wasn't a word he ever remembered using to describe a woman. Women were either fuckable or they weren't. Mary was both adorable and fuckable. He was surprised at himself.

"What are you going to do?" Mary queried him.

It was obvious that she was fascinated. That she might even want to be in Annie's place. Clever Annie, Lars considered. He now knew what she intended. She wanted them to seduce little Mary Finch together. The mere thought excited him. "Women suck cock," he said as he began to answer her question. "Men lick cunt."

Mary gasped at both the word and the idea, but she moved closer still to the bed.

Annie spread herself open, and Lars slipped between her legs, pulling them over his shoulders, his dark head diving between her thighs. Within just a few seconds Annie was making sounds of distinct pleasure. Mary couldn't help watching, mesmerized. His tongue was licking and flicking about Annie's wet flesh. Mary felt herself getting wet, like when she read sex scenes in romance novels. She knew she should probably turn away, go, but she just couldn't.

This was the most exciting thing she had ever seen, and it was very obvious that both Lars and Annie were enjoying it.

And then Lars lifted his head and, moving his body, revealed his penis, swollen to at least twice the size it had been before. Mary heard Annie murmur softly, "Fuck me, darling!" and Lars pushed himself into her. Annie sighed deeply. Practically hypnotized by the lush sensuality of it all, she watched as Lars began to move on Annie. It was beautiful, and when the couple's passion peaked with their pleasurable cries and they fell away from each other, Mary felt sorrow that it was over. Without even realizing it, she sat down heavily on the bed, for she didn't think her legs would hold her up any longer.

Reaching out, Annie drew Mary down and kissed her cheek lightly. "Wasn't that nice?" she purred at the spellbound girl. "Lars is a wonderful lover."

Mary nestled against Annie. "I never thought that sex could be so . . . so . . ."

"Wouldn't you like it to be like that for you?" Annie whispered.

"I don't know." Mary hesitated. And then she drew away from Annie and stood up, stepping away from the bed. "I'm going to my own room now," she said.

"We could make you forget what happened if you would let us. Replace that bad memory with a good one." Annie smiled at the girl.

"Would Lars make love to me like he did to you?" Mary asked softly.

"If you let me, I will," Lars said. "I want to make you happy, baby girl," he told her. "I want to give you good dreams, not bad ones." And to his surprise he realized that he did. This shy innocent touched him as no woman ever had.

"I think I would like that," Mary said slowly. "But I don't think I'm brave enough yet to let you. I always thought I would wait for my wedding night to have real sex, but now I don't think I want to wait. Does that sound silly?" Her look was anxious.

"No, it doesn't sound silly," Lars assured her quickly. He had seen the look of irritation in Annie's eyes. Annie wanted him to fuck the kid, but the kid wasn't ready, and if she wasn't, he wasn't going to do it. "You go on to bed, sweetie. It's been a long day for you. But when you're ready, Mary, let me be your first. I don't want some eager jerk spoiling your first time. I'll make it extra-special for you, I promise. Okay?"

"Okay," she promised him softly. "You can be my first, Lars. I think I would like it if you were." Mary smiled a little smile at him. Then she left Annie's bedroom, closing the door behind her.

"You'll have to be gentle, and extra-careful with that big stick of yours," Annie said with a mischievous grin. "It's going to hurt the first time you do it to her, and it's going to take all your persuasive powers to get her past that part."

"I know," he responded. "And I will be gentle with her, and I'll warn her so there are no surprises. I like the fact that I'm going where no man has gone before me." He grinned down at Annie. "But I also like an experienced woman, too. Just thinking about little Mary has me all hot and bothered again. Wanna do it again, boss lady?"

"I think I'm insulted," Annie told him, but she reached down to stroke his big cock with her skilled fingers. "But I'm also hot to be fucked again, Lars, so I'll overlook my hurt feelings, and you'll make me come and come and come. Deal?"

"Deal," he said, reaching for a fresh condom as he peeled the old one off.

"Let me," Annie said, taking the packet from his hand and opening it. His penis was turgid and swollen already. He must really be lusting for her assistant, she thought as her fingers stroked his thick length. She bent her head and nibbled the head of his dick with delicate teeth; then she sucked him briefly before encasing his penis in the condom. "There," she said. "Now we're ready to play, aren't we?"

"You've really changed," Lars told her, "since that first day you came to the Spa as its opening grand-prize winner. You were shy and very proper then. You aren't shy, and you sure as hell aren't proper anymore, Annie. You've turned into one wicked, sexy vixen. Maybe it's really true that power corrupts."

"I don't think I've changed much," she protested. "I'm just a working woman now, not a housewife. And everything I do is for my kids, so they can have a better life."

Everything?" he asked as he slid his cock into her wet vagina.

"Well, almost everything." Annie laughed. "Oh, God, that feels good. You are so deliciously big and hard. Now do me, Lars. Do me hard and do me deep. Make me scream and make me come. Not once. Not twice. I want to come three times."

"Whatever you want, boss lady," he told her. He pinioned her arms above her head with one hand, balancing himself with the other. Then he began to fuck her hard and fuck her deep. In short order Annie was moaning as she came once. He found her G-spot and worked it gently and teasingly. She swore at him as he brought her near, and then pulled back. His nails clawed him, and he laughed.

"Let me come, you bastard!" Annie swore at him again.

"You are such a greedy bitch," he teased her, but he gave her what she wanted, and she panted with her release. "Ready for number three?" he wanted to know as his cock began to flash faster and faster within her.

"God, not yet!" she begged.

"Oh, yeah, sooner than later, because I'm going to explode if you don't climb the mountain a third time, Annie." He homed in on her most sensitive spots, and in short order she was moaning.

He was the most skilled lover, Annie thought as she felt herself beginning to soar again. It really was a shame he hadn't wanted them to seduce little Mary tonight. But then, there would always be another time for that delicious treat. Lars liked good sex every bit as much as Annie had discovered she liked it. And multiple lovers were really the way to go.

CHAPTER TEN

But something had happened that December night, as Annie quickly discovered. Lars — big, stoic Lars — had fallen in love with Mary Finch that night. Annie almost laughed at the irony of it all. She had finally found a lover who wanted nothing more from her than good sex, and now, as he apologetically told her several days later, he was in love. "That's wonderful!" she said to him. "But please be good to her, Lars."

"I intend to marry her, Annie," he said. "I know she's younger than me — just nineteen — but she really is a good girl. We're going out New Year's Eve. I know that, having been in love yourself with your husband, you understand."

"I do," Annie replied. And she did, but it didn't make it any easier. Well, at least in the Channel her lovers would stay with her as long as she wanted them. She was probably better off keeping her sex life where no one else could know about it. Connor would have gossiped about her, she was certain. But after Lars had put him in his car that night and he had driven off, no one had seen him again. *Good riddance to bad rubbish,* Annie thought.

The holiday had passed without further incident. She had let Amy go skiing in Colorado with Brittany and her parents. Amy was rather pleased that of all the girls Brittany might have taken, she had chosen Amy. The twins were consumed with doing research for their science fair project, and Wills was happy with Nanny Violet, who was now teaching Annie's younger son to cook simple things.

"A man should always know how to make himself a nourishing meal," Nanny Violet said. "I'm going to teach him how to do laundry, too." She chuckled.

On January second Annie dressed with special care: a black lambswool sheath skirt and black cashmere turtleneck, over which she wore a bright red fitted wool jacket. She hadn't been so thin in years, and she was relishing it. She was wearing red tights and black leather boots. She had on gold jewelry, although she had finally put her wedding ring into her jewelry box. She wasn't married anymore. She was a widow.

363

"You look mah-vel-ous," Nathaniel said to her in a plummy voice. "What's the occasion, Mom?" He was home between semesters.

"Mr. Nicholas is coming today. He wants to see me in his office at ten a.m. I think I'm going to be made general manager of the Spa. Everyone thinks so," Annie told him. "Nora Buckley's been away a couple of months now, and no one thinks she's coming back. She isn't even in Egret Pointe right now."

"Wow! You really have been on the fast track, Mom, haven't you?" Nathaniel answered her. "Well, good luck then! But I suppose that means more time at the Spa, and less at home." He sounded a little disapproving.

"Probably it does," Annie agreed. "You can't run something like the Spa and leave it to your underlings all the time. I have to be there to make certain everyone is doing what they should be doing. And look what I've been able to do for the family because of my job. I may be letting Lizzie help you through Princeton, but I'm going to be able to pay for Amy's college. She talking about Yale or Skidmore. And with the grades she's been getting she's going to get in, Nathaniel. And at midwinter vacation Nanny is taking

Wills and the girls to Arizona to visit Grandma and Grandpa. I've rented them an apartment for ten days there. Amy has all the right clothes now because of my job. She had the most adorable ski outfits when she went off with Brittany. Everything I do is for this family, Nathaniel. No one suffers. Nanny is here for me so I can do my job, and not worry."

"The kids hardly see you at all, Mom. It used to be that you were at least home on the weekends, but since Ms. Buckley left the Spa you're there practically twenty-four/seven," Nathaniel told his mother. "If you want the promotion, I hope you get it. Just don't forget you've got a few daughters and a little boy who need you. We all got on quite well without all these things you talk about."

"We got on, as you put it, because your aunt and your grandparents helped us out. Part of me was grateful, but most of me hated taking their charity. It was almost like a rebuke to your father for not planning well and considering that he could die young. Now I pay all the bills. I send your sisters to camp. I buy their clothing," Annie said. "I like being able to do these things. I don't need anyone's charity anymore. Everything I do is for the family, Nathaniel. I could pay for Princeton now, but it makes my sister happy to do it. She has no kids and probably never will. And she's so proud of you."

"Okay, Mom, okay," he replied, and Nathaniel put an arm about her and hugged his mother. "So you like being a working girl, and now you're going to be a mover and a shaker. You deserve to be happy too, and I know Dad would be proud."

"Thanks for that," Annie said, realizing she felt a little teary all of a sudden. She fought back her urge to shed a tear or two. She didn't need to ruin her makeup. "I gotta run. Ask Nanny to do her shepherd's pie tonight with the leftover lamb, sweetie."

She arrived at her office at eight thirty sharp. She checked the guest register to see who would be checking out and who would be checking in today. She ran over the provisions list for the next two weeks that had been set on her desk, and checked the menus for the week to come.

"Good morning, Mrs. Miller." Mary was right on time, Annie noted. She came in at five minutes to nine every morning. "Can I get you something?"

"Green tea with lemon," Annie replied. Mary looked happy, she noted.

At ten minutes to ten o'clock the front desk called, and Mary came into Annie's office to announce, "Mr. Nicholas's car just pulled up. I can see the lobby from here, and he's coming in, Mrs. Miller. There's a man with him."

"A man?" Annie said, surprised.

"Yep. And is he hot," Mary noted.

Annie touched up her makeup, got up, put on her jacket, and hurried from her office. After knocking on Mr. Nicholas's door she opened it and stepped into the charming room. The fire was already burning, and she smiled. She'd given instructions that a fire be started at nine thirty a.m. so the chill would be off the room and it would be inviting.

"Annie, my dear, come in, come in," Mr. Nicholas said. He turned from the fireplace, where he had been warming his hands. "I do love a good fire," he said. "Sit down, Annie. I have some wonderful news for you."

Annie sat down before she fell down. The other occupant in the room was a tall, slender man with coal black hair and dark eyes. He was practically a mirror image of her Beast, except his hair was cut decently, and he had no scar to mar his handsome face. He was wearing a beautiful dark pinstriped suit. She forced her eyes away from him.

"Annie, my dear," Mr. Nicholas said, "this

is my nephew, Fyfe MacKay. He is to be the new assistant manager here at the Spa, because you are going to be the new manager. But I think you may have already figured that out." He chuckled.

"I did consider the possibility," Annie admitted candidly. "Where is Nora Buckley?"

"Oh, she is traveling the world for me now, my dear. The Spa has been a fantastic financial success, and we will be opening several more within the year. Nora has been selecting the sites, and she will now be overseeing the construction. An amazing woman, Nora Buckley. Of course, I never intended keeping her here in Egret Pointe, and we have been wildly fortunate in you, dear girl."

"Thank you, sir," Annie replied politely. She was general manager of the Spa! But she would really have liked to have picked her own assistant manager.

"Fyfe will report to you, Annie. He'll be living here. Your little apartment should be available now, as Nora's is yours," Mr. Nicholas said. "I will rely on you to break him in, but I must warn you that he won't be with you long. Fyfe is one of my smarter nephews, and I have bigger plans for him. You will be able to choose your next assistant manager as you see fit, my dear, but for now I appreciate your help."

"I'll be delighted to help out, Mr. Nicholas," Annie told him.

"Don't let my nephew intimidate you, Annie. He thinks that because he's handsome and wealthy, he can do as he pleases. He can't. You are in charge, dear girl."

"Knowing I have your support is important, sir," Annie responded. "I shall treat Fyfe as I would treat any employee."

"And I am certain he will, in the end, appreciate that, my dear," Mr. Nicholas said.

For a brief moment Annie had the distinct feeling that her employer meant something entirely different from what her words had meant. Then she shook her head. She was imagining things. Mr. Nicholas couldn't possibly know about her liaisons with certain members of the staff. Besides, she was through with that kind of behavior. With Connor and Devyn gone, and Lars in love, who was to say what she had or hadn't done? She was general manager of The Spa at Egret Pointe.

"I cannot remain with you long," Mr. Nicholas said. "Take today to help Fyfe settle into his new environment."

"Of course," Annie said. "I've ordered your tea. It should be here any minute."

"The week after the holiday has gone well?" he inquired.

"Very well. J. P. Woods is coming regularly. *Entertainment Tonight* wants to do a piece on us, but I've held them off until we could speak to you about it. I don't know if we need the publicity. We're fully booked just about all the time, Mr. Nicholas. If we disappoint too many people, the rumor begins that you can't get into the Spa, and then people start not booking because they think they can't get in," Annie said. "It's a fine line we tread."

"We will need the publicity for the new facilities opening this year," Fyfe MacKay said, finally speaking up. "Perhaps, Uncle, we could arrange to have *ET* do the piece when the island Spa opens up in April. They could start here, and then go on to promote the island." He turned and looked directly at Annie with those dark eyes. "What do you think, Mrs. Miller?" he asked her.

Annie felt a rush of moisture between her legs. The sound of his voice was an aphrodisiac. "I think you have an excellent idea, Fyfe," she replied in cool, businesslike tones. "Why don't you handle it for us? I'll give you the contact name, phone number, and e-mail." *God, you're gorgeous,* she thought to herself. *I want to fuck you.*

He looked at her again, a faint smile on his thin lips. *I want to fuck you, too.*

Annie flushed, startled, but kept her demeanor. He had not spoken, but she had heard his voice as plain as day.

There was a rap on the door, and Mary Finch stuck her head into the room. "The tea tray is here, Mrs. Miller. Shall I have the waitress bring it in?"

"Yes, Mary. And you come in and meet Mr. Nicholas," Annie said, grateful for her assistant's timely arrival. "Sir, this is my assistant, Mary Finch. Mary, this is our boss, the CEO of the Channel Corp."

"How do you do, sir," Mary said politely. She still retained the look of an ingenue.

"How do you do, Miss Mary," Mr. Nicholas said with a small, courtly bow from the waist. "You are happy in your work?"

"Oh, yes, sir! I love it here, and I love working for Mrs. Miller," Mary said.

"Then you will be pleased to know that Annie has now been made the general manager of the Spa," Mr. Nicholas told the girl.

"Oh, Mrs. Miller, congratulations!" Mary replied, as if she had not already been apprised of Annie's situation.

"And you'll come with me, of course," Annie said quickly. Then she turned to Mr.

Nicholas. "If Nora's Margaret is coming back I could put her with Fyfe."

"No, Margaret will remain with Nora, my dear. They are used to working together, and comfortable with each other's habits. We shall have to find someone special for my nephew. I'm certain you will get the right girl," Mr. Nicholas said.

"I'll find him a worker bee," Annie said with a small smile.

"Can she be pretty?" Fyfe MacKay asked dryly.

"It's more important that she be competent," Annie replied sharply.

Mr. Nicholas chuckled. "Annie's devotion to duty is commendable, Fyfe. You could learn a great deal from her."

"I hope to, sir," Fyfe replied, looking directly at Annie.

"If you don't need us, then, Mr. Nicholas," Annie said, "Mary and I will return to my office. Fyfe, when you have bid your uncle good-bye, please come and see me. Anyone can direct you to my office, which will now be yours. I'll get you started on your duties. Good-bye, sir, and thank you. I will do my best to justify your faith in me."

"A delicious piece of goods," Fyfe MacKay murmured when Annie and Mary had departed Mr. Nicholas's office. "Why did you want her?"

Mr. Nicholas smiled. "Actually, it was her sister, Lizzie, whom I was after. Annie was quite a surprise, and a marvelous bonus. Now I have them both."

"Totally?" his companion asked.

"Almost," Mr. Nicholas said. "Elizabeth Bradford had been angling for the Channel Corporation's business for at least two years. We've always used in-house counsel, as you know, dear boy, but it was time to retain a good outside firm. Hers is the best, but I didn't want one of the senior partners handling our business. Too staid, too settled, too cautious, too careful of their worldly goods and reputations. I wanted someone who was hungry, eager, ambitious, and willing to take chances, and, you will forgive my small attempt at humor, devil take the hindmost."

Fyfe MacKay laughed. "Uncle, you can be most amusing when you choose. But why Annie? She's pretty, but seems otherwise ordinary to me."

"It was simply too good an opportunity to resist. She won the contest we held just before we opened the Spa here. She was introduced to the Channel for the first time. She discovered she is a very sexual being both in and out of the Channel, although I believe she is reforming her ways outside of it now. No, Annie was easy to subvert and seduce. She was tired from struggling so hard to keep her family together, fed, and clothed. Her father, without meaning to do so, rubbed salt into her wounds by mentioning more often than not that he'd warned his son-in-law to have more insurance. Her mother always preferred Annie's sister, Lizzie, and made no secret of it. She was forever praising her younger daughter's success. And Lizzie, whose passion to get ahead in her career has caused her to block love from her life, dotes on Annie's children, giving them those little luxuries their mother has not been able to give them. Annie resented it, and then felt guilty because she did.

"When Nora Buckley brought to my attention that this exhausted widow was highly intelligent and had excellent people skills, I took a closer look. I realized that Annie would be an excellent servant for me. She has brought the same devotion she has for her children to her job. And she believes everything she does now is for their betterment. That is why I saw her supplied with the perfect nanny, enabling her to feel no guilt for neglecting them and putting all her energies into her work. She has earned the position of general manager here at the Spa. Eventually, as I have with Nora Buckley, I will move her into positions of greater responsibility, Fyfe. I can see you want to take her as a lover, but do not destroy her spirit and render her useless to me, *nephew.* Remember, she is a fragile human being."

"I want no long-term entanglements, *Uncle,*" Fyfe replied. "I just want someone to amuse me while I am here. How long will I be here?"

"Only until we open the island Spa in April, my boy," Mr. Nicholas responded. "Annie is very smart, and extremely clever. Learn what you can from her. You are the youngest of my *nephews,* and I have high hopes for you, dear boy. Now run along and find Annie. It's time you began your apprenticeship."

"Will I see you again soon?" Fyfe asked him.

"You will see me when you see me," Mr. Nicholas said.

Fyfe MacKay gave the older man a neat bow from the waist, then left him.

A young spa employee he stopped directed him to Annie's office. He found her speaking with her little assistant. "My uncle is leaving now," he told her.

"I'll go and see him off," Annie said. "Please wait for me. Mary will take you into my office." She hurried out. Mr. Nicholas's car was already drawn up beneath the portico of the Spa, waiting for him. Annie stood almost at attention by the lobby door, smiling as he came across the room. "Have a safe trip, sir," she told him.

"Send me weekly reports on Fyfe, Annie, and don't let him get away with murder," Mr. Nicholas said. "His mother has spoiled him, I'm afraid, and his good looks have allowed him to get away with more than he should. Shape him up for me, my dear."

"I'll do my best, sir," Annie said as she walked with him to his car.

"I'm sure you will," he answered her as he got into his vehicle. "Good-bye, now."

"Travel safely, sir," Annie said, and she stood watching as the limousine departed, easing down the driveway and out of sight. Then, returning to the lobby, she realized she had a meeting of the personal assistants in about ten minutes. Well, Fyfe MacKay could come with her and be introduced, and see what everything was all about.

"Mrs. Miller." The head housekeeper stopped her. "The florist says it's too early for daffodils. He suggested yellow and white mums."

"Tell him no, it's a lobby arrangement. If we can't do spring yet let's go tropical. Birds-of-paradise, those big green things with the long red whatevers. Exotic," Annie said. "Remind him we're making an impression on our arriving guests, and it's not a funeral home."

The head housekeeper giggled. "I will," she said. "Is it true? You're our new GM? The rumors have been all over the place this morning."

"I'm the new GM, and Mr. Nicholas's nephew is the new assistant manager," Annie said. "You can spread the word. No need to go formal at this point." She was smiling broadly.

"You deserve it!" the head housekeeper told her. "We all think so."

"Thank you," Annie told her, and then headed for her office again.

"Wondering when you would be back," Fyfe MacKay said. Then he went into Annie's office and sat down.

"I hope Mr. Nicholas got off," Mary Finch said cheerfully.

"Why don't you get someone to help you begin transferring our things over to Ms. Buckley's old office, Mary? It's ours now."

"Okay, Mrs. Miller," Mary replied. "I can't wait! I'm going to have a window!"

Annie had to laugh. "And I get a fireplace, just like Mr. Nicholas's office," she said. "We're really moving on up, Mary."

"Mrs. Miller, could I make a suggestion for the new hire?" Mary asked, and when Annie nodded she continued, "My friend Sandra is a wonderful secretary. She's been working for a temp agency locally. She would make Mr. MacKay a great assistant. There's just one thing: She's not the prettiest girl in the world."

"It's not a beauty contest, Mary," Annie said. "Have her come in, and I'll speak with her. It's her skills I'm interested in, not her face."

"I'll give her a call today, Mrs. Miller. Thanks!"

Annie went into her office, where Fyfe MacKay was lounging in her chair behind her desk. "Get out of that chair," Annie said.

"Isn't this my office now?" he drawled.

"Not quite yet," Annie told him.

He got up and strolled around the desk to seat himself in the chair in front of the desk. "Better now, boss?"

"You are going to have to ditch that obnoxious attitude," Annie said through gritted teeth. "Your uncle has high hopes for you, and I won't let you disappoint him on my watch. Do you understand that, *Mr.*

MacKay?"

He smiled a slow smile. "I'll bet you look great naked," he said.

"Do you understand?" Annie repeated.

"Do you ever lose your temper?" he wondered.

Annie sighed, exasperated. "No, Mr. MacKay, I don't lose my temper with my underlings, and for now you fall into that category. Now, for the third time, do you understand what I have just said to you?"

"Yes," he answered. Then he added, "You like order and discipline, don't you?"

"A successful business requires order and discipline to function efficiently. I am delighted that you understand that, because the Spa is a business," Annie told him. "If we weren't financially feasible your uncle wouldn't be opening more of them."

"My uncle enjoys catering to people's vices," Fyfe said.

"A little pampering in a spa can hardly be considered a vice," Annie replied.

Fyfe laughed. "A spa for women only, where the guests' personal assistants do whatever is requested of them, including kinky sex?" He laughed again. "Are you that naive, Mrs. Miller? I don't think so."

"Sex, kinky or otherwise, is not a part of our menu of treatments," Annie said primly.

"However, we cannot control our guests' needs, and I suppose as long as they are discreet we cannot judge them either."

"Oh, how politically correct, Mrs. Miller." Fyfe chuckled. "I do believe I am coming to see that my uncle's faith in you is quite justified."

"I have the weekly meeting with the PAs in two minutes. You will come with me, be introduced, and listen," Annie told him. "Is that clear?"

"Yes, Mrs. Miller," he answered her obediently.

"And no hitting on any woman who works here," Annie said.

"Agreed," he responded. "I understand that you don't want to share me with anyone else while I'm your subordinate. You want my complete obedience while you are in charge, but when I fuck you, I'll expect yours."

"Since that isn't going to happen, it's a nonissue," Annie said. "Let's go."

The personal assistants took immediately to Fyfe MacKay. He was a man's man, and he knew how to speak to them. Annie decided to put him in charge of the PAs while he was here. It would leave her free to attend to more important things. She had noticed that the gift shop was not as well stocked as when she had been running it. She spoke to Nancy, who complained that the suppliers were being difficult. Annie discreetly phoned several of the suppliers she knew personally. They complained that the Spa was not paying them for several months at a stretch.

"Tell Nancy I want to see her books," Annie told Mary. "And I want to see them now, not tomorrow or the day after."

Mary nodded. "I'll go right away. Oh, we've almost got all of our personal stuff moved over into the new office, and my friend Sandra could come in today at three."

"Good, I'll see her then," Annie replied.

They were moved into their new offices by the time three o'clock came around. Mary's friend arrived and was ushered into Annie's office. Mary had spoken the truth: Sandra Burns was not a pretty girl. She was tall and painfully thin. Her face was long, and so was her nose. She had thin, mousy brown hair and watery blue eyes. But she was well-spoken, and her skills were excellent.

"I'm hiring you to be our new assistant manager's executive assistant. He's tall, dark, and handsome. He's also the CEO of the Channel Corp.'s nephew, and he's as arrogant as the dickens. Are you tough enough to stand up to him? If you aren't, please don't take the job. While I'm the only one who hires and fires, I don't want you driven to tears by Mr. MacKay, who has just arrived to join us today. He doesn't know any more about running a spa than you do. Mary will be your guide. I rely on her entirely."

"I grew up with three older brothers, Mrs. Miller," Sandra Burns said. "I don't bully easily. And I never cry."

Annie smiled. "You're hired. When can you start?"

"Tomorrow too soon?"

"Not at all. Mary," Annie called. "Go find Mr. MacKay and tell him I want to see him now."

"Right away, Mrs. Miller," Mary called back.

While they waited, Annie explained the salary and the benefits that came with working at the Spa. "Before you go today you can fill out all the paperwork, and Mary will take you downstairs for your Spa uniforms. Then, when you come in tomorrow, you will be all ready to work. Ah, Mr. MacKay, come in. We've found you an excellent assistant. This is Sandra Burns. Sandra, this is Mr. MacKay, who will be your boss."

"You don't dillydally, do you?" Fyfe said.

"How do you do, Sandra." Could they have found a more unattractive girl? She had a nose like an eagle's beak, and a thin, prissy mouth. But he gave her his best smile. She would be more than competent, he knew, and the truth was, he would need someone who was capable and qualified. And if she was like all the women he knew, she would devote herself to him, because she would fall in love with him. She would want to protect him. They all did. Still, at least he wouldn't mix business with pleasure with this tall, spindly female.

"Time is money," Annie murmured. "Mary, dear, take Sandra to fill out her paperwork and get her uniforms. We'll see you tomorrow, dear."

Fyfe waited until the two girls had left the room. "She will do admirably," he said.

"Good," Annie replied crisply. "I told you I would look for office skills. You are both on an even playing field, as neither of you knows anything about the Spa. Mary will aid Sandra when she needs it, and I will direct you, Mr. MacKay."

"Will I see you tonight?" he asked her.

"Certainly not!" Annie said indignantly. "When I finish here I go home, unless my work causes me to remain."

"I meant in the Channel," Fyfe MacKay said.

Annie froze. She could not have heard him correctly.

He laughed softly. "You heard me," he said.

"I haven't the faintest idea of what you are talking about," she finally answered.

"I am Mr. Nicholas's nephew," he replied. "I am not just now coming into the family business, Annie. I have been in it for some time. I know everything there is to know about my uncle's enterprises."

Annie couldn't speak, even to remonstrate with him for using her first name.

"The Channel is an interactive network where women go to live out, to fully experience, their fantasies. It's a marvelous creation, and you would think that the whole world would know about it. But they don't, do they? It's a delicious and dirty little secret known only to the female of the human species." He laughed at the look on her face. "Now, how could that possibly be?"

"I think you must have a screw loose," Annie finally managed to say.

"Excellent! Very good!" he complimented her. "Your loyalty to my uncle, to the Channel, is to be commended. The old boy really does have a good eye when it comes to picking out new servants."

"I am not your uncle's servant," Annie said in a tight voice. "I am in his employ."

"As you will. Now, answer my question. Will you be joining me tonight?" The dark eyes looked directly at her.

"You are free to go now, Mr. MacKay," Annie told him. "I'm sure you want to set your office up to suit yourself, now that I am out of it, and I have work to do."

He stood up. "You will come," he told her. "Your curiosity will compel you to come, I suspect." Then, turning, he left her office.

Annie started to shake. He had frightened her. He had really scared the daylights out of her, although she had managed to hold herself together. Fyfe MacKay had to be totally mad. How had he found out about the Channel? Of course, she would admit nothing. Annie reached for her cell phone and punched the number one. It rang twice, and then she heard Mr. Nicholas's voice.

"Yes, Annie, what is it?"

"Your nephew, sir. He knows about the Channel," Annie gasped.

There was a long and deep silence, followed by a sigh. "Annie, Fyfe will eventually be my right-hand man. He is family. He has worked in other divisions of the corporation for a number of years now. His last position was overseeing the Channel for me when Nora Buckley took over opening the Spa. I had no one else available at the time."

"I thought only women knew about the Channel," Annie half whispered.

"I know, and Fyfe knows," Mr. Nicholas replied in his usual calm tones. "He has my complete and utter trust, Annie."

"I see," she responded, beginning to regain mastery of herself. "I told him I didn't know what he was talking about when he brought it up."

"You obviously have more sense than he does," Mr. Nicholas said. "Fyfe sometimes lacks discretion. He should have said nothing to you."

"He's appallingly arrogant, sir," Annie told her employer.

Mr. Nicholas laughed. "A family trait, I fear. Is that all, my dear?"

"Yes, sir."

"You were correct to come to me, Annie. You must always come to me when you are disturbed, confused, or concerned. I will always help you to solve your difficulties. You are an excellent employee. Good-bye now, my dear."

"Good-bye, sir," Annie replied. She closed her cell phone and sat back in her chair. Mr. Nicholas always made her feel better.

He was more supportive of her than her own parents, she thought. He had given her the opportunity to better herself, to advance within his organization, to take care of her children properly. But who was he? Really?

She had Googled him once when she first came to work at the Spa. There were very few references to Mr. Nicholas. Mostly he was acknowledged as the CEO of the Channel Corporation. There was little more. Was Nicholas his last name? What was his first name? Or was Nicholas his first name? Then what was his surname? The damned Internet could tell you almost everything about a person if the information was available. Hell, it could print out a map to your house. But there was virtually no information about Mr. Nicholas himself. Why was that?

"It's almost six, Mrs. Miller. I'm heading home," Mary Finch said. "Sandra is all ready for tomorrow. Her paperwork is done, and turned in to accounting. She's got her uniforms, and they've given her the keys to her assigned car. Is there anything else I can do for you?"

"No, thanks, Mary," Annie said. "I think I'm going to stay here tonight."

"Okay, then, good night." And Mary was gone.

Annie picked up her cell again and

punched in the number two.

"Miller residence," Nanny Violet's voice came over the phone.

"Nanny, it's Mrs. Miller. I have to work late. I'm going to stay up at the Spa tonight. Tell the children good night for me, will you?"

"Oh, dear, and I made shepherd's pie for you with the leftover Sunday lamb," Nanny Violet said. "Nathaniel said you wanted it."

"I did, and I'm sorry to miss it," Annie responded. "Tell my eldest that I got that promotion. I'm now the general manager of the spa."

"Congratulations, Mrs. Miller! I will certainly tell him. The children will be so proud of you," Nanny Violet trilled.

"Good night now," Annie said.

"Good night, dear. Please don't work too hard," the nanny advised.

Annie touched the end button on her cell. Then she punched in Lizzie's office number. She knew her sister would still be working.

"Hey, Annie, what's up?" Lizzie answered.

"I'm the new GM at the Spa," Annie answered her.

"Wonderful! Did you tell Mom and Dad yet?"

"Not yet. Lizzie, what do you know about Mr. Nicholas?" Annie asked her sister.

"Not a whole lot, really," Lizzie said. "Why? Is it important?"

"Maybe not, but I can't help but be curious," Annie answered. "I Googled him, and there's virtually nothing, Lizzie. Don't you think it's odd that someone who is the head of such a financially and seemingly large corporation is a virtual blank?"

"Look," Lizzie said to her elder sister, "some of these guys with money and power are a little bit eccentric. They don't want anything known about their background, or where they live, or if they have family. It's bizarre, but it goes with the territory. I've met Mr. Nicholas a couple of times now. He's courtly and he's intelligent. And most important of all to the firm, he pays his yearly retainer up-front without a murmur. Now, what's really bothering you, Annie?"

"He brought his nephew in this morning as assistant general manager. The guy is gorgeous, hot, and totally weird. He makes me uncomfortable, Lizzie. And he knows about the Channel."

"Fyfe MacKay!" Lizzie laughed. "Yes, handsome as sin, and the most arrogant man I've ever met. He was temporarily in charge of the Channel itself. I've met him. Did Mr. Nicholas tell you that you were in charge? Did he tell him?"

"Yes," Annie replied.

"Then trust me, you are in charge. Don't let Fyfe bully you or scare you with that 'I'm *his* nephew, and I'm mysterious' attitude. Show him you're the boss, Annie, because if you don't, you're going to lose control of your position. If that happens you'll be in deep doo-doo with your staff. They respect you. Don't let that change."

"Thanks, Lizzie, you always make me feel better," Annie told her younger sibling. "I guess I just got a bad case of nerves. It's been a long, extra busy day."

"Go home and get some rest," Lizzie advised.

"I'm staying here," Annie told her sister. "It's too noisy at home for me to rest. Besides, I have some work to do."

"Me too," Lizzie said. "You okay now?"

"Yeah, I am. Good night, sis."

"You, too."

Annie closed her cell phone, and then she pressed a button on her desk.

"Yes, Mrs. Miller."

"Are you alone on the front desk, Peter?"

"No, ma'am, Simon is here."

"One of you go to the kitchen. Get me a sandwich and a pot of tea. I'm in my office working late," Annie said.

"Right away, ma'am. And if I might say it,

congratulations!"

"Thanks, Peter."

A half hour later the young man from the front desk arrived with a tray. On it was a perfectly grilled Havarti cheese–and–bacon sandwich, a small meringue filled with berries, and a pot of black Irish tea. "Thought if you were working you'd need something substantial, and I know you didn't eat lunch today," Peter said as he set the tray down. "If you need anything else I'm on until midnight, Mrs. Miller."

"Thanks," Annie said as Peter hurried out, leaving her alone again. She ate slowly. The sandwich was hot and gooey. The black tea cleared her palate with every sip. The meringue shell and berries were the perfect ending. Finishing it all, Annie sat back with a gusty sigh. She felt so much better now.

Her office door suddenly opened, and Fyfe MacKay came into the room. "I was going to ask you to dinner," he said quietly.

"I've eaten," she said.

"My uncle says my ambition often makes me seem arrogant and eager to show everyone how much I know. I spoke out of turn today," he said.

Annie sighed. "You're part of a family corporation, and if your uncle shared the Channel with you, then he must have big plans for you. But I'll admit to being startled."

"Then I'm forgiven?" he asked.

"You're forgiven as long as you remember that until Mr. Nicholas says otherwise, I am the one running The Spa at Egret Pointe, not you. You will show me respect at all times, because right now I have my staff's respect, and I don't intend losing it to you or anyone else. It would lessen my value to the corporation, and I can't let anyone do that," Annie told Fyfe MacKay in a quiet, firm voice.

"I like it when you talk tough," he said softly.

"If there is nothing else, Mr. MacKay, I'd like to go back to work," Annie said.

"Then I'll bid you good night for now," he answered, and left her.

Annie spent the next hour going over miscellaneous papers she had put aside for a quiet time. She made some notes for winter excursions for the spa guests, and finally, feeling tired, she went upstairs to her new apartment. To her surprise all of Nora's furniture was gone, and in its place were furnishings more to her taste, warm and homey. And outside she saw that snow was beginning to fall. Tired, she washed, undressed, got into bed, and fell asleep. It wasn't even nine o'clock.

Several hours later she woke up. She felt refreshed, and, reaching for the remote, she pointed it toward the flat-screen television in the open walnut armoire. She would go to the seashore tonight, but before she could press the B button her finger involuntarily pushed down on A. *Damn!* she thought as she found herself once again hanging naked in the small round dungeon chamber. Two torches flickered from their holders in the wall. And instinctively Annie knew she was not alone.

His hands reached around her to cup her round, firm breasts in his palms. He pinched her nipples cruelly, causing Annie to cry out. "In this reality, Mistress Anne, I am the master, and you are the obedient servant," she heard the Beast's sexy, dark voice rasp. His hands ran down her torso, exploring her as if for the very first time.

She shivered at his touch. "What is your name, my lord?" she dared to ask him. His fingers wound their way through her thick, curly bush.

"You know my name, Mistress Anne," the Beast told her.

"No, I don't!" Annie cried.

He laughed a dark laugh. Then he unfastened the manacles that held her up, and when she stood on bare feet he walked about in front of her. He wore only one garment, tight-fitting black leather breeches, and from a slit cut into them his great penis hung supine. "On your knees, Mistress Anne," he commanded her. And when she knelt before him the Beast said, "Now cajole my cock to come out to play with you."

Annie took him into her mouth and began to suck. It was him. She knew it. Sensed it. Fyfe MacKay was the Beast. How had she ever imagined a man she'd never met? And yet since she had been a child listening to her grandmother read her the tale of "Beauty and the Beast," the image of this man had always come into her head. But her grandmother had died, and she had never again heard or read that story. And she had never thought of this man, this face, until the night she had first programmed her fantasy.

His fingers dug into her thick hair. "That's it, my beauty, make me want to fuck you. Ah, what a mouth you have! You are making my lust for you boil hot. Stop now!" He drew her up and kissed her hard. "On your back in the straw, Mistress Anne," he said. Then he slipped between her soft open thighs. "Take my mask off, beauty."

Her fingers reached up and undid the silk-

and-leather mask that covered part of his face. She pulled it off and gasped. "Where is your scar?" she cried as she looked into the perfect features of Fyfe MacKay.

"The scar was there for you when you did not know me," he explained. "Now you know who I am. Say my name, Annie."

"Fantasy end!" Annie cried, and found herself back in her bed, but Fyfe MacKay was still between her thighs.

"Say my name!" he told her again. "Don't you want to be fucked, Annie? And I'm not going to fuck you until you say my name."

"What are you doing? I ended the fantasy! I ended it!"

"And I came with you when you did. Say my name! I can keep us like this all night if you want," he threatened her.

"I'll scream!" she said.

"There's no one up here to hear you," he said, laughing softly. "Come on, Annie, you know you want my big cock inside of you. Say my name and I'll put it there. I'll go hard and deep and give you the best orgasm you've ever had. All I need is to hear you say my name, Annie."

"And if I don't?" she demanded.

"Then I'll tell my uncle that I don't think your sister is the best lawyer for us, Annie. I'll tell him I suspect she is skimming some of our profits to pay for her increasingly wealthy lifestyle. And I'll make it look just like that. Her reputation, and her firm's reputation, will be in shambles before she's found innocent," he said.

"You bastard!" Annie said angrily. "How can you do such a thing?"

"You don't get it, do you?" he said softly. "Haven't you figured out yet who my uncle is? Who the family is? Who I am?"

The reality hit her hard. *No!* It wasn't possible. It just wasn't possible! Was it?

He saw the confusion in her beautiful eyes warring with her common sense. "Say my name, Annie, and everything will be perfect for you, for your sister. Say my name!"

It was so little to ask of her, Annie suddenly reasoned with herself. What was so awful about saying his name? Why was she fighting with him over it? "Do you promise to give me the best orgasm I've ever had?" she whispered to him. "Do you, *Fyfe?*"

He smiled, his eyes catching hers, holding her gaze. "Yes," was all he said, and then he thrust his thick length into her heated vagina.

She felt him filling her, stretching the walls of her passage, throbbing. He drove her hard, and he drove deep into her hot, wet sex. His eyes never left hers, and Annie

396

couldn't seem to turn away from his blazing gaze, from the tiny flames that danced deep in his dark eyes. To her wonder she felt her orgasm building slowly, slowly, and then it burst, sweeping over her as Annie realized with perfect clarity just who her employer was, who Fyfe was. She screamed with a mix of fear and intense pleasure.

"Yes!" He laughed into her face. "Yes, Mistress Anne, my own innocent beauty, you understand at last the dangerous pleasures you have sought out, don't you!"

And he drove her harder until she began to swoon with her second great orgasm. But before reason totally left her Annie thought to herself, *It's for my children. Everything I've done has been for my children! It will always be for the children!*

EPILOGUE

"The Spa at Egret Pointe has proved so successful for the Channel Corporation that after three years they are opening another," the *Entertainment Tonight* reporter gushed. "I'm with Annie Miller, general manager of the first of these wonderful getaways for women only. How Annie came to run this luxe establishment is a fairy tale in itself. Will you tell our audience how you got here?"

"Well, my sister entered me in the contest that was the promotion for the Spa's opening. And I won! The rest is history, as they say," Annie said.

"I think you're being too modest." The reporter giggled. She turned. "Mr. Nicholas is the CEO of the Channel Corporation. Can you tell us how Annie became your GM here?"

"As a guest she showed an incredible instinct for what guests wanted and needed, the first of which was our gift shop. We asked her to run it, and she made such an incredible success we hired her as the then-GM's assistant manager. Annie had no experience, but we trained her, and when our first general manager left we asked Annie to step into her shoes, which she has done very capably."

"And she's trained your nephew, Fyfe MacKay," the reporter said, "and he's going to be running the newest Channel Corporation spa down in the islands. Mr. MacKay, are you excited about that?"

"I am, and I can't thank Mrs. Miller enough for all her help, her advice, and her kindness toward me," Fyfe MacKay said.

"And now, using the magic that only television can give you, we're going to switch over and go right down to The Spa at Fantasy Key."

"Okay, let's turn off the television," Annie said. "You've all seen my part."

"No," Amy said, "let's see more of that Fyfe guy. Jeez, Mom, he is so hot! How could you work with him and keep your hands off of him?"

The twins giggled.

"Amy, you're going to discover that there are lots of things in the world that don't have to do with just sex," Annie said dryly.

"Well, I guess you get to an age when sex doesn't matter anymore," Amy replied.

"Amy, dear, that really is dreadfully rude," Nanny Violet said disapprovingly.

Annie laughed. If her daughter only knew. But, of course, eventually one day Amy would. *It doesn't matter what I've done,* Annie thought, looking around the den at her youngest son and three daughters. *Whatever happens to me isn't important. It's all been for my children, and the kids are happy.* There were surely worse things than working for the devil. Weren't there?

ABOUT THE AUTHOR

Bertrice Small is a *New York Times* best-selling author and the recipient of numerous awards, including the 2006 Career Achievement Award for Historical Romance from *Romantic Times* magazine. In keeping with her profession, Bertrice Small lives in the oldest English-speaking town in the state of New York, founded in 1640. Her light-filled studio includes the paintings of her favorite cover artist, Elaine Duillo, and a large library. Because she believes in happy endings, Bertrice Small has been married to the same man, her hero, George, for forty-five years. They have a son, Thomas; a daughter-in-law, Megan; and four wonderful grandchildren. Longtime readers will be happy to know that Nicki the cockatiel flourishes, along with his fellow housemates: Pookie, the long-haired greige-and-white cat; Finnegan, the long-haired bad black kitty; and Sylvester, the

black-and-white tuxedo cat, who is now the
official family bedcat.

We hope you have enjoyed this Large Print book. Other Thorndike, Wheeler, and Chivers Press Large Print books are available at your library or directly from the publishers.

For information about current and upcoming titles, please call or write, without obligation, to:

Publisher
Thorndike Press
295 Kennedy Memorial Drive
Waterville, ME 04901
Tel. (800) 223-1244

or visit our Web site at:

http://gale.cengage.com/thorndike

OR

Chivers Large Print
published by BBC Audiobooks Ltd
St James House, The Square
Lower Bristol Road
Bath BA2 3SB
England
Tel. +44(0) 800 136919
email: bbcaudiobooks@bbc.co.uk
www.bbcaudiobooks.co.uk

All our Large Print titles are designed for easy reading, and all our books are made to last.